To Alex
Into the
greenwood
Awesome Con 2012

THE FRIAR'S TALE

A NOVEL OF ROBIN HOOD

JENNIFER R. POVEY

Jennifer Povey

Copyright © 2020 by Jennifer R. Povey

All rights reserved.

No part of this book may be reproduced in any form or by any electronic or mechanical means, including information storage and retrieval systems, without written permission from the author, except for the use of brief quotations in a book review.

1

The straightness of the road revealed its origins, dating all the way back to the time of the Romans. The surface, however, was not as it had been in that time. It was churned up into an unpleasant mud, heavy with the clay soils of the valley.

A single set of hooves plodded down the road, the sound echoing, and then a two-wheeled cart emerged from the trees. A particularly scruffy mule, so out of proportion that it looked to be the result of accidental congress between a small donkey and a warhorse, hauled the cart.

The cart's driver and sole occupant was a man of considerable girth. His rotund form was wrapped in brown robes, with a rope for a belt, and his head was tonsured. These features revealed him as a monk or, more likely, a friar. A closer inspection would reveal that the contents of the cart were road supplies and ale...more of the latter than one would expect a single man to consume.

From the fact that the extremely rotund friar was singing a hymn at the top of his voice, and with several of the words incorrect, one might also get the impression quite a bit of the ale had already been consumed.

The forest closed in on the road. The mule made its way along with basically no guidance from the driver. It simply walked along the road, towing the scruffy cart behind it.

Then, it exploded upwards into a crow hop. The cart overturned, spilling ale, food and friar onto the road...and the mule bolted, pulling the empty vehicle behind it. For a long moment, the friar did not get up.

The reason for the mule's rather sensible reaction, however, moved towards him, surrounding him. He looked up to see a ring of hard faces. Four men surrounded him, and his bulk would have made two of three of the four. All four were clad in rough clothing of hues of green and brown...the better to blend into the forest.

"Good friar. We have need of a priest."

He sat up, checking that all of his parts were still there. "Catch my mule and I'll give whatever rites you wish." The friar knew these men were outlaws. Wolfsheads. Those who walked outside of the law of civilized men. They might just as easily slit his throat for his ale as truly seek his services. On the other hand, he would almost prefer the company of outlaws to that from which he had come.

The man who had spoken whistled. The friar heard somebody moving through the trees, somebody he had not seen.

A rather large band. They might well have legitimate need of a priest...although most likely for a duty the friar would not relish. There was also the very real possibility he would yet need that duty himself afterwards.

Would they let him live after he had seen them? It depended. Some bands thrived on secrecy. Others liked to let people go to pass on their reputation so that their next victims would not fight.

On the surface of it, the friar saw no reason yet to fight. If they tried to kill him, then they would get a surprise, for the staff lying across the cart seat was neither decorative nor the tool of an old man.

"Come," the slender outlaw leader said.

The friar was not surprised to note that one of the outlaws...not the leader...had slightly broader hips than might have been expected. It would not be the first woman who walked and fought alongside men he had encountered.

Most especially recently. The leader, though? Definitely a man, although not a large one. He seemed to leave size to one of the others...a man well over six feet tall and broad through the shoulders.

The Friar followed, but not until he saw one of the outlaws returning with his mule and cart. Another started to pick up what casks of ale had not shattered and spilled.

He did not expect to see that again. They might leave him the mule, as unfortunate a specimen as it was. Possibly even the cart. His ale, however, would vanish into their stash, that which was not drunk by the end of the night.

He mourned it briefly. The outlaws moved silently. Most of the noise he heard came from himself. He was no woodsman. However, he could also hear the cart behind him. His staff was, he hoped, still in the cart. The trail was barely wide enough for it, and he suspected that their normal routes would be narrow deer trails, lined by brambles and stinging nettles.

If he could get to it, then he could win free of them. Assuming he needed to.

"What do you bring here?" A different voice, a rough one that spoke of age and ill use.

"A priest for Simon."

"A priest." The old man stepped out of the trees. "And what will we do with this priest afterwards, now he has seen *your* base?"

The emphasis on the pronoun showed bitterness.

The young leader narrowed his eyes. "Speak such again, Richard, and I will banish you."

Richard. The same name as the pitiful excuse for a king who preferred the crusades to his own people. Not the man's fault he shared it.

The old man snorted and vanished back behind the trees. "He brings up a good point. What should I do with you?"

"I place all I see under the seal of the confessional." Not that he was truly protected by that in this situation. "It would take torture to get it out of me."

He would not promise he could hold up under the ordeal. Few men could. He had his faith and he had a certain courage...he would not shy from a fight if forced on him, but he did not trust even faith to carry him through.

The lead outlaw nodded. "I am afraid it is a hard duty I ask of you."

"Last rites." The friar was not stupid. For this outlaw band to corner a priest and haul him to this place...it could only be for that. Even a wedding, they would likely go with the older handfasting should such be desired. A lychgate wedding, it was sometimes called. What property, after all, did such men and women have to pass on to the fruit of their loins? There was no reason for the bride to be churched.

Besides, any women with the band were unlikely virgins, having come here in pursuit of their men. If they were, it would be because they were sapphists. The friar had seen enough of the world not to deny the existence of such, which the church called vices. He was not so sure. "Show me the man."

The man had been stabbed in the stomach. A slow and unpleasant way to die. The sweet smell of corruption surrounded him. The friar listened to the man's sins. To guilt, to cowardice.

That was what he was supposed to do. Listen. Whether it had any power in the eyes of God, he had never been sure. It made the person speaking feel better, he had no doubt. He listened, and he spoke the words, and then he stepped out of the tent in which the man lay.

The young leader was waiting for him. "How long?"

"A few hours, no more." The friar might have suggested making that time shorter, but there were those who considered giving mercy a sin.

"Is there any hope for him?"

"No." The Friar was going to be honest. The best physician, the most experienced herbwife, could not save that young man...and the Friar did not believe that all herbwives were evil, unlike many men.

The young man nodded, his face set grimly, and made his way into the tent.

The friar had a feeling he knew what was about to transpire inside. He walked over to his mule. A couple of eyes followed him, but none tried to stop him. If he tried to leave, he knew he would be stopped. He might yet die here at their hands.

However, at the moment, they were paying little attention to him.

Or, perhaps, they were planning on asking him to do the funeral as well. Out here, they would seldom have access to a priest. He could imagine that at their most benevolent, they would yet seek to keep him a while.

One hand rubbed along the mule's ears. An ugly beast it might be, but it had served him well so far and hopefully would continue to do so. Besides, it was too ugly for anyone to be tempted to steal.

The outlaw leader approached him. He realized, now he had leisure to study the man that while he was young, he was more than a stripling. It was the lack of a beard that made him look young...most of the others had full beards, the only one without being the one the friar suspected was female. The hint of a nick indicated that he was shaving himself.

Perhaps he did not grow a beard worth keeping. Some men, after all, had that affliction. But a more accurate guess as to his age would place him in his early twenties. Still very young to be so obviously in charge.

Which meant either they were fools to follow him, or he was brilliant.

"Thank you, good friar. Might I ask your name?"

"Tuck." It was not his real name, but he had almost forgotten what that was. The nickname would serve better. "Might I ask yours?"

"Robin."

THE FRIAR SPENT THE NIGHT. The old man, it seemed, still wanted to see him dead. Robin, he suspected, had a different goal.

Robin wanted to cultivate him as an ally. A friar, associated with no church, he was the perfect person to tend to them on those occasions they needed a priest. Tuck sat under the wings of the tent, staring out into the rain, and contemplated the matter.

His ale was gone, his cart was a little banged up but workable. His mule, Brownie, was undamaged. Most importantly, his person was undamaged. This Robin...a pseudonym, surely...was a most honorable kind of outlaw.

Nobody else had stirred yet. The rain was enough to cause a man to take one look outside and then return to his bed. It fell in sheets of misery, dripping off the leaves of the trees, but inside the tent it remained dry. Not that much less comfortable than the average peasant hut...and far easier to move.

So. This outlaw. Honorable. Possibly devout. How had he ended up outside the law? Taken something from the forest, perhaps? Tuck snorted.

The forest laws had only become worse of late. A poor man could become an outlaw for allowing his swine to root in the wrong place. Not to mention what they forced these people to do to their dogs, crippling the poor beasts.

It might be that these outlaws had never done anything worse than shoot a deer to feed starving children. It might be that every last one of them was a stone-cold killer. The truth, likely, lay somewhere in between.

Almost certainly the food they ate was mostly stolen. The more honorable ones stole only from the crown.

Like Richard would care. Tuck snorted. John was an asshole by all accounts and Richard would be just as happy if the entirety of Britain sailed out into the ocean and sank one day. Neither of them was worthy of being king.

Well, you dealt with what you had. Tuck was more concerned about the reason he had left Newstead. The abbot. Now there was a worthwhile target for an honorable outlaw.

Fortunately, his own order did not run to such excesses...but they also did not run to always having a cell for a wandering friar.

He looked out into the rain again. The paths around would turn into mud and wet bracken. He was going to be wishing he wore boots not sandals soon. Still, that was the price.

Not that he had ever paid it by stinting himself at the table, or of alcohol. Maybe he could even steal some of his ale back. Not with breakfast, though. Even he did not start that soon.

The woman outlaw made her way across to his tent. He was now even more sure of her gender. She had a bow and her breasts had been bound so that they would not get in the way of her draw. Still, her hips gave her away, as did the fineness of her features. "Good father, can I get you anything?"

Clearly, the rest of the band knew, for she made no attempt to disguise her voice. "I don't know what food you might have. What is your name?"

"Clorinda," she introduced.

A Norman name when the rest seemed Saxon. Her hair was dark enough...like as not she was a mix. A herald of things to come...the English race was, after all, itself a mix of Saxons and the smaller, darker Celts.

"I can get you gruel," she offered.

He would not ask the origin of the grain. "Gruel would be fine." It would probably be bad gruel, but it would help wake him up. Of course, he would rather have a real breakfast. Eggs. Maybe they had eggs...but no. He would not ask.

He would not press their hospitality when at least one sought his life.

Clorinda returned in a brief time with gruel, sheltering it from the rain with her hand. To his surprise, it was not bad gruel.

He would, too, have laid bets she had not cooked it...and larger bets that any other stranger would have assumed she had. She was probably the lover of one of the men, but she moved like a woman who bowed to no one.

It was none of his business, unless he chose to stay. The outlaw leader would very much like to keep him. There might even be worse fates.

Certainly, he would rather not die. Perhaps it spoke of a loss of faith, but Tuck liked the things of the world. He saw no reason not to appreciate every aspect of God's creation. Even the rain which came down in sheets. He saw Clorinda vanish back into another tent. She had braved it to check on him, but once that was done, she was not staying out in it one moment longer. That was his guess, anyway.

Well, it had started early, and thus would end early. In fact, he could already see the sky beginning to lighten a little. No sign of the sun yet, but it would stop soon.

It never rained for that long here. Not like in the Holy Land, where it rained all winter, it seemed. And only all winter. Tuck shook his head. As far as he was concerned, the Saracens could keep the place.

A heresy he might voice here, amongst outlaws, but nowhere else. Besides, Richard was going the right way about losing it to them.

And then, abruptly, the rain stopped. Cautiously, he stepped out of the tent, glancing up at the sky. It was lightening rapidly. The ground underfoot was damp...mud, leaves and twigs intermingling into something even a pig would not have wanted to walk across. It had, though, stopped falling from the sky.

At least one braved it. The extremely tall man was returning through the trees, a dead deer across his shoulders and his bow in one hand. A crime, of course, for all deer belonged to the king.

It was probably lunch. The man was not the one Tuck worried about the most. He had learned that it was the smaller men who were the more dangerous. And the women.

He sometimes felt the Saracens had the right idea keeping their women locked up. Women who did not know how to fight could be dangerous only with their tongues. Those who did were ruthless. Some of the women who had ridden on the Crusades...

Most had been disguised, but he knew at least two, for he had taken their confession. Under the seal, they had revealed their secret. He wondered how many there really were.

He would never know. He glanced over at the big man and elected to avoid him. He did not want to be roped in to help dress the kill.

Instead, he went to the tent in which the dead man lay. He dropped to one knee next to the body. He was not sure where they would bury him, except that it would likely not be in consecrated ground.

Would God care about that? Tuck liked to think no, but most believed that he would be condemned to hell automatically. Of course, he might already have condemned himself.

He would do his best for him...but he would do no more. Not without the story. Not without knowing what manner of men these really were. If they were hardened killers, then he would seek his escape.

If they were unfortunates caught out by the Forest Law, then was that not Francis' mission...to minister to the unfortunate?

The question was how he found out. How he found out without hearing only lies, as the hardened might pretend to be the innocent. He did not know, at that point.

Then the young leader came in. "I dislike the fact that we cannot get him to consecrated ground."

"I will say rites for him. I doubt God could ask more from you."

"I am not sure how much attention God is paying," Robin mused. "It seems to me as if most of the time, God expects us to look after ourselves."

"No," Tuck said, glancing up at the clearing skies. "God expects us to look after each other."

He had planned for that line to be the last word, and he almost succeeded, for there was quite the thoughtful pause from the outlaw leader.

Tuck considered asking him outright how he had ended up in this position. How he was here, in the woods, not in some tidy village. There was nothing of quality about the man, but much of leadership. A solid yeoman, he suspected, not a man of high birth, but a man of integrity? He could hope so.

Finally, Tuck spoke. "Your older friend. Does he still want to slit my throat?"

"Oh, ignore him." Robin quirked up the corner of his mouth. "He is a bitter old man, and he has reason to be. Every reason to mistrust the church, too."

"I am a friar, hardly a representative of the bishops."

"Do I detect, in those words, a certain bitterness of your own?"

"I dislike those who claim to do the Lord's work but seek only a soft living." Tuck shrugged. "Not that I have always been best at keeping the vow of poverty myself. The occasional problem with obedience, too."

Robin laughed. "And chastity?"

Tuck shrugged. "I am not an attractive man. That one is a lot easier." He doubted Robin was particularly chaste. It was possible, even probable, the lithe, tough Clorinda was his wife or his mistress. Or simply his woman. Out here, it did not really matter. God, Tuck thought, read the intent in a man's heart, not the strict letter of the law. Marriage, in particular, should be in the eyes of god, not man. He did not speak to the depths of his heart and the fact that he had, in fact, never been tempted to violate that vow, either with woman or with man.

"Still. There was no gold or jewels in your cart. Admittedly, a rather large quantity of ale."

"When one finds a good brewer, it serves one to buy enough to last a while." Tuck shrugged. He was aware that he liked his ale far too much, his food far too much. But as the outlaw had said, he carried no gold or jewels. Had no woman. He did better than most.

Obedience, though? He tended to follow his own thoughts and his own ideas. Robin was a man who undoubtedly did the same.

"And when one finds a good priest."

"That I would have to think about. I am of the Order of St. Francis. Staying in one place is not much to my nature."

Robin nodded. "Nor to mine, to be honest. I will not hold you, except that if you reveal our secrets..."

He did not need to voice the threat, it was simply there. Obvious. Hanging in the air. Well, Tuck had expected no less. The man owed his people protection. He had a responsibility, and if that meant killing a friar, then he would do it with no hesitation.

Tuck respected that. It might not end well for him, but he did respect it.

2
_____

uck made his way along the trail. He was, for once, alone...although he was trespassing, it was unlikely that the king's men would arrest a friar. As long as they did not catch him with the king's venison.

That, of course, was the furthest thing from his mind. It was not escape he sought, merely solitude. They had buried Simon that morning, in a grave set by the roots of an oak. Not consecrated ground, but it would have to do. The words had been said, and Tuck was certain God had received the man's soul. Not into heaven, no, but least into purgatory, that place where souls learned those lessons they had not learned in life.

Nobody went straight to heaven except those rare true saints. Tuck had never met one. He had met many who thought of themselves as saints.

Hypocrites. He stopped at the edge of a stream. A small brown bird emerged from the water, something wriggling in its beak. He thought he could see small fish within the silver flow. Those, the king would not miss, being but they were sticklebacks...too small and too muddy to eat.

The king. To be fair, it was not all John's fault. The man was only following trends that already existed and doing his best in the absence of his brother. Not a good king, no, but not as terrible a king as some accused him of being.

Those some longed for Richard's return. Lionheart. Pfah. The man had no more courage than a common peasant. He was not crusading out of courage, but quite the reverse.

Tuck had met him, yes, on the road to the Holy Land. The man had thought an English friar would speak no French. Truthfully, Tuck's French was not what it could be. Yet, it had been good enough to catch most of the supposedly good king's tirade about England and his English subjects.

Barbarians, all of them, he had said. Not to mention the fact that it rained too much in England. That last, he would give him. The rain, of course, was welcome after the desert. Tuck had even lost weight...a difficult task for him indeed. Even if he did not eat well, his body remained heavy. God had meant him to be that way. His staff tapped the ground as he walked along the stream.

He opened his senses to the forest. His chosen life was not one meant to fall within the walls of a cloister. The Clares, the women who followed the path, did such. Even Francis had thought women unsuited to privation.

Tuck thought that Francis had needed to meet more women. But then, women were not as strong as men in some ways, nor as large. And, of course, they faced pregnancy and childbirth. It was his children a man sought to protect, not his wife. In many cases, anyway. Few were the men Tuck had met who truly loved their women.

That the woman loved her man was more common and might, he thought, be the great tragedy of humankind. The Clares were better off...of course, they would never know what joy children could bring, but neither would they die, worn from bearing, before their time.

His thoughts had taken him far from there, in fact. Had taken him to a little cloister where the Clares had let him stay in the guest house and sit in the back of the church. Even a sworn brother was not allowed within the cloister proper. Men were stronger and might take advantage of a sister, forcing her to break her vows.

He had known of men being raped. Rarer, yes, but it happened.

And he had once had to fight off a woman bent on taking her pleasure with him regardless of his wishes. He thought she might have had a thing for priests. For the unattainable.

Still, he had glimpsed the Clares at their work and contemplation. They prayed. He saw no reason they could not do other work, but that was as it was. They prayed.

He dropped to sit on a rock by the stream. He should pray, but he did not feel God's presence right now. Had not felt Him much of late.

Which no doubt meant he had been stepping down some path God did not wish for him. Out here, though. All creation is His temple, he reminded himself.

It did not help. Instead of feeling the presence of God, he felt the forest close around him. He heard the songs of the birds. Their voices echoed in his ears. Across the stream a fox, on business of his own, paused and lifted a paw, pricking ears towards the human.

"I mean you no harm, Brother Fox," Tuck said.

Not understanding his words, the fox loped off into the woods. He was fleeing without trying to look as if he was, for foxes had their own sense of dignity. Tuck shook his head. He did not see God in the fox. He saw only the fox.

What had happened to his faith? He reached out, but felt only a distant presence. Perhaps it was not his faith, but that God was busy elsewhere. Certainly the Crusaders were making plenty of work for Him. Not the best kind of work, either.

Or perhaps this was one of the old places, where powers other than God held sway. More likely, the fault lay with Tuck himself. A fault that he had to address, if he was to minister to anyone. Even a bunch of outlaws.

The water shimmered for a moment. He held his breath. It was not a fish jumping, but the water's surface itself. Changing, altering, and then back to normal. A sign? Certainly, but was it from God, Satan or somebody else?

Or just a trick of the light.

CLORINDA WAS MAKING ARROWS, sitting at the edge of the camp, as Tuck returned. Her deft hands secured goose fletching to the shafts.

Tuck watched her for a moment. It was not a skill he had ever had the chance or need to learn. Most men knew the bow, but friars and monks and priests were not expected to hunt or fight. More women than many thought. Her bow leaned against the tree near her. A longbow, albeit slightly smaller and lighter than most.

Tuck did not disturb her. He just watched her, her dark head bowed over her task. She was a woman who would have drawn some men to consider their vows.

"She is a temptation, is she not," came a soft voice from behind. Clorinda barely looked up.

This man was a little older than the leader, but not much. As close as he had approached, Tuck could see harp callouses on his hands.

That such a group would have a minstrel with them did not surprise him. He would dare and risk and then return to town, and the truths he told would be mistaken for tales. Or turned into them...exaggerated, linked to one man when they spoke of many.

"Who's woman is she?" Tuck asked, softly.

A blush colored the minstrel's cheeks. "She is mine, at least as much as such a woman belongs to a man."

He had thought Clorinda fought with the leader, but he saw now that he was wrong. He moved further away from her. "A temptation to some men, but not to me, I assure you.." Tuck shrugged.

The minstrel laughed. "Ah. You cannot tell me, though, that you don't have feelings."

"Would the vow be a discipline if I did not?" Tuck noted, heading further into the camp. He did not want to admit he was not tempted, for that had in the past invited questions, and he was not yet comfortable with this man. "I have not caught your name."

"Will."

"They call me Tuck."

"Not your real name."

The friar shrugged. "I prefer to keep the name my parents gave me unspoken, and my nameday Saint is a woman who's name does not lend itself..." He tailed off. He had a cloister name, of course, but he had regretted it within six months of choosing it. Tuck suited him far better.

"Like anyone here uses their real names. Or all of them." The minstrel shrugged. "But Tuck has to have some story behind it."

"A novice story, long told and mostly forgotten." He had had little choice but orders. No food for him, not for the fifth son. Not much for his brothers, either. In other, darker times, they might all have ended up as slaves. His choice was, thus, the orders or attempting to convince a wealthier family to marry him to one of their daughters. He preferred orders.

Will smiled. "But tales are my stock in trade. Come, you should tell me...and if it is exaggerated a little, so much the better."

Tuck laughed. "This evening, and only if you pay me in ale. My own ale, I would hasten to add."

He was still a little bit bitter about how rapidly his stash was vanishing. And what would replace it when it was gone? Bad home-brew? More likely something they stole or traded for, selling risky game to the villagers.

Like he had not eaten venison in a thousand places. As long as they were not caught.

"Yours, eh? Ours now. But then, perhaps you will stay?"

"I haven't decided yet. My feet wish to wander."

Will snorted. "You mean your sorry mule's hooves."

"Nothing sorry about him. He's loyal and reliable, so what if he's not handsome?" An understatement. Tuck was well aware the beast was as ugly as sin. "Besides, I swore a vow of poverty. Of course I had to buy a cheap mule."

"Shanks' Mare would be cheaper," Will pointed out.

"Ah, but I could not carry as much ale that way, and good ale is rare enough that acquiring plenty of it when one can is a good idea." Tuck shrugged. "I never was very good at poverty."

"So, I suspect you had no more choice about entering orders than most. It's small wonder half of you have mistresses."

"I find women less of a temptation than wine." A testing of the waters. Getting no immediate reaction, Tuck glanced at the sky. "But you're right. I had very little choice. Nor money behind me to get a good living." But he had freedom. Vow of obedience or not, he had far more of that than any other man he knew. Other than, perhaps, these outlaws.

"You could have become a minstrel."

Tuck laughed, and then chose to demonstrate the foolishness of that idea by singing a few bars.

Will clapped his hands over his ears. "Enough! Enough! Your point is made!"

"I sing better when drunk."

"You could hardly sing worse!"

Tuck felt the cameraderie between these men begin to expand to include him. He half thought he should fight the sensation. He was a friar, a man who belonged only to god and to no other place or person. He could easily come to belong here, and that would be dangerous. Dangerous to his soul.

He remembered the shimmer on the water. "So, you are all good Christians here?"

"Mostly." Will's response was edgy.

That meant, like as not, they had at least one believer in older superstitions amongst them. Possibly Will himself. The old gods had been pushed away into corners, but they still named the days of the week. People still dressed wells for the Celtic Brigid, claiming she was now a Saint. People still danced the May. People still locked the live-stock in on nights when the Wild Hunt was supposed to ride.

It was a small step from there to actually worshipping and making offerings to those old figures. Here, out in the countryside, it was more likely. It was likely that these people called on herbwives when one was sick or wounded, and if those herbwives made a quick prayer to Lugh or to the Norse goddess Eir, then who was to notice? "I am not somebody who wants to stomp on the old ways with a heavy boot," Tuck said, quietly. "I would rather men came to God in their own time and in their own way."

"And if that way is to call Him by another name?"

Tuck glanced at the sky again. "I will minister to those who let me. Those who would prefer I didn't interfere with their lives...life is too short to turn into one of those."

One of those who seemed to have more and more power. Of course, every time people sought an old fashioned handfasting or a lychgate wedding. Every time they casually forgot to baptize a baby, or simply avoided the two required masses at Christmas and Easter, the church lost money. The church needed money, especially with the crusades. More and more indulgences were being sold, and Tuck was pretty sure there were enough pieces of the True Cross around to build Noah's Ark. Possibly twice over.

"Good," Will said. "Because there are a couple of people here who have been known to invoke Cernunnos in a tight spot. And...well. You'll see."

Thou shalt have no other God before me. It went through his mind, of course, in the Latin. But that did not necessarily mean there were no other Gods. Tuck knew where his loyalty lay. He wasn't a very good friar, but he was still a friar. "As long as nobody asks me to join in such invocations. With the exception of those that have the church's sanction."

"The ones the church knows it can't stop, you mean." Will winked. "So. Tonight, over ale, perhaps you will tell us all your story."

"Get me drunk and I will tell you plenty of tales." He winked back. Not that he needed to be drunk, but the only way he was getting any of his ale back was to talk it out of them. "And perhaps a song?"

"Always."

Having been reminded of his mule, Tuck went to check on the beast. He was tethered with two scruffy forest ponies, the kind that tended to escape and breed on their own. Both had been recently groomed, at least. The mule was still the least attractive beast here. He found a small stash containing a curry comb at the base of one of the trees and liberated it. He was not about to ask anyone else to perform the task of grooming his beast, not right now. It might help him get into that state where he could feel God's presence. The one which kept eluding him.

It bothered him that he could not seem to reach God. Was this place forsaken? He had had that thought before, but felt it more likely to be some failing in himself. God was everywhere. God was even in an ugly mule who tried to nip him when he approached with the curry. "Enough of that, Brownie."

Why bother with a more original name? At his last stop he had been teased, both about the state of the creature and the name. People expected a churchman to ride a fine palfrey and wear silk under his robes.

Brownie resigned himself to being groomed, only shooting Tuck the occasional glare.

"I have a boy could do that for you," came Robin's voice.

"I like to do it myself." Tuck did not turn around, continuing what he was doing. He sensed that the man would likely not be offended.

"Good. You should always check your own equipment."

It had the air of a platitude. "So. Is there anyone here who would join me in divine service?"

"I can ask around. Some will, some..."

"Will warned me."

Robin circled around so he was standing on the far side of the mule, looking at Tuck over its body. "Will you stay, Tuck? We could use you, and I doubt you care any more for the so-called Mother Church than I do."

"For now."

3

They broke camp two days later. Tuck's mule and cart were pressed into service, with two other carts pulled by the shaggy ponies. He walked at the animal's head. It would do him no harm to walk, and there was enough weight on the cart with the tents and supplies.

He wondered if their initial thought in ambushing him had been to steal the mule to replace some beast they had lost.

Perhaps, but now he was with them...for the nonce. If they were caught he could say he had been captured and compelled to say Mass for them. It would be close to the truth. And Robin fell in next to him.

"So," Tuck asked. "What is your story?"

The man walked with his bow unstrung as a staff, apparently not too worried about attack in this part of the forest. "My story?"

"The story as to how you are here, not ensconced in some pleasant house with a pleasant wife."

"A wife." Robin's face shadowed a little. "Aye, I might have had one of those."

Tuck rested a hand on the mule's withers for a moment. "As might I, had my father not all but sold me to the friars. Too many mouths to feed. An unfortunate woman she would have been."

Robin laughed, lightly. Then his face darkened again. "Gisbourne. Gisbourne is my story."

"Guy of Gisbourne. He crusades. I met him in the Holy Land."

"So, you have...have you seen Jerusalem?"

"Yes. And I wish I had not." Tuck frowned. "No, I wish I had not seen how the crusaders act in the Holy Land. They call it Holy and then sack and despoil it."

"Gisbourne sacks and despoils everything he touches. He demanded taxes that were more than we could pay, and when we did not pay, he burned several houses. One of his men raped the woman I was to marry. She killed herself."

In such short terms did Robin give his story. Tuck saw no love for the woman in his eyes, only the sharp, cynical bitterness of a man ill-used. Of course, even a yeoman did not always wed a woman of his own desire. She could well have been the best available, and he bound to her for want of another option.

Or he could simply have been so hurt by it that he had set his love for her aside, tossed it away. "I believe Gisbourne himself raped several Saracen women and then informed them he was doing them a favor, giving them Christian children." Tuck frowned. Gisbourne was not a man he cared to deal with.

"When he comes back, I will find some way to hurt him."

"I can think of a number of ways." Tuck paused. "He spoke several times of a black stallion he is particularly fond of. Given the way I saw him treat his horses, we would be doing it a favor if we stole it."

Robin laughed a bit. "A black stallion, eh? Why is it that people like that always want their fancy colored beasts?"

"Because they think it makes them look like better horsemen. He whips his horse into a frenzy so he can show off his ability to control it." Tuck patted the mule again. "I might be no horseman, but I know that is wrong. Richard, now there is a horseman."

"What is the king like?" Robin seized on the name like a small dog on a rat.

"Very French," Tuck said, shortly. He could see the disappointment in the man's eyes. "If you think Richard would be a better king than

John, then you are setting yourself up for a fall. John at least cares something for England."

"And Richard does not." Robin's tone was flat.

"Richard is not crusading to be in the Holy Land, he is doing it to not be in England. I wish I could bring better news, but it would be a lie."

"So, the good king we are to look forward to...the one I saw in a vision...is not Richard."

A vision? Tuck did not dismiss it. Stranger things had happened. "Perhaps it is Richard's son. Or, more likely, John's. Or perhaps even further in the future."

It struck Tuck as unlikely Richard would leave any legitimate offspring. Most likely the king would die in the Holy Land. He was not one to shirk the front of the fight, after all.

"Richard..."

"I do not envision him ever returning to rule...and those who dream of it, do not know him." Tuck frowned. "Prince John's largest fault, from what I can see, is his grip on his purse strings."

"When people are unable to pay their taxes, you breed outlaws. When you mistake unable for unwilling, you breed even more." Robin glanced at the friar. "Perhaps a grip on the purse strings would not be so bad were it not accompanied by the desire to fill the coffers further."

"How much of that is the prince and how much is men like Gisbourne? And how much of it is the Crusades?"

"I had thought of going myself," Robin mused. "But..."

"I wouldn't recommend it." Tuck glanced at the young man again. "You would only be going from one kind of thievery to another, and a kind less honorable. They do not care who they hurt out there...and not everyone in the Holy Land is a Saracen."

"Truthfully?"

"There are Christians there, and Jews...not so many of the latter, for all that it was their homeland once." Of course, some would argue it was even less of a problem to harm a Jew than a Saracen. Tuck often felt men should be more respectful to Christ's blood kin, but...what men were respectful? Few that he had met, that was for sure.

"I would imagine that there would be Christians there still, but under Saracen rule."

"There are worse fates. The Saracens do not interfere with them." Tuck considered it for a moment. "In a way, they are better men than most here. They are more..." He tailed off. "Tolerant than most in Christendom."

"Still, they should not hold Jerusalem."

"It is sacred also to them. They consider Christ an important teacher."

Robin fell silent. Perhaps Tuck had said too much. Too much of his impressions of the Saracens and of the Holy Land itself. It bordered on if not heresy, then at least an unacceptable belief and attitude.

It was taken as read by all that the Saracens were evil barbarians bent on the utter destruction of Christendom. The truth was far more complicated. There was no need to take Jerusalem back from them...

But the Crusaders would, and it would be the ordinary people of that city who suffered for it. They who died.

They would make Jerusalem a wasteland, and once Tuck realized that he had turned his feet back to the west.

Back to England where, at least, there was no pointless war, no meaningless conflict. Or was there? Perhaps it had been his travels that had caused him to see the lack of perfection. To see the holes in the social fabric.

And now he walked with outlaws.

THEY MADE camp that night in a valley with steep sides. A quite defensible location, Tuck noted. He had, indeed, spent too much time with Crusaders. Once he would not have thought of such things.

He also saw the stream that flowed down through it, crisp and clear. Good water. He stepped around a fairy ring...friar or no, he was not about to risk an encounter with the Good People.

Robin. Robin was a fairy name. The outlaw had no doubt taken it for a reason, to reflect the ability to appear and vanish, to be part of the woods. But a fairy name nonetheless. He wondered if that would anger them.

The Church officially said fairies did not exist. Tuck had spent enough time in the woods not to believe it. He remembered the shimmer on the water. Had that been a sign from God after all? Nobody else stepped in the fairy ring either. It might as well have been formed out of solid stone.

It did not take long to make camp. Tents went up with practiced ease, but from any distance none of them would be visible. Forest greens and browns.

These people knew what they were doing. Tuck checked on his mule, then wandered a distance from camp.

As he did so, he heard footsteps. A broken twig. The passage of somebody no better a woodsman than he himself. Had that betrayed them?

No, he doubted it. But this person was...and then he saw him. A peasant, plain and simple. The dog that limped at his side was undoubtedly lawed. He carried a staff.

No threat, Tuck decided, except that there was a bounty on outlaws, and this was a poor man. After a moment, he came across a course of action.

Exaggerating a weave to his step, he crossed the man's path.

"Good brother!" the man called.

"Good day." He slurred his speech very slightly...attempting to appear ale-sodden. A state he wished he was actually in. They had drunk a lot of his ale...

"Be careful, good brother, there are outlaws in these woods."

"I doubt they would harm a man of the cloth."

"They took all of Abbott Moresford's jewels."

"Which he should not have had." He kept the slight slur to his speech. He wanted to appear drunk, but not so drunk he could not have a conversation. Drunk enough that he would not be able to lie. People forgot how to lie when they got drunk. Exaggerate, yes. Lie, no.

The man looked him up and down. "You have none. And if you had any ale, they won't be taking it now." He laughed a bit. "Just be careful."

"I am not so drunk as to stumble right into their lair...and if there's an outlaw lair, its far from here."

"Or invisible. Or you are too drunk to see it." The man laughed again. "The road is that way, good brother."

Tuck headed the indicated way, almost walking into a tree. Only when he was sure the villager was out of sight did he turn back. Invisible. These outlaws had quite the reputation. But if they had taken Moresford's jewels then he would cheer them on. "Should have taken his mistress, too."

A nearby tree responded. "He didn't have her on him."

He jumped, turned, and realized that he had somehow walked past the huge form of Little John. The Little, of course, being a sarcastic nickname. "Did he have her jewels on him?"

"Not that we could tell. Neat move."

"You won't let me get drunk for real."

"That ale is too good to binge on." John fell in next to him. "You need to be more careful about putting your heel down first," he added.

Tuck nodded. "I'm not a woodsman."

"Yet." The word sounded almost like a threat.

"Uh oh," was Tuck's only response. Turning into one sounded like far too much like hard work.

"Of course, there's a price to pay for any lessons."

"And what would you charge?"

"Your stories of the Holy Land."

"I think I would make that payment to Will. He can make more of them than I could. I lack the minstrel's gift. Or a good singing voice, for that matter."

John laughed, stepping back down into the valley. His long legs covered the ground such that Tuck had to scurry a little to keep up. "I am sure you can sing the services."

"Not very well." He could, any one in orders could, but by values of 'could' that anyone with a sense of pitch would argue with. "I sing better when drunk."

"You just want your ale back."

Tuck felt himself relaxing. The big man was full of banter...he was not the typical quiet that so many of such size were, but much more...truly laid back. No impression of trying to ward and hide his strength, not here. Of course, Tuck had noted the easy manner between him and Robin.

Almost too easy. If he was not sure and certain Robin was not a disguised woman...and certainly no woman would be the size of John...he would have thought them lovers. Perhaps they were anyway. A terrible sin in the eyes of the Church.

He was not going to ask. What he did not know about he would not have to preach against, and really, he was not sure he would bother. It certainly did less harm than robbing merchants...or abbots.

"John. Tuck." Robin approached them, his eyes flicking between the two. Then, softly, "Tuck, I would speak with you."

Tuck nodded. "Privately?"

"Yes."

John bent down and, to Tuck's shock, kissed the smaller man before withdrawing. It was not the kiss of friend or brother, but the kiss of a lover. Tuck blinked. Yes, a terrible sin in the eyes of the Church and one he should speak against, but he found he could not.

Instead, he followed Robin into the woods, to the nearby stream. Maybe he wanted to confess. Maybe he had something else in mind.

He crouched by the stream, glancing across it at the fairy ring. "Do you think they really use those as their gateways to our world?"

"I don't know. I'd rather not risk it."

"I have seen them," Robin said, softly. "And they are not what men think, or what men show in the May plays."

"I would imagine not. You still believe in God."

"I see no conflict between them and God, and I practice no magic." Robin paused for a moment. "But that was not what I wanted to talk about."

No. He had simply wanted to mention it, to gauge Tuck's reaction. Robin himself might not practice magic, but Tuck could definitely envision him visiting a witch.

Not Tuck's problem. Not unless he confessed it and had to be given penance. "What is it you need?"

"I need information. There is a village nearby named Cotman. I am known there...if I walk into the tavern, jaws will lock. They are too afraid of the sheriff and his men to speak to me. However, a somewhat drunken friar..."

Tuck nodded. "You wish me to spy for you?"

"Not spy. I don't want anyone's private secrets. Just the lay of the land."

"I'd need money." He could not go into a tavern and not buy himself ale or food. This was also a test. The perfect opportunity for him to flee these outlaws and move on. Robin wanted to know if he had a new man or just a companion of circumstances.

"You would get it."

"From the sale of the abbot's jewels, no doubt."

Robin laughed. "That set us up for a while. You do not seem to object."

"Chastity, obedience, poverty. I might be bad at poverty myself, but not that bad. And I hear Moresford isn't very good at chastity, either."

"Depends on your definition. I hear he married the woman."

Which was a violation of the vows, but in some ways a lesser one. After all, it was an acceptable vow to remain faithful to one's wife. "So, the lay of the land? Including the travels of any rich men."

"I have to steal to survive. I steal from those who can afford to lose it," Robin commented. "And from the king."

Meaning the venison that was even now cooking over the fire. "Money is of little use in the forest."

"True. I would also appreciate it if, while you are in the village, you would purchase bread and cheese."

Tuck nodded. "That I am more than willing to do. I should probably take the cart."

So he could carry more. So he could make a getaway. He was not even sure in his mind which it was.

Early the next morning, he set out. The cart was empty, but he had a list of things to purchase from the villagers. Bread, cheese, ale. Cloth and thread to mend clothes. If asked, he would say he was buying them for the poor. That it was an act of charity. Nobody would even look twice at that.

The village was not much. A few thatched roofs, a few rather desultory cows. He could see why Robin would not want to steal from these people.

No. He would give them good gold, which they could then spend on that which they could not make themselves. He hitched the mule by the green.

A couple of children were playing a game of tag across it. From their appearance, they seemed to be brothers.

Tuck wondered where they would be in a few years. Apprenticed, perhaps. Got rid of by some means, given some life that might not be to their choosing.

Nobody was free, he thought as he hitched the mule. He had more freedom than most, the vows that might under other circumstances have been a burden and a binding gave him the ability to go where he willed and do what he wished. Within reason.

But he was still not free. Kings were not free, peasants were not free. No man or woman could choose their own path.

It was odd that he even thought of it. Perhaps it was the influence of the outlaws, men who walked their own path and paid the price for it.

Would he go back to them? He would, he realized, because they had treated him well. How long he would stay with them was another matter. Until he felt the urge to move on. Maybe weeks, maybe years.

They, at least, would not invite him along on Crusade, and he a fool. A fool to go. All fools.

He forced his mood back to something more stable, and then looked around. There was no market today, but he saw a housewife making her way along the street, a small child attached to her skirts.

"Goodwife!" he called.

She turned. "Brother, what is it you seek?"

"When is the market?"

"On the morrow." She regarded him with little suspicion. Likely, she could not tell he was a friar, not a monk, and thought he sought supplies for some nearby cloister.

Well, he was not unwilling to let her continue to believe that. "In that case, where is the inn?"

"You have your back to it, good Brother."

He laughed a bit and turned around. He did indeed. The sign was of the three roosters. No writing under it, not in a place like this. "Thank you, goodwife."

He made his way towards the inn. For what it was worth, he would sleep under a roof tonight. If he was lucky, it might even be in a bed. He secured mule and cart and went inside.

The common room was not yet crowded, it being relatively early in the night. For a moment, there was nobody behind the bar, and then a large woman emerged from the back door.

She looked as if she partook too much of her own cooking and her own brew. Tuck had only once seen a small tavern keeper...and then he had sought food and lodging elsewhere. He did not trust a skinny cook.

"And with what can I help you, Brother?"

"Bed and board for one night, plus stabling for a mule."

She nodded, rattling off a price that included stew and half of a room.

He could have asked for common sleeping, but it was not his money. It was Abbott Moresford's money, ultimately, and from what he knew of that man, he had no qualms about spending it. "I'll take it. Could I have the stew now?" he added, sliding the coins across the bar.

"It's not quite ready. But soon. And I can give you ale. Or stout, if you prefer."

"Stout would be good."

She slid a pint across the bar to him. He took a sip. Not the best he had ever tasted, but not bad. Not bad at all. "This is a good place," he mused.

"We tend to think so. Of course, you have seen many places."

"I have just returned from pilgrimage to the Holy Land." That should break the ice. Anyone who heard that would be after him for stories.

"What is it like?"

He mimed mopping his forehead. "Hot. Very hot, very dry. The image we have of Christ's birth in a land covered with snow..." He tailed off.

"It does not snow there?"

"Very, very rarely, or so those who live there claim. Winter nights can get cold, but...that is also from those who live there. I doubt not that they would find our English winters freezing, and those experienced in the Germanies..." Tuck shivered. From what he heard, it got very cold in the central parts of Europe. Britain was a greener land. "But they are closer to the sun."

The sun did, indeed, seem to be closer in the south than it was in the northern lands.

"I wonder how that can be," the barmaid mused. He was, right now, her only customer, and she was taking advantage of the fact to talk.

"God makes it that way. Perhaps to make the world more interesting, by having some parts of it be green forest and other parts stark desert." Perhaps if everything was the same, God would be bored, but he did not say that out loud. "The people are short and dark."

Another incorrect image...the paintings of Christ as a tall man, often blond. Son of God or no, would he not likely resemble those around him? After all, he had lived quietly as a carpenter for years...would he have been able to do that if he stood out visually? "And there are some Moors."

"Is it true that Moors are the color of wood?"

Tuck considered that. "Close. They are very dark. Their lands are even further south and even hotter, perhaps the sun burns them that color, just as it darkens a farmer's skin in the summer."

Just more so. "Their hair is very curly," he added, thoughtfully. "They and the Saracens both use blades that are deeply curved and wear only light armor. The Saracen horses, although quite different from those we have, are extremely fine and very fast. They only ride the mares."

"Somebody once told me he heard from a Crusader that the Saracen sometimes ride these tall, ugly beasts with humps on their backs."

"Camels," Tuck supplied. "They are used as mounts in the deep desert and can go for days with no water and minimal provender. They are also hideous and ill-tempered. If I never come close to one of those beasts again..."

"Did it bite you?"

"No. It spit on me."

The bar wench shuddered a bit. "I can't imagine being spat on by a horse."

"Don't." He took another sip of his stout. "So, I came back, where things are green, where it rains regularly, and where people ride horses."

He wasn't about to reveal to her his real reason for returning so swiftly. That was between him, his conscience and God. Talking to outlaws about it was one thing. Scaring this young woman was quite another.

She would live out her life here, have her children, probably never leave the valley. Who needed to? He would move on...perhaps not as soon as he had originally planned, but he would move on. He envied her.

However, another customer came in. She moved to serve the man, a tanned farmer. More ordinary people. Tuck was sure now that he would learn nothing here to suit Robin's purposes. Well, that was not his problem. The outlaw would have to take what he could give him...and he would give him nothing that might hurt these people.

They were not prosperous, unless one measured it in good stout. Neither seemed underfed, but neither was well dressed, either. Their garb was that of those for whom money was a rare luxury, solid but not fancy. No doubt they managed ribbons for their sweethearts...sometimes.

He settled back and listened to the conversation between barmaid and farmer, but they talked of crops. Of the hard work that made him glad he was not a farmer. That he had not entered one of those orders that survived by raising sheep. Of course, those orders did more than survive. Many had more wethers than they could count and more gold.

Nobody could survive in England, after all, without wool. This farmer, though, was now talking about his pigs and the fact that one of them had slipped the swineherd and vanished into the woods.

Tuck doubted he would be getting it back, but it was information to pass on anyway. Perhaps the farmer would be grateful for its return by some means. Or perhaps not. He might have nothing to pay a reward with.

"Pigs are so stubborn."

"More stubborn than men," Tuck agreed.

The farmer started, as if he had not really registered the friar's presence. "Depends on the men. And not more stubborn than women."

The barmaid made as if to slap him, although it was clearly not aimed to hit. "I'd say it is men who are the stubborn ones, Robert!"

The thus-named Robert laughed. "I'd ask your opinion, Friar, but you have no wife to be stubborn around you."

"I think I'm going to stay out of this." He was often glad he had no wife...he had never been tempted to break chastity, and he had no desire to spend his life bound to another individual for what was in so many cases little more than convenience.

"Smart move. Maybe opting out of the entire thing is not such a bad move."

"Well, if I see your pig, I'll let you know."

"Or his wife," the barmaid said, slyly. "Or do you know where she is?"

Rather than being insulted by the implication, Robert simply laughed again. "At home. A six month old is more than a good enough leash."

At that, Tuck did feel slight envy. Women, he might not care for, but there were times when he regretted the fact that he had to remain childless. Even had he been tempted to break his vows, the life of a wandering friar was not one for wife or child.

Hence, no doubt, why Francis had insisted on celibacy in the first place. He wondered if Clorinda was using some form of birthbane. None of the herbs used for such were fully reliable, but she would obviously not wish or seek offspring.

No, that would be a bad thing for both her and her husband. And most of all for the child.

The barmaid laughed again. "Six moons, is it? I thought it had been longer."

Robert shook his head. "Six. And a healthy boy he is, too."

"You're lucky." Tuck leaned against the bar. "That he is healthy, that is." And lucky to have a boy as the first one, and based off of the farmer's age it likely was. He'd want a second, of course...six months healthy proved nothing. It was rumored the Greeks did not name their children until their first birthday, so they would not get too attached.

Of course, if everything said about the Greeks was true they were an odd people indeed. It was rumored that, while Christian, they still celebrated Passover.

"Oh, I know, and that my Ruth is well too, for all that I sometimes wish to make her not well."

The tone of voice indicated he loved his wife, in any case. "I have yet to meet a husband who did not feel that way. Or a wife. Helpmeets women might be, but I sometimes think God sent them to test us."

Of course, staying apart from them was supposed to be the greater test. Tuck was not entirely sure of that.

"No, God sent men to test *us*," the barmaid supplied.

Tuck could not help it. He laughed.

4

He learned nothing, however. No rumors of wealthy travelers that might be worth robbing. Tuck would not support stealing from these people.

Gisbourne would do that cheerfully come tax time, for Gisbourne was indeed the liege of this place. Now him, Tuck would cheerfully rob blind. Were he not still on crusade.

Their opinion of the man was no better, although their complaints were muted and at least once he heard the conversation change as he approached.

Even getting "drunk" and loudly declaring what an idiot Gisbourne was would probably not help.

A good lord could tolerate his people speaking ill of him and, indeed, invite it to his face. Gisbourne had not so much as shown his face in his holdings for years. Supplies, however, he was able to purchase readily. Bread was the most important. It was hard to live without bread, and impossible to make it in the greenwood. He also bought several casks of the stout...almost as much as the villagers could spare.

No questions were asked. He had a story ready but ended up not needing it. Of information, though, he left empty handed. Or would that be empty eared? That thought carried him out of the village.

The road was quiet, but he did not worry, this time, about robbers. Maybe about somebody jumping him for the fun of it, but outlaw bands tended not to overlap one another.

They tended not to get on. He could not believe, at some levels, he was in this situation. With these men, who lived outside the fabric, tugging at the edges of society.

Most of it was Robin. There was a reason he was a leader so young...a strength of charisma such as Tuck imagined a saint would possess. Not that he was not a long way from being a saint. Charisma alone was not enough. What had he sacrificed? Possibly quite a lot. A woman, he knew that. An inheritance, possibly. Or he might have been an impoverished younger son.

The mule abruptly stopped and planted all four hooves in the road. Horses will balk at their own hooves, shadows and imaginations. Mules did not balk without a reason.

"What's up, Brownie?"

The only answer was a snort. Then, Tuck saw the woman. For a moment. Standing in the middle of the road, clad in a fine gown of blue, her dark hair entwined with jewels. Then she was gone. He would have thought it a hallucination...but Brownie had clearly seen her too.

Her. He crossed himself by reflex. Either he had seen, for a moment, some noble of the fae or... The alternative was even more frightening. The mule began to walk forward again, as if nothing had happened. She was clearly gone.

Tuck realized his hands had turned white and relaxed off on the reins so no tension would communicate to the beast and make him start again. A woman clad in the sea. It could have been, but if so, of what was it a sign?

To turn back, or to go on? He could have taken the supplies and left, but he was bent on returning to the outlaws. Had she shown up to warn him not to?

Somehow, he did not think so. And there remained the possibility that, mule or not, it was his imagination. Novices had visions all the time, or claimed to. Some monks and nuns made a business out of it, spinning their tales. He could have simply imagined or dreamed her.

In truth, he had never encountered any miracles. And he was not sure whether or not he believed in fairies. He had been told over and over again that they were a kind of demon, or something only the superstitious peasantry believed in.

He wanted to believe that had not been what she was. He wanted to believe she had an existence outside of his own mind, but he saw nothing more until he turned the wagon between two trees and came upon the camp. His arrival triggered no changes other than Robin coming out of a tent...with Little John behind him. Both men appeared in mild disarray.

"Anything?"

"They're too scared of Gisbourne. They seemed to think me one of his agents."

Robin frowned. "I was afraid of that."

Tuck hopped down from the cart as one of the young men...little more than a boy...went to the mule's head. He started to open his mouth to mention the vision, then closed it again. He would not have believed himself; how could he possibly expect anyone to believe him? Besides he had yet to puzzle out what it meant. He waved off another of the outlaws and stalked to the edge of camp, pulling his cloak around himself. It was cold enough to need one, that was for sure, and poverty did not have to mean freezing to death.

When had it got so cold? When the sun had dipped below the horizon. The forest was darkening into night. He heard a toowhit and then a little later a toowhoo, a pair of owls keeping touch in the dusky sky. Beasts living their simple lives. He doubted the owls knew or cared about the affairs of men.

He thought about the fact that there were two common kinds of owl. The ones that gave those calls and the white and gold ones that haunted churchyards and convinced the weak minded they were ghosts.

They were only owls. He forced himself to focus on the woman. Three possibilities. One, his own pure imagination. Novices commonly had visions of women, even when given monkswort to tame their adolescent libido. Tuck had never experienced that, nor visions of men.

On the other hand, most men, even the sworn celibates, had such dreams on occasion. He had no doubt that women did as well, if no woman would ever admit to it. Some thought those dreams came from demons...incubi and succubi...to tempt people into indiscretion. He thought they were just...dreams. Not to be sought out or appreciated or enjoyed, no. But just dreams, not from the devil.

What if the woman, though, had been from the Devil? Or even from the old gods, if they had ever existed? The common church wisdom was that they did not exist.

The common wisdom of the people was that they existed but had been essentially defeated by the true God. That they were now but shadows, in the corners.

It was possible, he thought, that they were both wrong. He had studied the Latin. The Saracens did indeed claim there was only one God. The same God he served, although they called Him something a little different. They were not the heathens most claimed, not if one actually listened to them. They simply did not accept Christ was the Messiah. Like the Jews, albeit different. They followed the teachings of a prophet, a man of God who claimed to be speaking his word.

The Bible did not explicitly state there was only one God, only that one should only worship one God. He had never voiced his thoughts on that matter.

There was the other possibility for who the woman clad in the blue of the sea had been.

Mary.

THE NEXT DAY, several of the band left to hunt. Robin was among them, as was the lovely Clorinda. Avoiding the bitter old man, Richard, Tuck sat at the edge of camp. He would be useless on a hunt and he at least knew it. Even if he were a better woodsman, he would still be a lousy shot. That skill he had attempted to improve on enough occasions to know he was on the edge of being a hopeless case.

Well, it was not his fault. Some people were simply better at things than others. He was good at talking and listening and good with beasts. Those were far more important to a friar than being a good shot. He could always trade the talking for food and ale. It had worked many times...more now that he had tales of the Holy Land.

Somebody came up behind him. "So, Brother, you remain."

The old man.

"You don't trust me."

"I trust you more than I did." He lowered his creaking form to sit next to the friar. "Still. You are a churchman."

"What did the Church ever do to you?"

"What have they not done, at some point, to somebody? Annulled a loving marriage and ruled the offspring bastards. Or perhaps taken a man's land and livelihood to add it to the holdings of a monastery."

From the first of the sentences, the Friar divined the man's personal problem. "I am but a friar," he said, spreading his hands. "I have no control over the actions of the Church."

"And the one who does, no doubt, has a mistress and satins."

There was no word on whether the Pope had a mistress or not, but Tuck would be surprised if he did not. "You're probably right. But there's nothing we, here, can do about it."

Tuck could, himself, set a good example, but... He added, "And I admit, I'm a poor figure of a man of God myself."

"No, you are a very good figure of one, which I suppose is what you refer to."

The reference to his bulk did not go over his head. Rather than allowing himself to get upset, he chose to laugh it off. "Even on poor provender, I will never be as skinny as Robin. I think I would starve before actually losing weight."

The old man actually laughed. "I knew somebody like that, except far more unfortunate. A fat man, at worst, is called a glutton. A fat woman..."

Tuck found himself relaxing. Turning it into banter had worked. "So, that is why you are out here. To strike against the Church? Not, I would hope, against God."

"I have little interest in a God who would have followers such as that," the man said, bitterly.

Had he found one of those few, elusive, followers of the old ways? Or simply a man who hated God. There were more of the latter than the Church would like, and even amongst the laity it was common belief that such consigned themselves to Hell. But it was easy to hate the Church. Easy, therefore, to hate God.

"God gives us free will. That includes the freedom to make fools of ourselves. I have no doubt but that He is highly embarrassed by the actions of some of those who claim to be his men." Tuck had had that thought before.

"Maybe. I am skeptical. When the bad outnumber the good... But you. Why are you out here?"

"I have nowhere better to go."

Richard laughed again. "Aye, I suppose not, as your Order has no permanent cloister."

"We have some buildings, but they are used only for the instruction of novices." He remembered those days for a moment.

"And I doubt you had any choice about becoming one."

"It was novice or seeking a bride. Novice appealed more at the time." Had he regretted it? Occasionally. But what he regretted more was not having had the money to apprentice a guild. "Perhaps a huge part of the Church's problem, though, is that so many don't have the choice." How could somebody be devout when the Church had been chosen for them?

The common wisdom, of course, was that you were doing your son or daughter a great favor by dedicating them to God, much as Samuel had been bound to the temple. The offering of the first born, that. A sacrifice...letting one's heir become a priest.

"You're probably right. But then, who the heck would choose to be a monk?"

"You might be surprised there. I have known some who are genuinely devout. But they're outnumbered by the unwanted younger sons and ugly daughters." Most of the nuns Tuck had encountered had been rather unattractive.

"I'm sure Christ appreciates his brides being ugly."

The man riffed off of one of the common euphemisms for a nun. "Well, they are women." Women never had much choice, with a few rare exceptions. Some women managed to be independent within guilded professions, especially brewing, and some kept stores or taverns. "If they can't attract a man, what choices do they have?"

The old man snorted a bit. "More than I think they think."

"Not if they don't want to play the man." Tuck tailed off. He wondered, for a moment, if the world couldn't use more women like Clorinda. But then, women had their special duty, the one men could neither understand nor share.

"We all have more choices than we think." He walked away, leaning on his cane.

Tuck shook his head. The man was either an idealist or a fool. He knew of no men who had actually truly chosen their path. He thought of Lionheart, chained to a throne he did not wish and leading men to die in the Holy Land just to avoid it. He thought of the villagers, who seemed happy, but no doubt only because having a choice would not occur to them.

Most people did not think that way. They accepted who they were, married a suitable man or woman, followed their profession and bred children. It was not wise to seek more than that, except through the vehicle of the church. And the church demanded much sacrifice.

Maybe that was the real reason the Crusades were so attractive. They broke the pattern. They opened a place for people who did not fit in. Of course, they would all likely end up dead. One day their tattered remnants would return to England, leaving the Holy Land to the Saracens and the vultures. Tuck was sure of that.

The Holy Land had a lot of vultures. Most of them were human.

5

*T*uck had not yet had reason to mention his vision of the woman to anyone. They moved camp again, and he dismissed the incident as his own overactive imagination.

He had begun to learn the rhythms of the place. He learned who appreciated his services and who would prefer to avoid him. Clorinda and the old man were both Old Way. In the case of the latter at least it was probably why he was an outlaw. In the case of the former, it was likely she had seen this as her only escape from marriage to a man she did not care for and many children she would not have been allowed to raise in her beliefs.

The church had eclipsed their path, and it was a weed now, growing in the corners where the gardener did not check so often. Given what he had heard about some of the habits of the Druids, if true, it was probably a good thing.

Still, he gave the two his respect. They were, as far as he was determined, harmless. And Robin, the leader, was quite devout.

So he was not entirely surprised to come across the man on one knee, praying. He stopped, a distance back, simply watching.

Robin was incredible, Tuck thought. If he did not become a legend, it would not be for want of deserving deeds. Likely he would be one of those men who accumulated stories rightly attached to others. Such was his charisma.

He should have been born a king. Yet, Tuck could hear the words of his prayers and the hair on his neck began to rise.

"Mother of God. Hear me, Star of the Sea, and grant my prayer."

He was praying to Mary, but not in terms of Mary as intercessor. As he stopped, he stood, and then he turned.

The two were face to face. And Robin had turned...pale.

Tuck knew why. Robin was a heretic. He was invoking Mary as an entity capable of granting prayers in her own right. As a goddess. And now he had been heard to do so by somebody who, whilst perhaps loyal to him, was yet a representative of the church.

Tuck wanted to ask him why. He wanted to ask him, too, if this was why the man was an outlaw. Heresy was serious, albeit often ignored if one was merely a yeoman and not too loud about it.

"Tuck..."

"I didn't hear anything," Tuck said, after a moment. He would let God judge Robin, not man. If only more would do the same.

A weak smile came to Robin's face. He knew full well the friar had heard. "Thank you."

Then, very softly, "I think I saw her. On the road. I am not sure." A woman clad in the sea. It was possible. Even without believing the heresy, she was the special one, the mother of God's son. The archetype of true, uncomplaining womanhood.

He tried to imagine Clorinda not complaining with a gaggle of children attached to her skirts.

"Not sure?"

"It could have been my imagination. I thought it was. But I saw a dark haired woman, in blue. It occurred to me, too, that she could have been fae."

Robin paused. "These woods are close to Faerie. It's perhaps more likely. I have seen them, and I have heard the Hunt ride."

The hair on Tuck's neck rose again. The Wild Hunt, not a superstition he wanted to believe in. "I thought the Hunt went after those out of doors."

"It did not bother us. After other prey, I suppose."

Some tried to bring the Hunt into the auspices of the church by claiming it was the Devil who rode that night. Not the fae. Or, as some claimed, an old god, be it Celtic Cernunnos or Norse Odin. But Tuck could not help but shiver. Even if he did not rationally believe in it, there was something visceral about the possibility of its existence. Something worth being afraid of. He told himself *Robin* had an overactive imagination and forced himself to dismiss the possibility. He had enough to worry about without adding phantoms to the mix. "But I am not sure. Like I said, I might have imagined her."

"She has always watched over me. I know what you think..."

"Like I said. I didn't hear anything." Of course, he suspected most in the band knew. But he would not let it pass his lips.

Robin glanced around. "We are safe here. And you don't judge me." He seemed almost surprised.

"It's not my job. It's God's job to judge people."

"What about hearing confession?"

"If people confessed directly to God, they would not be shriven." He paused. "Or maybe they would just not *feel* shriven. God is not responding to their words, or they are not ready to hear his response. One or the other."

Softly. "Will you hear mine?"

A couple of hours later, Robin vanished into the woods. Tuck was the one slightly troubled. The thought he had voiced about confession was vaguely heretical in and of itself. The idea that confession was for the benefit of the person, not God, implied that priests did not have the special status they were granted.

But what if it was true? Did God really need a priest to hear people confess for him? After all, He was omniscient.

Tuck did not doubt that fact. Sometimes he doubted whether he should worship God or serve Him, but he never had doubts about His nature.

Yet, at the same time, he did doubt whether He was the only God in existence. He sat down on a stump and prayed.

For once, it went well. The woods seemed very close around him, but that was not a bad thing. God's creation was a better temple than any cathedral. He wondered what Joseph of Arimathea must have felt when he found these green shores and planted his staff at Glastonbury. He'd seen the thorn. He'd seen thorns that looked very like it along the edges of streams in the desert. Until then he had thought the legend might be a picturesque story.

Now he actually believed it. Those particular trees could be propagated by cutting. Somebody might well have brought a cutting here, to bring a little of their own land with them.

But he was not sure why they would wish a reminder of that dry desert. Then he thought more. Because it was home to them and they loved it. Just as he loved the greenwood, and preferred it to any city built by man.

That was why he stayed, he realized. It was an excuse to be out here, where the only sounds were of birds and water. Where human voices were rare and far between. Where, for that matter, human smells were. The village had not even had a bath house, as it was said once every village did.

No amount of perfume could fully disguise the stench of a body that had not been bathed in months, if not years. At least out here there were fewer bodies and more space. He stood up, heading back to the camp.

There had to be some ale around here somewhere.

"So, then he fell right off the back of the thing and landed on his back in the sand. We thought he'd broken something."

"So, they're as tall as horses?"

"Taller," Tuck supplied. "They kneel down for you to mount...and then lurch upwards. Which is why the knight fell off."

"I have sympathy. Horses are hard enough to sit on. Why do they use those things?"

"Because they can go for a week without a sip of water. They're used by the tribes of the deep desert, where oases can be that far apart. You can't carry enough water for a bunch of horses. Hard enough to carry enough for the humans. But they are the ugliest creatures in both body and mind." Tuck reached for his mug of ale and found it empty. When did that happen?

"I'm glad I don't live in the desert," Clorinda murmured.

"You should be. The Bedouin...as they call themselves...treat their woman as precious, fragile treasures."

"In other words, they never let them do anything."

"They believe God made man naturally superior to woman. Women are not even allowed to ride...they stay in the oases and walk if they must travel." Tuck shook his head a little.

"Then they're idiots. Worse idiots than most." Clorinda reached for an arrow and started to sharpen it, making her point in a rather literal manner.

Will laughed. "Well, most men are afraid that if they let their women out of their sight..."

"Who else is there? I'm certainly not going to leave you for the Friar here!" She laughed, setting the arrow down.

Tuck laughed with her. "I wouldn't let you, anyway." He hesitated. "I never had much interest in women."

Now it was Will's turn to laugh. "The only one I'd worry about losing her to is Robin. Don't deny it, Clorinda, I've seen you look at him."

"Well, his heart is held by others. I'm not going to try and compete with either of them."

"His...devotion." Was Robin, in some odd way, in love with the Virgin or the idea of her? He knew some men who felt that way.

"And his lover," Clorinda added, flickering a mischievous grin to Will.

"That I don't want to know about."

Will laughed. "You've *seen* them together, Friar. I know you aren't blind."

He thought of the two men coming out of the tent, and of other things he had seen the edges of, and nodded. He was trying his best to be okay with it, but he didn't really want to think about it. At least he had never experienced *that* urge. It was getting harder to judge, though.

"Most men don't. I've always wondered if they aren't afraid they might like it." Clorinda's tone was amused as she placed, firmly, the final piece to confirm his suspicions.

And he sure as heck knew stuff went on between the novices. Monkswort helped most of them, but not all. Some, he suspected, simply should not be there. Some men could not handle celibacy and should be married.

And some men... He tailed off. "I have absolutely no interest in finding out. Besides. Vow of celibacy."

"And obedience. What happened to obedience?" she teased. "I don't see you following the dictates of the church."

He laughed. "I follow the dictates of my order, not the church as a whole. Hence why I'm out here wandering the streets barefoot."

"In a mule cart."

"It helps me perform acts of charity. Like donating all of my ale..." Not that he was really still sore about that. But it gave him ammunition.

He was coming to like Clorinda. He had not thought it would be possible to work with a woman as an equal, but with this one? He could manage it. She was no frail flower who needed protecting, but one of the best hunters in the band.

Will clearly saw much in her that Tuck could not. Did that make it easier or harder?

"I only drank one mug of it!" Clorinda protested, cutting into his thoughts.

"What, was it that bad?" Whatever she said, he was not about to let her win the conversation, even if there was no prize. It made him feel more part of the group, more...involved with everything that was going on.

"No. John grabbed the rest of the keg before I could and drank the entire thing."

Tuck laughed. He could easily see John draining a small traveling keg as if it was a mug. The man was a walking tree. And dangerous with a staff. Far more dangerous than Tuck himself. Yet, Tuck felt perfectly safe with him.

He was surrounded by sinners and heretics...and he had never been happier in his life.

6

_A_bbot Moresford was on the road in style. Tuck was pretty sure, from his vantage point, that the swaying carriage contained the Abbot's wife or mistress. Whichever she was. It did not matter...his vows forbade him either.

On the other hand, he had been the younger son of some lord and used to style, when he had been forced into the cloister. Tuck could not bring himself to judge him too harshly.

He did not entirely forgive him. Not when he saw the fine pair of matched bays drawing the carriage. The fine blacks ridden by the outriders. It seemed the Abbott was in the carriage with his woman right now, his own horse being led by an outrider. It was not a small horse, and not quite as fine as the blacks. Perhaps a personal favorite?

Robin, nearby, hissed, "I say we take the horse."

He had perhaps come to the same conclusion. And it was a fine animal, but somewhat nondescript. It would be easy to sell on.

They had run out of gold from the _last_ time they had robbed the Abbot. Tuck had no intention of actually participating in the ambush. He intended to watch. To learn, perhaps.

To see if Robin kept his word and left the Abbot and his woman alive. If he did not, then Tuck was gone. Or he would try to leave, anyway.

They had tested their trust of him. He could leave at his leisure, for they assumed that he would stay. He was not sure Robin had not, in fact, accepted that the friar might not. That he might leave at any time, head off into the forest.

He thought Robin understood the kind of man who became a friar better than some of the others. That little choice he had had.

He might have lived in a cell in Moresford's cloister.

The arrows that hailed across the road did not hit either the driver or the outriders. Not this time. Them, Robin had not promised to leave alive, but he was apparently in no hurry to kill them.

Tuck felt himself relax. He had his staff, just in case, both hands closed around it. A quarterstaff was the weapon of the lower classes. Of those who did not have the leisure to devote to learning the sword.

The outriders had swords. The driver, though, seemed to be unarmed. He made the best decision, however, shaking the reins to try and send the horses into a gallop. That was what one learned to do if ambushed.

To run for it. Sense, not cowardice.

Then both horses stopped and threw up their heads. They danced to the side, not at all willing to plunge into the barrier of brush and bramble that had been placed across the road.

Good. Tuck would have hated to see such fine beasts lamed...and they might have been, had they gone onwards.

Two men stepped from either side of the barrier.

The driver looked frightened, but the outriders were urging their trained mounts forward, their swords unsheathed.

Both men had staffs. One of them was John, who seemed almost tall enough to go eye to eye with the rider on the smallest horse.

An illusion of perspective, surely. He was not quite that huge. Quite. The other was Alan, a man not much smaller and as blonde as the sun.

"We'll be taking your gold and your jewels," came a voice. "And I think that good riding horse, too. Might take your woman."

Robin's voice. Tuck thought he had been next to him, but the voice came from further up, closer to the barrier. Try as he might, he could not see the outlaw.

A shriek came from inside the carriage, definitely the woman. Tuck knew if Robin did take her, it would be to demand more gold from Moresford not to harm her. The only woman Robin would harm would be one stupid enough to fight...and then he would be almost as likely to recruit her.

Tuck held his breath.

"On second thought, she doesn't sound worth the taking."

The two outriders surged forward. Tuck did not see much of the fight, for it happened far too quickly. At the end of it two swords and one rider were on the ground, one horse running back the way they had come. Alan had a shallow wound along one arm. It dripped blood, but he did not seem overly bothered by it. The second rider was too busy trying to control his mount to fight on.

Horses, even trained ones, still tended to try and escape battle. Except for bred warhorses, who would engage in it even when asked not to.

Tuck held his position. He was still just watching. They did not need his inexpert help, that much was clear. Robin was moving to untie the riding horse from the wagon. It was not being very cooperative, shaking its head and snorting.

Two more were 'helping' Moresford out of the carriage. He stood there, shaking a little. Not quite an autumn leaf, but certainly not a solid man, either. For all of his bulk.

Tuck had seen him before, but in his own turf. In his own church, going through the motions of the mass. It felt like that now.

Going through the motions. Of course, Tuck went through the motions for a lot of his life. But then, he did not have a flock to worry about. Rarely did he have the charge of any soul other than his own.

His own, he cared about, but he did not think he had ever committed a mortal sin. Maybe the occasional edge of gluttony.

Not like this man, now being stripped of his jewels. Clorinda had pulled the mistress out of the carriage too. She was taking her rings. One of them she slipped onto her own finger. It hardly seemed worth it.

It hardly seemed likely it would fit and she did not intend to keep it, surely. Perhaps a token, a demonstration of exactly how she felt about the matter. A demonstration of power, Tuck decided.

When they let them go, they had the horse and the jewelry, but no gold. Apparently, the Abbot had learned better about moving his treasury. They moved off through the trees quietly, the horse's hooves muffled.

"We'll get a good price for this beast, and probably be doing him a favor too," Robin murmured once they were clear of the road.

The horse did not seem particularly concerned about any change in his fortunes. He merely walked behind the man leading him, his head down a little. He honestly looked more bored than anything else.

Tuck sometimes envied horses. It seemed to him as if they were most fortunate creatures, not in any way, shape or form required to think. They did not know of tomorrow or yesterday. Of course, that made it all the more cruel to ill-treat them, for they could neither remember better nor hope.

Such was the common wisdom. He personally thought they remembered very well. A horse might bite an abuser months later or prick his ears towards somebody known to bring apples, even if he had not seen them for a year. They remembered.

Still, they were horses. They did not worry about the state of their souls, for they had no souls. Some vital, animating force, certainly, but it was not a soul. Perhaps that force returned to the earth when they died.

He almost tripped over a root.

"Woolgathering, Brother?" Clorinda, turning the abbott's wife's ring around on her finger. It was at least a size too large.

"Guilty as charged. I was envying the horse and his lack of concern for anything in this world beyond his next mouthful of hay or grass."

"There's no sense being concerned about anything else. Why worry?"

"Because..." He paused for a moment. "Men should have larger concerns."

"But I'm not a man," she teased impishly before darting ahead in the line to fall in next to Will.

He shook his head. She was far too childlike at times. But not simple. Perhaps that was her secret, after all. Her secret was that she did not allow herself to worry about anything. She might even have a point.

Worrying was, after all, not the smartest course of action for any man or woman. It could age one. Yet, Tuck found he could not often stop himself from doing it. Stupid, and he knew it was stupid, but what else could he do?

He was supposed to be a friar and he had days when he was not sure God existed. Or worse, not sure God cared. Clorinda seemed far more carefree. Clorinda, whom he knew prayed to older gods. To false gods.

What did that say about him? Nothing good, he decided. He glanced up at the forest canopy. God was in the trees, he knew that. Maybe God was in the horse. Maybe it was only humans who were thus separated from him. Separated by knowledge and by sin.

It was the tree of knowledge that had condemned Adam and Eve, he reminded himself. If you did not know what was good and what was evil, then you would not worry about it. You would exist in a state of innocence. Like the horse.

They picketed it next to his mule, removing its saddle. The marks of saddle sores were made visible. Robin frowned, disappearing in search of some physick.

The abbott could afford jewels, Tuck thought, but not a saddle that fit his horse? Maybe he did not care. He could afford another horse, after all. He went over to his mule. "I promise I'll never put ill-fitting gear on you."

Brownie snorted at him, exhibiting a distinctly low opinion of the promises of humans. Being a mule, he had an opinion on everything, and none of his opinions were good. Despite that, though, he appreciated the rough affection the animal gave him. It felt like the mule didn't like him, but didn't like him *less* than he didn't like others, and that might as well be friendship.

He scratched him at the base of his shorn mane before heading to find some ale.

WINTER WAS APPROACHING. Winter in the greenwood would be unpleasant. For the first time in a good while, Tuck questioned whether he should stay.

Nobody would suspect him of having been involved with outlaws...and he could even say, quite truthfully, that they had coerced him.

Besides, a priest had a certain obligation when it came to things like last rites. One did not turn a person down, even if they were a criminal. It was a basic right, and he, for one, would not deny it to anyone.

Yet, he had chosen to stay this long. Cold rain fell down on him...which had started with him a good way away from camp.

His own stupid fault for not watching the sky, he chided. Mud had caught under his sandals.

Ah, yes, there was the road. If he could get on the road, he would be wetter, but less likely to get caught in some kind of unpleasantness. Like, say, the deep mud hole he had just barely avoided. At least this was not the moors, where the mud holes could be deep enough to drown a man.

They said the only safe way to cross Dartmoor was riding a pony bred on the moor, because they could smell the quick bogs and avoid them. He had never even tried to cross Dartmoor. There was nothing there except ponies and sheep.

Yes. There was the road. An old road, built by the almost legendary Romans. Supposedly, they had known ways to build a road now forgotten. He had seen Rome, where their ruins dominated the skyline. Especially the great theater where, the stories had it, men had fought to the death for the entertainment of others.

At least these days people only had roosters do that. The sky was starting to clear.

Then he saw the riders. Four of them, on quality horses. All men, of course. The horses were not quite war horses, not quite palfreys. The kind of light mounts, almost, favored by the Saracen. Who had ridden rings around the knights on their chargers.

Quite a few of the Crusaders were making plans to bring some of these animals back with them. They were willing, even, to give gold to the infidel for them. These horses, however, were stockier than that. Garrons. That was the word.

"What ho, Brother? You look as if the rain does not like you much."

Tuck laughed to the rider. "I should have watched the skies." He was quite willing to mock himself for his own folly. "You look no better," he added.

The rain had darkened the horses' coats and soaked the riders. He wondered where they were going.

Then again, he was far from the only man to have ever failed to check the skies properly. Or, perhaps, they did not wish to delay several hours for the rain. On a long trip, that could easily translate to an extra day.

"God seems determined to ensure we end the day damp," the rider admitted. "We hear there are outlaws in these woods."

"Not my concern." Tuck showed one hand empty...the other was curled around his staff. "I have nothing worth stealing."

"No, not much point robbing a friar. Unless, of course, you have gold hidden in the seams of your robes."

Tuck laughed. "I have a few coppers, and they could have those. Far from worth my life." So, they were hunting the outlaws? Or just expressing a genuine concern for his wellbeing.

His eyes drifted over them. They did not have anything worth stealing either, as far as he could tell, other than the horses and maybe their weapons. Traveling light and fast. Perhaps they were returning Crusaders, attempting to get home before they got too wet.

"Well, they won't be here much longer, at any case. You're lucky you're a friar...we're supposed to be pulling in any vagrants."

But they would not suspect...or touch...a man of the cloth. Relief flowed through him. He had never directly done anything. Robin had not, yet, asked him to fight for him. Only to watch and remember, and say Mass for those who cared for it.

"Well, I am a friar," he said, cheerfully. Of course, some of the vagrants would put on brown robes. If they were found out, they would be whipped or worse, but... "And I haven't seen any outlaws or any vagrants. They're probably all hiding from the rain."

The rider laughed again. "Like anyone with any sense. I think I'm going to head for shelter myself."

They rode on past Tuck. He shook his head. At least he knew they were out there, however. He could warn Robin. That mattered a lot, being able to give that warning. He kept moving along the road, however, determined not to leave it until he was sure the riders were out of sight. He could not risk being seen acting in a way they might consider suspicious.

Suspicious, ha. He still did not think of himself as an outlaw. He was a friar, and friars could get away with things normal men could not.

They were long gone and he ducked back off the road, following a deer path he knew would lead him to those he was starting to think of as his people.

7

"Four riders, you say?" Robin inquired. Nearby, Little John was fletching arrows with surprising dexterity, given the size of his hands.

Everyone in the band could fletch. Tuck was even starting to pick up the skill himself. The best feathers, of course, came from geese. Not always easy to find in the greenwood.

Clorinda had left earlier that day to acquire more. He was not going to ask how. The fact that she had not returned yet was no cause for concern. She had probably waited out the rain. "Four riders, on good garrons, armed."

"Not good," Robin mused. "They have the sense not to try and use full size war horses in the Greenwood."

Tuck laughed a bit, having seen what happened when knights tried that. It was one reason some sought to bring back Saracen horses. The other being their incredible endurance.

"It is not funny. We may have to move on to avoid this hunt...and I was hoping to winter here."

Tuck nodded. "What was funny was the image of a knight on a charger trying to get through here. Not them." He had often thought it was best to laugh at one's enemies. That it weakened their power.

He was not going to push, though. If Robin was worried, then there was reason to worry. He was not a man to do so often.

"Tuck. Could you please pass this all on to Will?" He vanished through the trees, presumably to tell others.

Tuck found Will hanging strips of venison for drying. Jerky was one of those essentials for this life, something without which they would be struggling to survive.

"We have trouble."

Will nodded, pointing to a stack of the strips. Trying not to roll his eyes, Tuck moved to help him. Surprisingly, though, hanging out with the outlaws had caused him to do the one thing he had thought impossible short of a starvation diet. Lose weight.

Not much weight, but there it was. They would not let a set of hands stay idle.

"What kind of trouble?" Will asked.

"Four armed riders, good garrons, they warned me about the outlaws and said they were going to get rid of all of them."

"If there's only four..."

"I am sure they are not so stupid as to think they can clean out the Greenwood with four riders. No, they're advance scouts for a much larger force. Robin thinks we may have to move on."

Will nodded. "Well. We've handled people hunting us before."

"Robin seemed worried." Tuck secured several pieces of venison to the rack. "If he's worried...."

"Then he knows something, likely. Put something together from what you said. Could it be Gisbourne back?"

"Gisbourne seemed determined to be Lord of Somewhere In the Desert. If he's back, I'd be surprised." Gisbourne cared little for his holdings except for expanding them. Of course, Richard had promised land in the Holy Land mostly to younger sons. Gisbourne would find a way to earn his share. Somehow.

"Doesn't mean he's not back. Perhaps not for long, though."

Perhaps Richard was back. Would that be a bad thing? Likely it would change nothing. "I still doubt it."

"Gisbourne would not stop until we were all dead. He would not stop, too, until the yeomen were so afraid that they would not breathe without permission."

Tuck thought that an accurate assessment. "I keep hoping to hear he caught a Saracen arrow."

"Not a very Christian sentiment."

"He's not a very Christian man."

Will laughed. "Well, if it is Gisbourne, we'll rob him blind, send his men on a wild goose chase and make him decide the Saracens are easier to deal with."

Remembering Robin's worried eyes, Tuck found it hard to share Will's sentiment. If the leader was concerned, then the men should also be concerned. "I hope so."

Will set another piece of jerky on the rack. "I know so."

"Where is Clorinda, by the way?"

"Still out foraging."

For some reason, Tuck felt a wave of concern. A certainty that something was wrong. "Well. I passed on the message."

He knew he should not look for her on his own, but he also knew that few men would follow another based off of a hunch. Even if that hunch was getting stronger with each moment. It pulled at him, it niggled at him. It was starting to rise towards a sort of inner scream. If something was going on shouldn't Will, who shared her bed, feel it?

It was a hunch. It was his overactive imagination yet again. Said imagination never could or would shut up. As he left, he thought he saw blue behind the trees. Had it been the Virgin or somebody else? Something else? Part of him still suspected the fae. This was their country, after all, only grudgingly shared with man. Only the fact that most now carried cold iron kept them at bay. He thought he saw a sparkle in the air, a shimmer.

"Where is she?" he asked, out loud.

No response other than a growing sense that Clorinda was in trouble. She was the one who would be in the worst situation if caught. The others would merely be hanged. She would likely be burned as a witch.

Which he was not entirely sure she was not, and he was not entirely sure he cared. True, the word of the Lord was 'thou shalt not suffer a witch to live', but if he was going to tolerate outlawry? It was between her and God, whether she acknowledged him. Whether she acted like a normal woman or, yes, a witch.

It was not his place to judge her and certainly not his place to kill her. The greenwood seemed dull right now, autumn clouds rolling in again. More rain threatening the skies. Well, if he got a bit wet, it would be worth it.

This was the way she had gone. He was learning to track, and Clorinda's feet were smaller than anyone else's. Smaller even than Robin's, and he was not at all a large man. At one point another trail crossed them, and he almost lost it. Then he found it again, on the far side of a small stream. A squirrel scolded him from some branch overhead as he passed.

"What did I ever do to you?" he asked it, cheerfully.

Then he saw it. Signs of a struggle. An arrow, one of Clorinda's...she used distinctive fletching...on the ground. Her bow, the string broken, cast to one side.

Clorinda had been taken.

It was a council of war that met under the great oak tree. Will leaned against it. He did not appear inconsolable, but rather wore the set face of a man bent on revenge.

Tuck would have to talk to him. Revenge was all very well, but he could do Clorinda no good if he got himself killed.

That they would take her for a witch was highly likely. In some quarters, 'witch' was another word for 'woman who doesn't know her place'. Clorinda had made her own place. That meant they had to find her quickly. They would bother with a trial, but it would be brief and a foregone conclusion.

They had days before they would be retrieving a body. Less if they decided to put her to the ordeal...where the innocent drowned and the guilty were hanged.

More if they decided to use her as bait. "They might use her to lead us into a trap," Tuck voiced.

"They might. But I don't leave any of my men in prison." This was Robin much as he had been when Tuck first saw him, all of his light heart faded. That time, he had been obliged to give mercy to a dying comrade. This time...he had a rescue to plan. The same focus.

The same almost frightening intensity. Even John was staying back from him right now.

"I'm not saying you should. Just..." Tuck tailed off. He could not bear the idea of Clorinda dying, possibly a highly unpleasant death. By many standards, she *was* a witch. She was also his friend.

Could the blue lady help them, whoever she was? Perhaps she already had. It might have been a lot longer before they realized Clorinda was gone.

Even now two of the best trackers were following the trail from the place. They had to be sure.

They did not have time to chase any wild geese.

Will, finally, spoke. "It's my duty to go after her."

"You're compromised," Robin said, softly. "If you do it, you won't think straight and I'll have to rescue both of you."

It was harsh, but likely accurate. Will loved her, which made him the last person who should go. "I'll go," Tuck found himself saying. "If nothing else, I can get in to give her last rites...and if all else fails."

If all else failed, he could at least ensure she did not face the gallows.

"Two brothers might be better for that," Robin mused.

"If somebody is willing to have a bald spot for a while." It took a long time for a tonsure to grow out...which was why it was done. So a monk or friar was well and truly marked, in a way that did no harm to him.

"I'll do it myself." Robin flickered a weak grin. "After all..."

Robin rarely let anyone outside the band see him without his hood up. He could easily hide the cut for the few months it would take to fully disappear, and he was young enough to be sure it would grow back.

Tuck nodded. "I'll coach you. How's your Latin?"

"Lousy. You'll have to do most of the talking."

The next day, they set out. None of Tuck's habits would fit Robin, of course, but they had a couple. Stolen, presumably, from the laundry of an abbey somewhere, for just this kind of need.

Without prompting, though, Tuck was not sure Robin could have pulled off being a friar.

"So," he said, on the road.

"Let me do the talking. Don't be offended if I tell them you have no talent for languages." That was the best way to explain a friar with poor Latin. Tuck's was not that great. Unlike a parish priest, he did not use it all the time, or had not before joining the outlaws. But it was better than Robin's.

Robin nodded. "And?"

"Keep your head down. Don't meet worthies in the eye. You'll look either scared or humble...or both. Either way, not a threat. At least you shouldn't be recognized." Tuck was not sure who had taken care of Robin's hair, but it was no less neat than his own. And nobody expected friars to be neat. They slept under trees most of the time, after all.

Robin nodded. "I know how we're going to get her out. If we can. If we can't..."

"Let's hope it doesn't come to that. Now, hush, I hear hoofbeats."

The rider went chasing past. A message rider on a fast horse, Tuck noted. He kept walking, returning to the road once the horse was past. He did not, however, feel it safe to return to the conversation.

They walked in silence. What Tuck was doing would require a major penance if he confessed it. Assisting somebody in imitating a member of his order? Breaking a witch out of jail? Actually, he decided, that he would probably be defrocked. Or they could try, anyway. He felt he was doing the right thing in the eyes of God, if not in those of Man.

Clorinda had never poisoned anyone and if she was a witch, she had cast no spell on him. Maybe one on Will, but that was the spell any woman could cast. It was a woman's power, after all, to lure a man into her bed.

Often, it was the only power they had, and if they claimed more, they were witches.

Tuck knew what was expected of women.

He thought, for a moment, of the Lady In Blue. As he did so, he thought he saw something larger than a butterfly, but winged like one, cross the path.

"Robin."

The young man stopped. "You saw it?" he whispered.

"I did." Not a hallucination, then. Not if they had both seen it. A pixie, the least of fairies. A creature that did nothing but dance and laugh. Harmless.

Unless you believed the church doctrine that all of the fae were demons. The Sidhe might well qualify...those who stole children and sometimes men and women, releasing them only after decades had passed. The purpose for which they took adults was generally considered to be passion.

Some in the church said the stories of changelings were invented...that the human child had not really been replaced by a fairy. Or that the child replaced by a lump of wood was the work of a mortal woman desperate for a baby of her own.

Some women would steal children. It was a known sickness, not uncommon amongst women who were unable to conceive or those who had experienced a recent miscarriage or stillbirth. It was a sin, but generally not considered a crime. In fact, it was not uncommon to resolve the issue by giving the thief an orphan to raise.

"I call that a good omen."

"I do not know what I call it, except that from what I hear." Tuck glanced at Robin. "Where there are pixies, there is likely to be worse."

"You do not consider them demons, then?"

"I don't know what I consider them. They're not exactly benevolent, unless you can convince a brownie to move in with you."

"No, but not always malevolent, either. And it was only a pixie." Robin fell silent, for now they were approaching the outskirts of a village.

Two friars discussing having seen a fairy would have been suspicious. Rather than find a new subject of conversation, Tuck too became silent. He observed his surroundings with some thought.

The town they were heading for was half a day further. He would have suggested stopping here for lunch, but he doubted the villagers had anything to spare.

This was Gisbourne's territory, and deep within it. Whoever was looking after things while he was on crusade had tightened the purse strings. He saw only thin, hungry faces. Their clothing had seen better days. One little boy ran across the street wearing what looked like his father's shirt and nothing else.

Then again, that was not uncommon even when there was some money. Children grew out of clothes so quickly that few parents would take much care. There was a reason the rich dressed toddlers in dresses. Easy to let down.

A thin dog followed him. It appeared to have mange, and it limped as lawed dogs always did. Tuck could count the unfortunate creature's ribs.

No doubt they had no food for him, and a lawed dog could not forage for itself. Not with no front claws. Which was, of course, the point.

Tuck flinched. "These people need help."

Robin nodded. "They need a better lord than Gisbourne. But the prince would not likely replace him."

"I hear his son is already no better." The young Gisbourne was no more than fourteen and already set fair along his father's path. "His death in the Holy Land would not help them." He kept his voice quiet. Even in such a place, Gisbourne would have agents. Or at least loyal followers. Some men would support even a lord who ill-used them.

"That is what I hear too. We should not impinge on them for alms."

Tuck nodded. "We can eat the bread we have. These people need to be given alms, not asked for them."

A goodwife had come out of one of the buildings. She seemed a little better off than most. "Good brothers. I could perhaps..."

Tuck turned towards her. "We would not take anything from you that you need yourselves."

"You truly do not seek alms?"

"We have extra from the last place we visited." Tuck glanced at Robin. He was letting him do the talking. "It seems you have little or nothing to spare."

The woman seemed completely...nonplussed. "Truly?"

"Truly. We are poor friars, we have very little need." Which was true. In terms of needs, Tuck needed food, a place to lay his head and, every so often, a new habit. Of course, he also had a few wants. Like ale. "If I had anything to spare, I would give it to those here who need it."

It seemed almost an alien concept to her. The concept that somebody would not demand of her what little she had left? That thought flowed behind her eyes.

He could see her thinking. "What we might ask is if there is a good log or stump hereabouts on which we might rest for a few minutes. We are hoping to make Nottingham by nightfall."

She nodded. "Then you have quite a walk, but I suppose you are used to it. Take the east road. It's quicker."

She seemed more relaxed, now she knew she would not have to provide lunch for them. And willing to offer that which she could afford. Tuck thought about the fairy.

Maybe the fae could help these people. It was, however, unlikely that they would. The fae seldom helped anyone. Except, of course, themselves. That made them little different from humans.

They found a log in the village green, and sat down, eating bread.

"I forget how poor these people can be," Robin mused.

"There is not much we can do for them. If they had food to sell, we could buy it from them, but it seems they do not have even enough for their own stomachs." He could see the mangy dog, or one from the same litter, rummaging through some trash at the side of the street.

He did not want to think about what might be in it. How much of this poverty was Gisbourne's fault, this close to Nottingham?

Robin threw part of his crust to the dog.

"Probably shouldn't have done that. It's likely to follow us now."

"Good point." He stood and stretched. "Let's go."

There was almost a please in his tone. He did not want to be here. He did not want to think about being here.

Tuck was inclined to agree. They could talk about it later. Later when the greenwood surrounded them and no ears that might belong to lord or abbott were around.

For the rest of the day they walked along a road that slowly improved. It was the goose road, where the geese would be driven for the autumn fair. It followed, in part, the line of an old Roman road.

Ahead of them was the city, and above it, the castle. It was the latter one first saw, perched on the rock above the city. Sheer cliffs fell down from it, riddled with caves. The people kept ale in some of those caves, brewed it in others. Lived in some. The caves were a part of the city.

Nottingham had no true wall, only an earthen barricade. This was a relatively stable place, seldom touched by war. There was no need for the more extensive defenses of York, which to this day got raided by the occasional viking.

"That castle always seems..."

"Watchful?" Tuck inquired, glancing towards Robin.

"Vigilant. Not always in a good way. They use some of the caves as a prison. She will be there."

Which meant...the caves. Not all of them were interconnected, but most were. Tuck could certainly not make his way through the smaller gaps, the ones that did not officially exist. Robin, not much larger than many women himself, had a far better chance.

"So, we go into..." And then Robin's eyes lit, his entire face. "I know exactly how to get there."

Tuck was almost frightened by the man's intensity. He had not previously experienced that level of drive from the leader, not aimed at him.

Now he understood why men and women would follow him through the fire. Perhaps even why he, himself, had not yet left. That fire leached through the man and flowed off of him. It drew Tuck onwards.

The town of Nottingham was clustered around the base of the rock. Around it were water meadows and fields. The road led first through those fields, then past a few poor houses, then through the barricade.

Inside, houses leaned against one another like drunken brothers. The upper storeys shaded the streets.

"First, we go to the inn."

"Which one?"

Robin shot him a look. "The only one in this place worth visiting."

Tuck frowned but followed. They were heading towards the base of the rock. The streets were somewhat muddy and at one point they had to dodge a chamber pot being emptied into the street.

Tuck suspected the much-vaunted Romans had a better way of dealing with that, but that had been many centuries ago. Rome, these days, had a quite different meaning. A black cat looked out from an alleyway and mewed softly.

"Good luck," Robin muttered.

Tuck nodded. Black cats were sometimes considered to be the familiars of witches, but could also mean the best of luck to those who saw them. Magical creatures, and magic could go both ways. For all that some in the church said otherwise. "We need it."

Some sort of basket could be seen being pulled up the cliff. "What's that?"

"Ale for the castle," Robin noted. The basket vanished into a hole, some kind of chimney cave no doubt. "Why put up with the brewing smell in your castle if you can hire a brewmaster who works directly under you?"

"In this inn you mentioned." Tuck knew Robin. He was not just after good ale. Was he after the basket? It looked too small to hold a man. But not too small to hold, say, a message.

"Yes. And don't worry, you will have time to get a mug, my friend."

Tuck laughed. From any distance, their banter would seem to be that of two brothers traveling together. Nobody was that close. A white goose crossed the road in front of them, chased by a small girl in a home-spun dress. If she was going to be a goose girl, she had a lot to learn.

The inn was set against the cliff, possibly built into it. No doubt at least the cellar was. The sign outside was a pilgrim with a staff. "The Pilgrim," Tuck translated.

"Yes. Owned by the Templars and the start of many a crusade. You did not leave from here?"

"I was in London when I decided to make pilgrimage, but now I seem to recall this place being mentioned." He did indeed. It was a half-timbered building, with a large cobbled yard outside. None were gathering for pilgrimage or crusade now, though. A couple of men leaned against the outer wall with tankards in their hands. "I think they called it both the Pilgrim and the Trip."

"Pilgrim is the official name."

But names could change and drift, and Tuck wondered which one would stick...as long as the brewhouse lasted, anyway.

Robin headed for the door, ignoring the two men. Tuck caught a snatch of the conversation, "And a fine boar it was...but it would not cover spotted sows, no sir."

He laughed to himself, having heard of such discrimination in horses, but never in pigs. Probably, it was an Irish tale, exaggerated in the telling and exaggerated further by the drink.

Inside, the inn was small and dark. The back of it was a natural a cave, and the tallow lighting did little more than cast shadows. The rich smell of hops drifted through it, making a man hungry for ale. A barmaid who would have been attractive in better lighting leaned over one table, carefully pouring a refill.

Tuck followed Robin to the bar. No doubt, the small outlaw had a plan, he could see it in his eyes. He had not, however, voiced it. It did strike him as if the passages that led up through the rock, though, could give admission to the castle.

Perhaps Robin simply sought to fortify himself with alcohol against the mission ahead. A lot would take away performance. A little could aid courage.

"Two of your best," Robin asked the barkeep.

"Of course, good brother. Do you go on pilgrimage?"

"Maybe. We have been thinking about it."

Tuck remained silent. He was not ever going on pilgrimage again and had he thought Robin was serious...

He knew he was not, although pilgrimage could turn an outlaw into a citizen once more. To make it was to earn remission from all of one's sins. Which was a fine idea, for it was a hard trip, had the pilgrimage, of late, not turned into... He tailed off, forcing the image of what had happened to those villagers out of his mind.

They had been Christians. That had been the last straw, that and the knowledge that they would do the same to Jerusalem itself. They would turn the Holy City into a charnelhouse. Even had they only faced Jews and Saracens, it would have been wrong.

"I hear," Robin added, conversationally, "rumors that Gisbourne has returned."

"Not that I know of. The sheriff is still in control, certainly. If Gisbourne is on his way, he is not yet here. Or perhaps he has been and gone."

Robin nodded a little. "Perhaps."

Tuck shuddered. Gisbourne's sheriff had a terrible reputation. It was rumored his tastes led to leaving serving girls with scars. Boys too, on occasion. Supposedly, it was the death of his wife and son in childbed that had turned him this way. Tuck thought it more likely that she had been the only thing keeping him from acting out his fantasies.

If all of that was true. But he had a worse reputation than Gisbourne himself. And what of Clorinda?

"I hear," Robin added, "that the sheriff might have his hands on a pretty young witch."

"Ah, that I hear...a woman who dresses up as a man." That, alone, was enough to get a woman branded as a witch. "I hear he daren't touch her. The abbot wants her tried for heresy, not under civil law."

Moresford and the sheriff fighting over jurisdiction.

"But its the sheriff who has her...and whoever gets her, she will hang eventually." The eagerness in Robin's tone would have been frightening had Tuck not known it was feigned.

Of course, there were plenty out there for whom watching a pretty young witch hang would be highly enjoyable. Tuck shuddered inwardly, hoping his robes concealed any outward echo of it. He could not show disgust at a traveling companion.

"Oh, the entertainment will come soon enough...but not too soon, with the wrangling. I would say a couple of weeks."

Robin nodded, taking his ale. "Well, I am certainly not planning on leaving."

Anyone who heard the conversation might, Tuck thought, suspect that they were here to rescue the witch, but they might not. And if they did, they would remember two friars. Not outlaws. Nobody would think of that until it was too late. He hoped.

If caught, then they might both burn for heresy. Pretending to be a priest certainly qualified, even if Robin's true beliefs were not revealed.

Tuck found himself hoping the blue lady...whether she was Mary or one of Clorinda's goddesses...was watching over them. He tried to chase the thought, which would certainly condemn him to fires hotter than the sheriff could light, out of his mind. He did not succeed. It remained there, hovering in front of him, an image he both feared and longed for.

Perhaps, though, he was already damned. Or saved.

8

$\mathcal{T}$he sun flared against the red stone of Castle Rock, giving it a glow that would have been attractive, even distracting, at better times. As it was, the only thing Tuck cared about was the cliff's height and the fact that scaling it would be near impossible.

"We have time, and she is in the castle."

"You know that for sure?"

"The barkeep told me. Oh, not in words. He looked up when she was mentioned."

Tuck might have seen that gesture, but he had not really noticed it. "At least he didn't tell us the trial was tomorrow."

"If it was, we would have gatecrashed it in force." Robin flickered a grin. "I've done it before."

Tuck nodded. "The downside to it being in two weeks is they won't let us in to see her. Yet. And I'm not leaving her in the hands of that..."

That had been the initial plan...to offer her last rites and sneak her out in a third habit. It was not going to work...although they still had that item with them, and a hood to hide her face and hair.

They were going to have to break in. Robin glanced at the sky, nodded, then headed for the bottom of the passage. It came out near the inn, a different one from the vertical shaft they hauled ale in. This one wound its way around Castle Rock. It was used as a sally port by the castle personnel. Robin was hoping that it was too little known to be well guarded.

In any case, they both had staffs. One or two guards they could take and it hardly seemed likely there would be an entire company at the top.

Robin went first, lightly climbing the few rock 'steps' into the passage and vanishing within. He did not have a torch.

Tuck had noticed he had the night vision of a cat. About all he could do was follow and hope he did not stumble on something in the dark and cry out.

Up. The other side of the rock was an easy walk. This one was a cliff, one that provided the castle with much of its defenses. From the top, there must be a spectacular view.

No doubt Clorinda was not enjoying it. She would be in one of the cells in the basement of the keep or a side tower. Most likely a side tower. Contrary to popular belief, keep basements were seldom dungeons. They were usually wine cellars.

The sheriff likely drank well and ate well. Most of his kind did. They might even have permission to take the occasional swan.

Tuck had tasted swan once. He had not thought it worth all of the fuss. He would rather have venison, or even really good beef.

Up. The passageway was steep and twisty. Occasionally the outside of it opened up, letting in light. Hopefully they would not be visible from the ground. A runner might get ahead of them. A message in the ale basket certainly would.

He began to seriously wonder what he was doing here. He was not an outlaw not a fighter; he would be executed if caught. No sense doing anything else, not to a man trying to break a witch out of jail. They would not even hesitate. They might not even bother to capture him.

If they did not get Clorinda out, somehow, she would be burned. If she repented, they might be nice and strangle her. He did not see her repenting. He did not see her pretending to renounce her gods. If she had any sense, she would be silent about her beliefs.

Then there was a chance they would simply flog her as an uppity woman and let her go. A small chance. It did not seem likely. They had decided they needed a witch to hang or a heretic to burn. Every so often, it kept the peasants in line.

Tuck had doubted the Church for a long time. Recently, he had thought it might be better for everyone if it did not exist. Of course, it was also possible they realized Clorinda was one of those troublesome outlaws.

She might be bait. They might be going into a trap. He did not say anything. He knew that Robin would be *more* aware of that possibility than he was. He was leaving things to the expert.

In many ways, his part of the mission was done, but he could rap guards on the head with his quarterstaff.

And that would be the top. An iron gate blocked the passageway and he saw part of a man's back beyond it.

A guard who needed, Tuck thought, to pay attention to what he was supposed to be guarding. With his back to the gate, he could be readily surprised. However, he was not alone. There was no question of that.

There was also the gate.

Robin pulled out a thin dirk, moving to the gate to try and pick the lock. If the guard turned around. If the lock squeaked, then it was entirely probable the guard would just shoot them through the gate. In the narrow passageway, it would be impossible to avoid getting hit. Tuck flattened himself against the wall to minimize the risk as much as he could, but he knew that if they fired, it would only be a question of how badly he was hurt.

The lock squeaked. The guard started to turn. Tuck hesitated only a moment before throwing himself against the gate.

The half-picked lock gave, and he stumbled through it, between the two guards, off-balance. They drew swords.

Swords. Zounds! Tuck thought, blasphemously. Everyone always tried to use a sword against a staff. He swung the staff around, knocking the blade from one of their hands. Robin was moving swiftly to get behind the other one while they were both focused on Tuck.

He spun the heavy length of oak as if it were a child's baton. The disarmed guard actually showed the whites of his eyes before the staff slammed into his midsection, knocking the wind out of him before he could yell for help.

The other got "Int..." out before Robin hit him on the back of the head. He went down, quite probably dead.

"Should I finish this one?" Tuck asked, softly.

"Knock him out."

Tuck brought the staff down carefully on the side of the man's temple. If he had it right, he would wake up in a few hours wishing he was dead. Robin wanted these people to remember...well. That was fine by Tuck.

He was starting to think like them, he realized. The intimidation, the quick movements, were as much part of it as the weapons. Reputation was a weapon in and of itself.

They were in the outer bailey. Walls lined it, somewhat lower on the cliff side than on the side from which an attack could readily come. There would be guards on those walls, and it was getting lighter.

Not for the first time, Tuck wondered how Robin planned on getting them out. Possibly bold as you please with hostages. More likely, they would change into the habits they carried and walk out the front door as friars.

Hostages struck him as a smart idea. They moved close to the bottom of the wall, where the soldiers on that wall would not see them. Hopefully those opposite would see shadows. He did not ask Robin if he knew which tower to go to. He trusted the man to have done his research, or at least his thinking. Their route took them past the mews. Sleepy hawks peered out at them. It was not light enough for them to be awake enough to cause a problem. Tuck hoped the kennels were a good distance away. There was no way dogs would not notice them and make a ruckus.

He thought he saw them on the other side, sleeping noses resting on sleeping paws. Those dogs would not have to limp along on missing toes. They would be treated, he thought, better than most humans.

He thought letting them out might make a good distraction. If they needed one. Robin was approaching the base of the tower.

"Are you sure this is the right place?"

"Not entirely, but I have to make a call at some point." He frowned a little. "No entrance on this side, and if we go around..."

If anyone on the wall heard them, this could easily be a killing zone. Tuck was reminded that he was, after all, far too large a target. Any idiot should be able to hit a man his size.

Maybe, he thought with bitter humor, Robin should use him as a shield. Then Robin was moving, darting faster than any man had a right to around the tower. Tuck did his best to follow. He prayed...knowing that Robin would invoke Mary and Clorinda her own gods. They had everything covered. That was another bitter thought.

And a heretical one, of course, but he did not really care about that. If he had to spend an extra year or two in purgatory for thinking it, then so be it.

Somehow, he made it into the shelter of the wall. From above, "Ho! Who goes there?"

They had been seen or heard. He flattened himself against the tower, crawling around it.

Robin was working the lock on a door. He frowned. "I can't get it open," he murmured.

"Given they know we're here now, how about the old-fashioned way?" Tuck tapped the side of his staff meaningfully.

The air seemed for a moment to turn blue. For a moment, Tuck felt her presence...goddess or saint? He was not sure.

Robin's eyes widened for a moment. Then, softly, "Do it."

Tuck was the larger and stronger of the two. He brought the end of his staff into the hinges of the door once, twice, three times. On the third blow they broke, the door falling inwards.

Inside, the base of the tower was dark. Robin ducked through and Tuck followed. He could still sense her presence. He still knew she was there. Supporting them, being with them. Being part of what they had to do.

Cold flowed through Tuck for a moment. Was this Clorinda's goddess leading Robin to *believe* she was the Virgin? Tricking him into damnation?

He did not want to think of Clorinda as damned. "Up or down?"

"Up. There's a guard room, then the cells. Down is just storage."

Another myth pushed into nothingness. Again, the dungeon, not where the prisoners were kept. Tuck knew now she was in here.

Barely aloud, he whispered, "If you're using Robin..."

No answer, but the slightest smell of roses. Rose of the sea. It proved nothing. Roses were associated with immortality, along with apples. Whatever was in here with them, though, it was not human or mortal. Not anymore, if it ever had been. It was no mere woman.

Up the stairs. Guard room. There would be more guards in there, by now, they would know the goal of their intruders.

"We need a hostage," Robin muttered.

"One of the guards should do. I'll take care of it." Tuck wondered why he had offered, except that he had far more chance of holding another man, physically, than the woman-sized Robin.

Had he not seen the man topless, he would have wondered. But no, Robin was definitely not a woman...and probably not one of those rare unfortunates who partook of both.

Unfortunates because nobody ever knew how to handle them. Tuck had spent part of his novitiate with a future friar who wanted to be a woman. Longed to be one. Felt that being one was his destiny. He had chosen orders because a friar could be genderless, could be neither one nor the other, and it was the closest he could get.

Tuck failed to understand why anyone would choose to be a woman, supposedly a weaker vessel, further from God and closer to sin. Unless they had met a woman like Clorinda. She had cured him of those feelings.

Maybe she, too, was between the two, maybe she was part man. No... The door opened from the other side.

An arrow lodged in his robes, somehow missing his flesh. Lousy shot, he thought, to miss a target his size in such a confined area. Well, he supposed he should be grateful.

"Lousy shot," Robin called upwards, echoing his thoughts. He was trying to provoke them into anger.

Angry men were lousy shots on the whole. Another arrow spiraled past. This one did not even come close. "I noticed!" Tuck called, joining in the mockery. "Maybe you need to go back to shooting straw men...oh wait, you'd miss them too!"

An incoherent shout came, and the guardsman attempted to tackle Robin, who stepped to the side.

The man landed in a heap at Tuck's feet. He put his staff on his neck. "Welcome, my friend. You'll be enjoying our hospitality for a brief while."

He fully intended to let the man go. If one did not release hostages, the technique became valueless. Worthless. The Saracen were fond of taking hostages.

They were fond, in fact, of taking an enemy's child and raising him within their own household...a tactic which genuinely fostered peace. It was hard to hate and fight those who had cared for you as a child.

Tuck thought that some of the quarreling lords could do well to learn from that particular idea. That they could exchange a few children, find understanding. Of course, they would not. It was Saracen, and therefore automatically bad.

He pulled the man to his feet, dragging him up the stairs by his collar. He had dropped his weapons, and did not struggle. Perhaps he realized his life expectancy was far greater if he did not argue with the outlaws.

"Where is the witch?" Robin demanded.

The man made an incoherent sound. Tuck thrust him up the stairs ahead of them. If he took an arrow, then so be it.

The other two guards seemed to have realized archery was not their strong point. Both had swords out at this point. Tuck noticed that they did not seem to be incompetent. Unfortunately. It was only shooting they could not do.

They hesitated, though, rather than charge towards their comrade.

Robin spun his staff across his hands. Tuck could not quite juggle staff and hostage well enough to bring his own into play. He focused instead of using the man as a shield...although if the guards were good enough they could probably reach around the guy and still get to a good part of the rotund friar.

Instead, both of them charged Robin. He was not the staff fighter John was...Tuck had seen that man handle a quarter staff well enough to give nice sets of lumps to four of the other outlaws at once...but he was competent. Even the best swords had difficulty cutting a well-tempered oaken staff. One got lucky, nicking Robin's weapon a couple of times.

He retaliated by swinging it into the man's gut.

"Stand down," Tuck called. "Or I'll inflict some serious pain on your friend here."

They all knew he could not kill the man, because then he would have no protection. Beating him up, though, was well within the realms of possibility. The man knew it, Tuck heard him swallow, felt him tense up. Smelled his sweat.

Well. If all went well, he would live, although knowing the Sheriff, possibly without a job. Heck, if Tuck was the sheriff and they got away with Clorinda, he would fire the guards involved too. He could not afford to show them any compassion.

Better they lost their jobs than Clorinda her life.

They were hesitating again. "Where is the witch?" Robin hissed. "Tell me and let me pass...and nobody has to get hurt."

His voice carried a strong conviction, but the guards apparently wanted to keep their jobs. They launched at him again. This time, he swung the staff low, knocking the legs of one of them out from under him. The other managed to get past Robin's guard, his blade drawing a thin line of red down the outlaw's arm. He hissed but did not cry out.

The second one was getting up. Tuck tossed the hostage into the wall, freed his staff, and hit the man from behind. He went down like a poleaxed steer. The hostage had apparently lost all will to fight. He lay against the wall, visibly unwilling to attempt to move. Possibly, his bell had been rung by hitting the wall.

Robin flickered Tuck a grin and then almost casually knocked out the second one, the blade falling to the ground.

"She's on the next floor," the hostage gasped. "Just don't kill me."

"Coward," Tuck informed him. He dragged him back to his feet, pushing him ahead up the stairs. In case he had lied.

There was a central chamber on the next floor and cells set around it. "Which one?"

"Number three," the poor guard choked out.

Maybe he would be better off losing his job. He clearly wasn't very good at it. "You need a new line of work. Pig farming, maybe."

Robin walked over, pulled the keys from the guard's pocket and unlocked the cell door.

"What took you so long?" came the voice from within.

THE UNFORTUNATE GUARD was tagging along behind, afraid to follow and afraid not to follow. He was clearly not sure whether it was better to be conked on the head by Tuck or fired. Clorinda was miserably thin, and had clearly been roughed up, but was otherwise fine.

Remarkably so, given she had been in prison on charges of witchcraft. Maybe she'd had the sense to pretend to be a stupid, silly girl who had fallen in with the outlaws over some affair of the heart.

Somehow, they made it to the passageway without being shot. Tuck pushed the guard ahead of them now. They'd had plenty of time to arrange an ambush at the bottom end, he thought.

Robin spoke, softly, "Did they do you permanent harm?"

Clorinda shook her head. "Nothing that won't heal quickly enough."

Tuck had noticed as they ran across the courtyard that she had a split lip and a black eye. She was probably lucky if she still had all of her teeth.

But she would heal. He was sure of that. And if she did not, then they would come back and do something permanent to the sheriff.

Tuck assigned himself a good two dozen Hail Marys as penance for *that* thought. It was not right to be quite so angry. Even if the man did deserve it, by all he had heard.

And yes, there was the ambush. The guard gave a slight sigh as an arrow struck him in the chest.

Damn, Tuck thought. He had not intended to get the man killed. He thrust forward, continuing to use him as a shield...he could tell from that sound that he could be hurt no further in this world. A couple more arrows hit the dying man, and then Tuck was able to throw him aside and thrust his staff into the first of the archers. It happened to hit somewhere lower than the gut and the man went down, screaming in agony.

Tuck's own balls tried to contract up into his abdomen in sympathy, but he did not have time to stop. He had to get clear of the passage so that the two behind could come into the fight. He swung the staff again, and felt an arrow graze his arm. This time, it bit more than his clothing. The pain was delayed, hitting a moment later, and faded by fight adrenalin. His fingers all still worked on that arm, so it was not bad.

Not bad, and his next blow hit a man in the chin, snapping his head back with the sickening crack that accompanied shattering vertebrae. Another death, but Tuck had no time to regret it. Clorinda relieved the first man, now groaning on the ground, of his sword. He was surprised that she seemed able to use it well...he had never seen her with anything other than a bow. He had assumed she was only trained as an archer.

Surprised, and then somebody had grabbed his staff. He shifted his grip, twisted it free from the attempted disarm. Robin hit the man in the shoulder from the other side, and he stepped back, reaching up to clutch it.

"Let's go." Tuck needed no second bidding. He made sure nobody had arrows trained on him, and then ran. Towards the town.

If they could get into the crowd, then...no, these people had already killed their own man to get to him. They would not hesitate to shoot into a mass of peasants to get the outlaws.

Tuck assigned himself a few more Hail Marys, preemptively, then cursed them at satisfying length.

"No, this way. They won't follow us." Robin was ducking towards the caves again, then vanished into one, powering down the passage. Tuck pushed Clorinda in front of him before following. His arm stung. He managed to take a second to glance at it. A long, thin rip through his habit and a gouge in the skin beneath that bled sluggishly. He was lucky.

No. Lucky would have been not to be hit at all.

Robin took one turn, then two, then three...and Tuck realized why they would not be followed as the odor from further into the caves struck his senses.

Stale urine. There were people down here tanning leather. It was all he could do to keep running. Tanners, it was rumored, often permanently lost their sense of smell.

He wished he could lose his! The scent of the mixture of urine and oak bark was the worst he had ever encountered, worse than a charnel pit. Worse, even, than a camp latrine. The tanners looked up, then back to their work. Several of them had scars, for the mixture could cause burns if it splashed on a person.

They ran across a kind of catwalk above the tanning pits. Clorinda was coughing. But the sheriff's men had not followed them. That was what mattered the most. Their lungs and noses would recover later.

It did, though, seem as if they moved through the tanning pits forever. When they came out, they were practically the other side of town, at the edge of the water meadows.

"Phewf. I think that was worse than the jail."

"More temporary, though," Robin pointed out. "Or do you want to go back?"

Clorinda tried to laugh, ended up coughing again. "No...absolutely not. But I feel as if I got my share of brimstone!"

Tuck shook his head. "How about we make ourselves scarce, before somebody comes up with the bright idea of going around the tannery instead of through it?"

Robin laughed again, but quickly followed Tuck's suggestion, heading across the water meadows towards the river itself. Tuck divined his plan instantly. They could not, of course, cross the Trent here unless they wanted to swim, but their tracks would be hard to follow in the marsh along the very edge of it. A couple of cows protested at their presence, although they did not approach. A shaggy pony turned out with them did, for a few strides, perhaps hoping the fruit of the garden was in somebody's pocket. Then the wind shifted and it fled.

They probably smelled of tannery, even if they could not detect it with tired noses. Certainly, the pony had acted as if its senses were distinctly offended.

Besides, there was no need or reason to steal it, although Clorinda looked tired and limped very slightly. Hopefully just a sprain. She still had the guardsman's sword.

A trophy Tuck felt her well entitled to. And then they were plodding through the marsh, the far side of the levees that controlled the flow onto the meadows themselves. It was unpleasant, but far less so than the tannery.

For a moment, he thought he saw a glimpse of blue.

9

The feeling of the Blue Lady's presence did not leave them until they got to camp. The next day, Tuck sat at the edge, carving a new staff.

The simple activity kept his hands occupied. His mind, however... His mind recoiled in fear from the possibility that she was one of Clorinda's gods. That she was real and he had done her bidding.

No. He had done it for Clorinda, not her. The Church, though, considered Clorinda a witch.

The Church and God were not the same. The Church was made up of humans, fallible mortals who made errors. On the other hand, if the old gods were real? No. He had always known they were real, in some way, at some level.

Real, but not significant. They had faded under His power into mere shades. Not to be worshipped or respected, but occasionally, perhaps feared.

Certainly not to be loved.

Robin's intent was to love the Virgin. If the Blue Lady was not she, then Robin had...come to logical conclusions. To be fooled by such was certainly no shame. To be Marian was to be wrong...which was ultimately what heresy was.

Tuck finally realized why Robin's heresy did not bother him. It was quiet. Most of the heretics Tuck had encountered had the strong desire to teach the rest of the Church the error of their ways. They preached, cajoled, and occasionally threw riots. They did not simply live their lives and mention their beliefs only to those who asked.

Which proved only that loud heretics were the only ones you noticed. Sensible, quiet heretics kept their mouths shut, ensuring they would not face the fires.

Robin could believe what he wanted to. He wasn't corrupting anyone.

But the presence of the Blue Lady meant something. Tuck sought out the old man. Richard.

Richard was sitting in the doorway of one of the tents. He looked far worse off than he had been. He seemed worse off every day. His health was deteriorating.

He might die this year or next, Tuck thought, with neither sorrow nor rancor. He disliked the man, but wished no ill on him. However, he would not much miss him.

He moved to sit down nearby.

"The brother, not avoiding me?"

Tuck decided to be blunt, "I don't like you. I'm fairly sure you don't like me."

"I don't like your God."

"But others here do." Tuck shrugged. "What god, then, do you serve?"

"I serve the Great Mystery and the gods."

Tuck's eyebrow arched upwards. "You are a *druid*?" That was supposed to be the term they used for God. There also were not supposed to *be* any druids.

"One of the few. Now do you understand why I don't like your God? The Romans cut down our groves and demanded we worship in temples of stone. Then the Christians knocked down the temples and demanded we worship no more."

Put that way, his enmity made far too much sense. "Who is the Blue Lady?"

"I am not sure. She has not appeared to me. Only, as far as I know, to Robin, Clorinda and Will. If she has appeared to John, he has not spoken of it. She seems not to care for the rest of us."

"She has appeared to me. Robin thinks she is the Blessed Virgin."

"She may be." Richard held up a hand. "My religion does not deny the existence of your God, only his supremacy. It is not impossible that his beloved mother would come to men in visions. After all, who does a man love the most? Especially if it is true he did not marry."

Common Church wisdom held that Christ was single. Some few tried to make a case that he had wed the former prostitute, Mary Magdalene. Occasionally, so-called miracle workers claiming to be descended from that union showed up and caused trouble. They usually ended up burning as heretics. "I keep an open mind on that one."

"A God who was born to a mortal woman, would he not elevate her to immortality? So, yes, it could be her. Clorinda, however, believes otherwise. She believes it may be either Aine, the goddess of love, or possibly the old Roman goddess, Diana of the hunt. Who is also considered to be a virgin."

Tuck considered that. "No way to tell by looking at her. I have only seen her once, but she was there during the rescue. Apparently, Clorinda matters to her."

"Well, Clorinda is rather likable, is she not?"

"So, do you still want me dead or vanished?" Tuck asked, resting his staff across his knees.

"I would rather you were not here. Yet, you could have betrayed us to the Church at any time. Why have you not?"

"Because I don't particularly want to see any of you executed for heresy. Even you."

Richard laughed sharply. "Even me, eh? With my Norman name and my Celtic ways."

Tuck was Saxon to the bone. He shook his head. "What is Clorinda to you, anyway?"

"She is my granddaughter."

Why had he not realized that? Why had he not seen the similarity? Not physically, no, clearly Clorinda favored some other branch of the family. But there was something about the way their minds seemed to work that held within it a great similarity.

"Nobody expects *me* to give such things up," he added.

Tuck shrugged. "In all honesty, I have never been tempted by women. I might make a good father, but I think I would be a rather bad husband."

"Ah, but you have not been given the choice."

Tuck shrugged. "How many priests keep their vows?" It was smaller, he knew, than the number who did not. A lot smaller.

"True. But be warned. It might be that the Blue Lady's interest in you has something to do with you being the only virgin in the camp. If she is Diana, you are safe. If she is Aine..." Richard laughed. "She may have decided you are a challenge."

A goddess of love might well want to see a man break his vows, Tuck thought. "And if she is Mary after all?"

"Then you are probably very safe."

IT WAS HARD WINTER, the band camped in a hollow where they could store food. The trees shielded them from a heath where the rain fell horizontally, streaking through everything and everyone in its path. Snow dotted the high country.

Tuck had not left camp in some time. He had little to do.

He might have written something, but he lacked parchment and ink...quills were not a problem, goose feathers being as suitable for that as for arrows.

Maybe if he asked Robin they could arrange to steal some ink from the abbott, who remained one of their favorite victims...well, except that there had been none in evidence last time they robbed him.

The abbott, Tuck thought wryly, had things to do other than write. More physical pursuits. He supposed the woman was attractive enough.

What kind of woman agreed to a secret marriage with a Church-man? Had she been after his money, or did she love him?

Tuck was glad of celibacy once more. He did not have to experience the vague guilt of being wed to a woman who had no interest in him, or the certainty that he would not be interested in her. That had happened to his oldest brother. He had been married to a tradesman's daughter. A nice girl, attractive, even, but they simply...despised each other.

The Church would not grant an annulment. They lived apart, linked together only by their two sons. There would be no more children.

Yes, Tuck much preferred the life of a friar. He did not wish to share his home with a miserable person, even if she was only a woman

Only a woman. The words echoed through the wind that blew through the tops of the trees. He thought of Clorinda and chased them off. Women were not, in the end, inferior to men.

To the south of the hollow was a huge oak, which Richard kept walking circles around, muttering. Druids really did, it seemed, talk to trees. Well, there were worse things he could have been doing.

Tuck found himself drawn towards it. The trunk was large enough that if a couple of children climbed through the crack in one side of it, they could play house comfortably inside. They would, too, if they found it. Children loved climbing in hollow trees. Despite being hollow, the great oak seemed remarkably healthy, albeit bent and bowed with age. "What have you seen, I wonder?" he asked it.

Oak trees lived for generations. God had granted them a span greater than any man's. Tuck wondered why. Why would an oak tree live four hundred years, a man three score and ten, and a dog maybe a decade?

It seemed very strange. True, he was not to know the mind of God, but he doubted He did anything random.

Tuck looked into the hollow trunk. Then he laughed. Somebody had hid their ale stash in it. He was tempted to steal some, revenge for the time he had met the band and they had taken what had been meant to be a three-month supply. After a moment, he decided to be a better man, and stepped away, turning around.

She was standing between two of the trees. This time, her presence was not a suggestion. She was clad in a blue dress of a style that might be worn by a noblewoman, assuming she was not planning on doing anything important that day. Extremely fine, but simple. Her dark hair was worn loose, as would be appropriate for a maiden, and flowed over her shoulders. A circlet of silver was set within it.

She might have been Mary...she was dark, her eyes dark, she could have been a woman of the Holy Land. Yet, she could also have been a woman of, say, Wales, or a Pict from the far north of Scotland. Or a Roman maiden.

There was something about her that was all of those things and none, that might indeed encompass the blonde of Saxon and Norse without being of it.

Ambiguous. All goddesses, no goddess. Maybe she was Sidhe after all. "Lady..." He tailed off. If she was Mary and he did not bow to her, as the Mother of God, she might be angry. If she was not and he did, then he committed heresy. So he just stood there. Waiting for her to speak. Waiting for her to do something.

She did. She stepped forward, brushed his lips with her fingers. The scent of roses filled his nostrils. Then she was gone.

Whatever she wanted from him, it remained uncertain. The druid had said she might consider him a challenge. If she was Aine. That she might set out to find him a woman, he supposed he meant. The idea terrified him.

He had never let a woman touch him like that. His heart pounded in his chest, then settled. No. He did not want to be touched like that. Not by a woman. Not by a man. Not by *anyone*. Had she been testing him?

What was she trying to tell him? He wasn't sure he wanted any understanding of this, only the relief that for now it was over, the fear that she would return.

What he could no longer doubt was that she was real, and perhaps that had been the only message she sought to send.

If she was... He murmured the words not of the Hail Mary, but of the Jesus Prayer. Normally such gave him some comfort, but not now. If she was some alien, ancient goddess, some power older than the Church? Even acknowledging her existence bordered on blasphemy, yet he had done it before. He had not tried to convert Clorinda, when all the rules of the Church said he should. To save her. To ensure that she did not burn forever in hell.

It was hard to believe that woman was associated with Hell. But then, perhaps she was Mary after all. The scent of roses, the garb of the sea.

Perhaps. He sat down heavily on a stump.

Quiet footsteps behind him. "Tuck. Are you alright?"

Robin. He did not even turn. "I'm fine." He could share it with this man, who had also seen such visions, but he found himself oddly unwilling to do so. It felt as if it had meant to be a moment for him alone.

"Remember that village we went through?"

"Yes."

"The sheriff is going to be there. Collecting taxes they're 'refusing' to pay." The cant Robin put to refusing made it clear how he felt on the matter. "I think we may want to collect some tax from him."

The man's tone was grimly mischievous. Robbing the sheriff was akin to robbing his master, and that went all the way up to the king. But they stole from the king all the time.

"We should be careful. He'll..."

"Have plenty of guards with him. I know. I have a plan."

Tuck sighed inwardly. "What do you want me to do?"

10

*I*f anything, the village seemed worse on their return than when they had left. The dogs seemed thinner and Tuck could hear a woman's sobs from a building nearby. It was not his business, but the temptation to go and comfort her was strong.

What comfort could he give? Those sobs were of a woman who had lost a husband or, perhaps, a child. More likely the latter. Children died all the time. Especially when they did not get enough to eat.

Robin glanced at him. "Are things this bad everywhere?"

"Bad, but not like this. Gisbourne's not the only lord to empty his coffers for the Crusades, but from what I saw on the way here, he's one of the worst offenders. Most are at least making sure the peasantry have enough to grow next year's crop." Not for the sake of the peasants, mind, but for their own. Tuck wondered if Gisbourne even planned on coming back. If he was not thinking of joining those who were carving out far larger holdings for themselves in the desert.

Far larger, but not as pleasant. Then again, there was a wealth in silver and silk and spices out there. Enough for the younger sons who had nothing to inherit.

Nothing would satisfy the likes of Gisbourne. At least the King went on Crusade out of avoidance, not greed. Of course, then he demanded John send him funds. Weapons, men, horses. They'd be better off acquiring horses from the Saracens. "Gisbourne is running things into the ground."

"That he is," Robin murmured. "But here they come."

Hoofbeats did, indeed, echo through what passed for a street. Robin and Tuck had positioned themselves at one side of the desultory village green. Even the tree in the center of it seemed tired and wan.

The knights who rode in were well-equipped and well-mounted. Better than Tuck had expected. He had thought the sheriff would use the dregs to quell people such as this, and then he realized Gisbourne himself rode with them, on a fine palfrey.

A dog padded over towards them, thin and with visible teats. One of the knights dropped his lance butt next to her, and she yelped and trotted away.

At least he had not actually hit the creature. Tuck gave him a few points for that. A man who would beat animals was one step from beating, say, his wife.

He thought with amusement about what would happen if anyone tried to beat Clorinda. Of course, a lot of people felt a man had a right to beat his wife. She was only a woman. Three women, speaking of that, came out of one of the houses.

"Where are your menfolk?"

"In the fields, sir," one of them said, dropping a relatively neat curtsey.

It was Gisbourne himself who spoke, his dark Norman features seeming to darken further as he regarded the woman. "Ah. Yes. Well, then, I will just have to deal with you. You have not paid the levy."

The woman made frightened gestures towards the village. "We don't have it, my lord."

"We'll see about that."

He would take it in whatever coin he could find, Tuck knew. He felt his hands tighten on his staff. It seemed that every day something happened to make him more and more angry with these people. What happened to Christian charity?

The woman's face was thin and drawn, and so pale she looked like a great lady who never stepped outside, not a peasant.

She was perhaps afraid they would take coin in the form of her and her body. He had heard of that happening. Rare, but it occurred. Of course, it occurred far more in the Holy Land, where the woman might, after all, get a child of Christendom out of the deal. Of course, nobody asked the *woman* what she thought about it.

Gisbourne was ordering his men to dismount and secure their horses. They would take anything of value, leaving these people with nothing. Tuck had seen it before.

The difference was that this time he did not plan on standing and watching.

Wait, though. Wait until they...yes. One of them was pushing past the woman into her house. She made a token effort to stop him, not wanting the contents of her pantry to be ravaged. Another was coming right towards Tuck and Robin.

"A friar, eh? You are free to go, but your friend must remain."

Levy could be taken in labor, too. Labor, of course, that the village likely needed itself, and it was not as if they would be fed. Supposedly they were paying for Gisbourne's protection. Who would protect them from Gisbourne?

The king. But John did nothing, seldom left his castle, and Richard would likely never set foot on England's turf again.

"I'm not leaving."

"Suit yourself," the soldier said, stepping towards Robin. "Can you shoot, Yeoman?"

A light came into Robin's eyes. "I would bet I can shoot better than your commander."

Tuck hid a smile. It was likely Clorinda could beat them in a fair contest, let alone Robin. The only one who would have no chance against them was Tuck himself.

"Ah, and what would you bet?"

"If I win, you take no levy here. Honestly, what do these people have? If you win, then the levy includes my service for a year."

Gisbourne, stepping over. He had overheard. "This peasant thinks he can beat..."

"I think I can beat every man you have brought with you, in fair trial. Standard distance and target."

Gisbourne looked at Robin and laughed. "Well, perhaps he will be good enough to be useful. And we are not even getting entertainment here."

Tuck let out a breath. If he had to rescue Robin because of this stunt...when they had enough men hidden to rob Gisbourne back...

Well, that also meant they had enough men hidden to welsh on the bet if needed.

The men were already moving to set up a target on the rather sorry green. Villagers poured out of their houses. They might be on the verge of losing whatever they had left and starving until the crops came in, but this was still entertainment.

Robin blew on his arrows.

"You had better know what you are doing, my friend."

The first of the men was beaten easily, his arrow barely resting in the target. Robin put one in an inner ring over and over until only Gisbourne himself was left.

"Win or lose, it seems."

"I beat your men." Robin smiled.

"You have to beat all of us."

A nasty murmur went through the village. That had not quite been the terms, and they knew it.

Robin simply smiled and shrugged.

Gisbourne picked up his bow, lifted it, and fired. In an instant, Tuck realized he had misjudged the man.

It was a perfect shot. Allowing for all of the wind, and all of the air, and the arrow sailing through the air to strike the very center of the target. He lowered his bow. "Are you even going to bother to shoot, peasant? You can make no better shot."

Tuck let only a small frown show on his features, but Robin actually winked at him.

Then he lifted his bow, drew, nocked and fired in one smooth motion, as if he was hunting deer. The arrow flew, twisting in the air a little, and...

...it struck home. It struck the very shaft of Gisbourne's arrow, splitting it.

"I would call that a better shot," Robin said, calmly.

Laughter and applause echoed through the village.

Gisbourne turned several interesting shades of red. "Seize him!"

Well, that was hardly unexpected. Tuck's staff spun into a ready position. And the men hidden amongst the village houses stepped out and drew their bows, almost as one.

Gisbourne's men did not move. "I said..." Then he looked around, realized he was surrounded. He leapt on his horse and fled, his men following. No arrows flew after them. Killing Gisbourne, after all, was far less fun than humiliating him.

Besides, there would be other chances.

THE INN WAS small and dark, but the stout was very good. Tuck sipped at it, listening.

"And then he and his men vanished back into the woods."

"I wouldn't believe it. Not shooting like that."

Tuck hid a smile behind his glass. He was not about to let these men know he was there and saw the feat of which they spoke. Which was not even being exaggerated. It did not need exaggeration.

Of course, Tuck suspected there was no more than a handful of archers alive who could duplicate it. He had known Robin was good, but that good?"

"Believe it. My sister saw it with her own eyes. Gisbourne was so embarrassed he fled."

"I don't think he needs to be embarrassed about being beaten by somebody *that* good."

"A peasant."

"Who thus has more time to train, I reckon. Less time spent hawking, hunting with dogs and sleeping with mistresses."

Sharp laughter followed. Tuck drank more of his stout. For Robin to have a reputation for being almost supernaturally good? That was something they could use.

When had the band gone from being the people he hung out with to his people? Sometime over the winter, he thought, when they had been confined to camp. When he had joined in the bickering.

He had been part of that, part of the light banter that kept people sane in confined surroundings. Of course, he had experienced it before.

Yet not like that. He belonged here, as little as he wanted to admit it. More of the stout vanished. Now, the question was how, indeed, did they make use of Robin's reputation? How did they support it, use it? Had Robin been thinking it through this far when he had challenged Gisbourne?

It had been a risk, but a risk that came off. "I'd imagine," Tuck said conversationally, "Gisbourne has quite the bounty on that outlaw's head."

"Oh, a large one." The man glanced over. "He's embarrassed, for one thing."

"You don't sound as if you're too upset about that."

"I...eh."

"You should be careful. He's probably got spies." Which was almost certainly true. Tuck only cared to a point. Friars had a certain level of protection from the secular authorities. Part of it, of course, came from nobody taking them seriously. They wandered around and prayed.

Of course, that would make one the perfect spy. In a way, that was what he was doing. There was as yet no price on his head, and far less chance that anyone would set one. Even Gisbourne, who might vaguely remember that the crazy outlaw had been accompanied by a friar.

People seldom looked past the habit.

"Spies in friar's clothing, perhaps?"

Tuck spread his hand. "I'm not his man. But I don't want to see anyone strung up. Gisbourne does like his gallows."

"He does indeed."

Tuck's glass was dangerously close to empty. For a moment, he was not quite sure how that had happened. Surely he had not drunk that much? Well, apparently, he had. "So, perhaps a change of subject would be wise."

Not that the story would not circulate. Gisbourne could not stop it, and there was no sense worrying about it getting back to him. But Tuck did worry that the line would be crossed. That somebody would end up, as he had put it, strung up.

He didn't particularly want his neck fitted for a noose either. Would Gisbourne dare? Quite likely, if he realized Tuck was the same friar. The thought made Tuck reach for his glass again. The men had changed the subject, to the charms of a certain young woman. They discussed her as if she was a prime brood cow, and Tuck shook his head a little. If he was the serving wench, he would 'accidentally' spill ale on them.

Instead, she approached him with a pitcher. "Refill, brother?"

"Of course."

She was glancing over at the table. "One of these days, those two will discuss the wrong woman and get slapped."

She was likely right. Some women did not mind being treated like objects. Others would object in the most vociferous terms. "Well, you're safe from me."

"Indeed?" she teased.

"Admittedly, you would tempt me to break my vows, but I have managed to keep them so far." He voiced it carefully. She was a pretty young woman, and not acknowledging that might offend her. Acknowledging it too much might lead her to think he *would* break his vows with her.

She mock-pouted. "You'd be better than them. Eric there has been trying to get me in his bed for months."

"Slap him," Tuck suggested.

"I did. It seemed to make him more enthusiastic."

Tuck lowered his voice, "Slip monkswort into his ale."

She giggled...she knew what monkswort did, alright. Of course, she probably knew it because some farmers used it on mares, to calm their cycles and make them easier to handle.

He winked at her as she headed back off again. Maybe she would. It would certainly do the man no harm, other than making it harder for him to get either desire or performance for a few hours. Eric, he noted, was looking daggers at him. Jealous, perhaps, if he was that keen to claim the woman.

He was probably married to somebody else. Likely, in fact, he was not ill-favored. Then again, ill-favored was not always on the outside. Tuck had met many handsome men who were cruel and beautiful

women who were ruthless. It did not always follow...outside appearance was simply not connected to the heart. Wasn't there a lesson
about that in the Bible, somewhere?

Something about King David. He shook his head. He had not
managed to read the text in some time. But then, laity never got to,
they had to rely on sermons. Tuck had even given a couple to the
outlaws...from which Clorinda was always noticeable by her absence.
Will, too, seldom attended. Out of respect for her or his own feelings?
Tuck found it hard to care.

11

*I*t had taken him a little while to really grasp that he was afraid of the Blue Lady. He was afraid that she would turn out to be something that might damage his soul. A demon? He did not think so. He would have thought he would have known a servant of Satan when he saw one. Or would he?

A fairy? Some said they were servants of Satan. Most agreed they were dangerous. That one did not want to catch their eye. The greatest danger was for a man who attracted the eye of a lady of the Sidhe.

However, that did not seem to be happening here. Robin had seen her, and he was dedicated to his lover; and despite his talk about his grief for his wife, Tuck suspected he had little interest in bedding women. Clorinda had seen her. Tuck had seen her. The pattern was obvious. The Blue Lady was being seen only by those who would *not* want to sleep with her.

She was not, therefore, a fae lady after a night in the hay with a mortal man. A night in the hay that could be a hundred years for the mortal concerned. And if things were reversed, it was rumored, strange children could be born. Half-mortal, half-fae. In some versions of the old legend, Merlin was such. In others he was sired by a demon.

Not much difference, perhaps. Yet, the Blue Lady...definitely preferred those who would not be tempted by her beauty. That pointed towards...something. Perhaps she was a goddess in truth, and not the one Clorinda thought. "What do you want?" he asked the air. If she was the Virgin, surely, she would hear him.

Whether she did or not, she offered no response. Not even the scent of her presence. As if her attention was simply elsewhere.

Which was again evidence that she was fae, not divine. But if so, what did she want? Perhaps these woods were her kingdom?

None of it made sense. He focused his mind, trying to pray, but it eluded him. There was no sense of the presence of God, either.

Which implied that the failing was in him. Perhaps he needed to fast for a couple of days, to cleanse himself. Perhaps he had drunk too much stout the night before. Too much alcohol could dull the senses, after all. Maybe he should stick to smallbeer for a few days, or the fresh water of the forest.

Or maybe it was the niggling demon Doubt, flowing through his mind. The fear that the old gods were not just real, but potentially benevolent. That the church was, quite simply, wrong. He did not want to accept that, even as the most remote of possibilities. It went beyond heresy, beyond even blasphemy.

Believing it even for a moment could cause him to spend thousands of years in Purgatory. Accepting it would condemn him to Hell. He knew these things, deep in his self, in his mind. He accepted and embraced them, and thus his fear.

If they were wrong, but they were not wrong. They could not be wrong. He slumped to the ground, his back against a tree, his eyes closed. It might look as if he had fallen down drunk...early in the morning, even. If anyone saw him, they would mock.

How could he reconcile everything he had been taught? Robin's answer was the simple one. Assume it was Mary. Believe it was Mary. Convince himself it was Mary. Unless she told him who she was, he could not prove it. He should not be contained within this raging river of doubt.

He opened his eyes. There was a light in front of them, a small glow. A small fairy, a lesser one, and this time he saw it clearly. It more resembled a glow with wings or a large insect than a winged woman.

The wings were, it seemed, the most significant part of the being. "Hello."

No response. The fairy hovered in front of him, her glow dimming a little until, indeed, she seemed like a small girl with wings. Girl, not woman, her breasts tiny and her hips narrow. She looked barely ripe, not yet marriageable.

And she was silent. She was simply looking at him as if not quite sure what to do about this large intruder. "Hello?" he tried again.

Then, he just heard a glass like sound and she zipped off. He decided, after a moment, it was laughter.

Perhaps he was right in his first guess. That this was a magic place, a fae place. A place where Oberon and Titania might take a moonlight ride. Whatever the Blue Lady was, he was almost sure she was not a demon.

He wanted to find a church, or a cloister. To hide in it until he no longer felt threatened, until he no longer felt uncertain.

It was a very long time before he got up, and when he did, he was in no hurry to return to camp. He was in no hurry, in fact, to go anywhere. There was no more sign of the fairy, or of the Blue Lady, or of...anything. The only person he could think of to talk to was Richard, and Richard owned different truths. Or lies.

Or... Tuck managed to restrain himself before swearing, glancing around the clearing. The people...he loved the people here, but it was perhaps time to move on. In another place, he could forget the Blue Lady, could restore himself to sanity. If he stayed, he would drift into heresy at best.

He should leave, and he should leave now, without a word to anyone. It was a betrayal of sorts, but if he talked to anyone, he would stay. If he even went back for his mule, he would end up staying.

Thus, instead of walking towards the camp, he turned his footsteps away. Away from the outlaws. Away from Nottingham. He was resolved not to return.

∾

THE SOUND of hooves disturbed Tuck from a reverie. He was alone, he was on foot, and he was going to need alms. For the moment, however, he was getting out of the road. It sounded like multiple riders and it sounded as if they were coming at speed. He did not want to get accidentally ridden down.

They were knights, he realized. Three of them on palfreys, three squires behind on mules, leading the war horses. Their armor was secured to the war mounts, they were dressed in civilian clothes, but armed.

They were heading towards Nottingham. Tuck wondered if there was going to be a tourney. He felt, for a moment, very alone. The laughter between them, the banter, was enough to make him turn around. Go back. Beg Robin to let him back, tell him he'd needed some time alone.

"Brother!" one of the knights called.

"You seem in good spirits, sir," Tuck commented, stepping out as the horses were reined in. They might be, their mounts were not. The palfreys seemed tired and he saw spur tracks on the war horses.

Typical. Infidels often, he had noticed in the Holy Land, took better care of their mounts. "And why should we not be?"

"Because you have been long on the road."

"Ah, but that only means we are almost home."

Home, then, was Nottingham. As Gisbourne had returned from Crusade, so now those who had followed him trickled back. "So, what of the Holy Land?"

"Dusty, unpleasant, and I'm almost inclined to say the Saracens can keep it. Almost."

"I had that impression myself." He was not going to deny or hide that he had been on pilgrimage. "If the legend that Christ came here as a child is true, then why did He go back?"

The knight laughed. "It is, indeed, a far more pleasant country we have here. On the other hand, I dislike that Jerusalem yet remains in the hands of the infidel. We will have to return."

Tuck, secretly, did not dislike that at all. "Ah, then my guess would be you came back because you had forgotten the faces of your wives."

The knight laughed again. "A brother who knows how to banter with soldiers. I would say you had forgotten the face of your mistress, but..."

"I am a wandering friar. Even if I were inclined to break the vows which bind me, I would not inflict this life on a woman."

"Then you are a better man than most Churchmen."

Tuck shrugged eloquently, but it took all of his willpower not to pointedly look at those spur tracks. One could judge a man by how he treated his beasts. The evidence was that they were not better men than most knights. "Besides, I am happy enough on my own."

Which was the first lie he had told them. He kept looking around for a friend to tell them something, he kept looking for signs of the camp. He kept wishing...he was even missing Richard, even missing the ones he did not know well. Missing Alan and Will and Reginald.

Missing, most especially, Robin and Clorinda and John.

"I suppose one would have to be, to lead your life and stand it. Well. We must be home by dark."

The knight spurred the palfrey onwards. Tuck managed not to flinch until the group was past. He missed the mule he had left with the outlaws. It had been a good beast, but he trusted Robin to either look after it or sell it to somebody who would. Some farmer could make good use of it.

The greenwood seemed to close around him, though, after they were gone.

12

The inn was a small one, and he was four days walk from Robin's turf. It did not surprise Tuck to hear somebody declaiming the story of Gisbourne's humiliation at the outlaw's hands.

It seemed as if he would have to go back to the Holy Land to truly escape reminders, for every time he thought of Robin, he thought of the Blue Lady. Every time he sat down in an inn, every time he exchanged greetings on the road, it seemed that Robin came up.

Robin was probably...would Robin look for him? Or would Robin accept that some things, and some people, could not be held? Not that he was not held. He almost might as well go back to them.

How could he explain that it was her...the lady, the goddess, the maiden...that he fled? Not the outlaws, not Robin, not Clorinda, who was his friend. His friend. He had never called a woman friend before.

It was she above all whom he missed. He shook his head. Perhaps a retreat? Perhaps a shorter pilgrimage. To Glastonbury, say, or to Lindisfarne in the far north. Lindisfarne, he had heard, was worth it for the mead the monks brewed alone.

No. Glastonbury. He would go to Glastonbury, where the thorn grew and where the legendary king was buried.

The resolution calmed his mind. He left the common room early, to bed down in the barracks style room this inn had as cheap board. He woke early, took what breakfast the cooks had, and left before he could hear any more word of Robin.

He might make it there before winter, he thought, if he hurried. Then he could winter in the monastery. In a comfortable cell, not a tent. Then why did he long for the tent?

The road, for now, was obscured. Deep fog...not quite the pea soupers common in this valley...but deep enough that it made his passage harder than it needed to be. He followed the road by the feel of it under his sandaled feet, not by vision. A desultory bird attempted to sing, the fog muffling the sound. After a couple of stanzas, it gave up and fell silent. At least this early the midges would not yet be flying.

Now there was a reason not to live out in the greenwood. At least not anywhere close to a lake or a slow river. Between the midges and the mosquitoes...

South and west he began to bend his feet. He heard the sounds of a carriage and stepped aside. Emerging through the fog, pulled by two good bays, with outriders on black palfreys. It was clearly the carriage of somebody rich. Inhabitant, driver and riders alike ignored him.

The part of his brain that had spent entirely too much time with the outlaws made note of how lax they were. They were all but asking to be robbed, he thought. Possibly, too, it was some lady inside. Who could be ransomed.

He had to get out of here...but then the outrider saw him. Their eyes met. Gisbourne had been cruel. This man was so cold Tuck wondered if he even had a soul. Or if he had already sold it to the Devil.

Not that he had ever met or directly heard of anyone who really had. It was one of those things that, for him, hovered between reality and myth. To deny the existence of the Devil was one step away from the ultimate heresy.

"You will come with us."

"I am a brother of the Church," Tuck said, softly. Technically, secular authority had no power over him. In reality, of course, he had to be careful.

"Screw the Church." The man drew his sword, lowered it towards Tuck's throat. The horse spooked a little.

Tuck considered his options. He had nobody he could directly protest to, and the outrider had him at a disadvantage of height. By the time he got his staff up... No, he was being abducted, but there was little he could do about it.

Little, possibly nothing. He followed after the rider, one hand on his staff. Could he fight? Yes, if there were fewer of them. He watched for an opportunity for escape, but he saw none.

This was not Gisbourne's territory, not any more, so it was not that lord, realizing this was the same friar who had caused all the trouble. Unless word had spread. It might have. He had heard of a 'friar' with Robin. Perhaps this guy was pulling in every friar he found for questioning.

If so, he could probably escape this by playing stupid. It was often a good technique when dealing with the truly evil.

Which was what he sensed here. Gisbourne was selfish and unpleasant. Whoever these men were, they were evil. The same kind of evil that had led them to sack that village. When he had turned and fled back to England.

The evil had followed him. The castle to which he was led was a small one. Not designed to deal with anything more than peasants trying to rob the storehouse. Perhaps to take back what they needed to survive.

Tuck forced the anger down. Play stupid. It was his best chance of walking out of here. If it was not too late.

They pushed him through the castle gates. He glanced around. There were some good horses...better than he could steal for the simple reason that he was no kind of a rider. He knew men who could. He wished they were here. He also missed the mule, whom he had left with the outlaws.

He would have been glad to know they knew he was in trouble. He would even have been glad to see or sense the Blue Lady. She could help him.

No. He had to place his trust in God and his Son to get him out of this one. Not in any goddess, whoever she might be, or Fae lady, or...

He was pushed into a tower, up some stairs and into a windowless room. It reminded him of where Clorinda had been held.

The door was locked behind him. He took stock of his surroundings. Whoever this lord was, he was taking a great risk arresting churchmen, without even bothering to voice a charge. Unless he was not even going to try...Tuck would likely just disappear. He was only still alive because this man wanted something.

Perhaps only to scare him, to exert some authority over the Church. He would be far from the first secular power to attempt to do so. The Church was feared...for it alone had power over men's souls.

Or did it? Tuck paced the cell, seeing no immediate means of escape. He sat down on the narrow bunk and attempted to pray.

It was a larger and more spacious cell than he had had as a novice in the friary, more comfortable than many places he had spent the night. Were it not for the locked door. God could open doors. He truly believed that. Not that he expected God to walk up to the door and unlock it.

No. He worked more subtly than that, he was as a thief in the night. Part of Tuck hoped to see a literal thief, but there was no way Robin could know about his plight.

Had he not left...well, no. He could not have predicted this, he could not have second guessed it. He was, besides that, still alive. Which meant he could escape. He knew far more of such things than a friar would be expected to know.

He assumed he would be fed at some point. When he was not, he curled up on the bunk and slept.

He supposed it was morning when he awoke. With no windows, not even arrow slits, he could not tell. Nor could he be sure what had awakened him.

A vague sense of alert flowed through him, a sense he could not readily shake off. Something bad was about to happen.

They had, of course, taken his staff. No big deal in the long term...he could always make another. But it left him unarmed. He was not good at fighting unarmed. He took stock of the room again. No furniture other than the bunk, and that too heavy for him to lift. They were careful.

The two guards came in a moment later. And that was when he clearly felt her presence. He didn't want her. His soul or his life, was that his choice?

He sensed, almost heard, the words 'Trust me.' But he was not sure if he did, he was not sure if he could. She was...whatever she was...and he was a friar and devoted to... Possibly Her son. Perhaps. But the fear that flowed through and around him was the same fear that had driven him here.

The fear he could not shake, and now it mingled with a very real fear for his life. It was all he could do not to soil himself...he who had been brave in so many other situations.

They grabbed his arms and all but pushed him down the stairs.

"What do you want with me?" he protested. "I am but a traveling friar!"

"We have to be sure of that."

Then, perhaps, it was the stories of Robin to blame for this. Or perhaps somebody else had had the idea of pretending to be a friar. By chance, though, he had the right man. Tuck only had to prove otherwise.

Play stupid. Pretend to be somebody pushed into orders because he was of no other use. That was what Tuck had to do. He could not quite manage to be the drooling fool, but he could certainly convince them he was slow.

As they pulled him across the courtyard, though, he remembered everything he had learned with the outlaws. The stables were there. The worn pattern towards the base of the third tower indicated the likely presence of a sally port. That, of course, was a better escape route than the main gates.

Of course, right now, to escape he would have to grow wings and fly. Even with the Blue Lady's help that seemed unlikely. If he accepted her help...

She was there. He could feel her, sense her, he knew her. She asked only that he trusted her. Not worship, trust. How could he, though, when he did not know what she wanted of him?

He started a little. The sound that came from one of the towers seemed very loud, but it was only pigeons taking off. He guessed it was mid morning. It was hard to tell, for the sky was deeply overcast, threatening rain.

Rain would be good if he could get to that port. It would conceal his tracks and pursuers that were wet and miserable were likely to give up sooner than they would on a pleasant day.

But he needed more than a bit of rain. He needed Robin. Or real, true magic, of the kind that existed only in stories. Of the kind that helped a man split another archer's shaft? No. Robin had been both damn good and damn lucky that day. It was not exactly a feat he could repeat regularly.

Tuck wished for his staff, but one did not drop out of the sky either, and then he was being hustled up the steps into the keep.

The great hall was dank and mostly dark. It was lit no more than it needed to be, and there was a faint smell. In fact, the prison cell smelled better. Perhaps it had not been occupied recently.

No. It was the smell of hound. Three of them, flopped at the base of the dais in various angles of repose. They were huge hounds, the kind one would use to pursue wolves. Two were dark grey, the third a solid black.

His chances of escape had dropped considerably. Such hounds could equally easily be used to hunt men. Behind them, sat a man with an aquiline nose.

He looked as if he might be distant kin to the king...no, it was not John, not here in this godforsaken place. But some Norman cousin, no doubt. Pure Norman, for sure, there was nothing of the English about his features. He was dressed in black.

"So. Are you the fake friar?"

"Fake friar?" Tuck played it as casual as he could. "Somebody has been impersonating a member of my order?"

"Somebody has. And as a result, I no longer permit friars in my holding."

"Not something I was supposed to know." So, he was being assumed to be a spy. Well, then, he would be one. "I had heard...a rumor, but it seemed to be a minstrel's tale, much fueled by ale."

"Exaggerated, Brother. But not untrue."

"My mother house is in Cirencester. My identity can be checked with them." He kept some fear in his voice. It was easy, as the black hound lifted its head and looked right at him as if assessing how much meat his bones might carry.

It was only a large dog, he reminded himself. No doubt well trained, and he doubted the man would feed him to his dogs. Whilst it happened in minstrel's tales, a dog that had once tasted man flesh would be useless for all purposes, for he would grasp the possibility that his handler might be a meal.

However, no doubt that these dogs would be trained to corner him if he tried to run. They were certainly big enough to pin him.

"Cirencester. I would say you are a long way from home, but it is the habit of your order to wander far, is it not?"

"I have been to the Holy Land." It might be coin he could barter with. As a former pilgrim he would be respected.

"Indeed?" There was skepticism, though.

Perhaps it had backfired. Perhaps this man did not believe him. Tuck glanced around again and realized something he should have grasped before. He might have fine horses and trained men, but there was something distinctly threadbare about the castle itself. Bringing attention to the signs of poverty, of course, was not a smart move. It might well be taken as an insult.

Still, the only thing he had seen worth stealing was the horses. Of course, that was a good priority for limited funds, in most people's minds. "I have. But being a friar, I brought back nothing but my memories."

The man leaned forward. "Then, what is it like?"

"Hot and dry. Much of it is desert. I was glad to get back to England. I was forgetting what the color green looked like." No, dumb was not the way to play with this man. To play as if he could expect a confidence...

"Except for those who wear it."

"You know that no cloth can match the deep green of a forest."

"No." The lord looked thoughtful. "Unfortunately, I see no reason to believe you are not the friar concerned." He glanced to his guards. "Flog him, then escort him to the edge of the property. If you see him again...kill him."

How did he get out of being flogged? He saw no way right now...and if they took the lord at his word, then Tuck knew he would likely not survive. He would be in no state to be on the road. Nor could he run.

He placed himself in the hands of God, but it was her presence he felt. The Blue Lady. Asking him to trust her.

Asking him to let her in, to let her damn him if she was not the Virgin after all. "Mary," he murmured.

Perhaps what reaction he sensed would help him.

"Ah, now the friar prays."

Tuck looked at the man. Softly. "You will not prosper." Which he was not, already. It was a reasonable prediction. A reasonable guess.

"Take him out of my sight."

The guards grabbed Tuck, starting to pull him out of the hall. Well, trusting her had got him nowhere so far.

Until they got to the entrance to the keep. Outside, rain streaked down and lightning occasionally flared in the sky.

"Screw this," one of the guards said. "I'm not going out in this even for Himself."

Break and run into the storm? But they still had him pretty firmly. Perhaps if he tried to drag them out there.

The sky was an ugly color. He had not seen a storm this bad in, easily, a couple of years. It almost seemed unnatural. It was unnatural, but how could he use it? Then the guard let go of him.

He had decided no sane man would step outside in this. The sally port was...not that far. Of course, once outside, he would have to survive in the storm.

Trust me.

The rain poured down on him, soaking him to the skin in seconds, the sodden robes slowing him. The inside of the sally port. It was barred. He lifted the bar easily, and was out into the field beside the castle. He was fortunate there was no moat.

He picked up his skirts and ran.

he rain poured around Tuck as he ran for the eaves of the greenwood. One did not go under a single tree in a storm. A forest was a different story.

Inside, it was a little dryer. He gasped for breath, but the guards...had not followed. Perhaps they had decided that it was not worth it, that he would have the sense not to return to this place. What sane man would?

He laughed. He had just proved he was not sane. He was sodden, clad in soaked wool, but it was still better than being flogged. Except that if he did not get dry soon, he would surely catch something.

He plodded deeper into the forest. Under its eaves, it was definitely somewhat dryer, but he was already so wet it did not matter.

Eventually, he decided the best thing to do was to strip naked. It was unlikely any woman would be out here to see him, and any swine-herds would be heading for shelter themselves with their charges. Or at least huddled somewhere. With his wet robes over one arm, he continued to plod into the woods. The ground squelched beneath his feet.

How did he get dry? Then he found it. There had been a charcoal burner here. Recently. No doubt he had fled for better shelter too. The fire still smoldered, and the rain was easing off.

He tossed a couple more branches on the fire and settled down close to it. If the burner came back, he could apologize. Whoever it was would probably understand. This storm had come, after all, out of all but nowhere.

He was doomed now. And he wanted to go home. Would Robin take him back? Would he accept that he had needed time alone to think? Or would the outlaw, quite reasonably, decide the friar could no longer be trusted? He had, after all, run out on them.

That was when the plan formulated. He had to have something to offer when he went back. The habits of this solitary lord would not be enough. The man was not worth robbing.

Tuck needed intelligence he could return with. Intelligence the band could use to their own ends.

He had to go to Nottingham. But not yet.

It took the rest of the day to get his robes somewhat dry. The charcoal burner did not return. In the end, he spent the night there, curled up close to the embers of the fire. In the morning, he began to head back to the north and east, making a careful circuit of the castle and avoiding the road.

He was not sure where the property ended, but if he was caught again, they would kill him. He was surprised they had not tried to shoot him in the storm. Maybe they had, and it had gone so wide he had not even noticed. Anything was possible.

His robes were still not entirely dry, either, but once he saw a crossroads, he traipsed back onto the road. It felt like a penance, to be retracing his steps like this. It was, but not one he owed to God.

One he owed to his friends, whom he had deserted in what he now recognized as fear and panic. Well, he was still afraid. The adventure with the lord would stay with him...the evil he and some of his men had shown.

He had not seen evil like that in some time. Perhaps something needed to be done about him anyway. Not worth robbing, no, but perhaps worth removing. He was less dangerous than Gisbourne, perhaps, but...

Gisbourne was not evil. Just selfish, arrogant and not particularly, in Tuck's mind, smart. But as he approached Nottingham, he wondered if there was something in 'Better the devil you know'.

Of course, he would have to be careful if people all over were looking for a large-built friar. He did not have a knife. He did not have money, either, but that problem could be solved. He hated to ask for alms, but he had no choice. Not right now. He was not about to go to Abbot Moresford for help. Perhaps one of the smaller...and then he recalled.

There was a house of Poor Clares just outside Nottingham. The Sisters would help a friar who had 'lost everything to robbers.' It was even the truth. He had been robbed, and the fact that the thief sat in a castle made it less ethical than it would otherwise have been. They might even have a spare belt knife for him.

The decision made, he changed course, walking deliberately a little bent, trying to look more exhausted even than he felt. A tired friar was a threat to no one, especially one that carried no weapon. He was no threat, to be honest. He doubted he could fight. He was even rather hoping the Clares might have a spare cell in the guest house for him. Even he would not be allowed within the cloister itself. The women protected their virtue thus, by excluding all males. Most said it was because men could not be trusted.

Ha. It was as much to keep the women, especially the novices, from temptation as that. Not that he was much of a temptation, especially as it started to rain again. Quite hard. By the time he got to their door he would resemble the proverbial drowned rat.

Nobody offered him alms as he crossed through the edge of the city and then across the meadows. Nobody approached him at all. He probably stank, thinking about it, more than even most people did. Most people did not notice.

He remembered the escape from the castle through the tannery and wrinkled his nose. Now there was a stench he was sure he could never get used to.

The convent was a relatively small building with an attached chapel. There was a service he could perform for the Sisters. While he would not dare say Mass for them as he had for the outlaws, he could take their confession...a service they could not perform for each other. Women, being further from God, could not represent him in any way. They were, after all, the fallen ones, bound by the curse of Eve. Folly, Tuck had come to think. Clares devoted their lives, instead, to prayer and contemplation. He knocked on the door.

THE SMALL HOLE in it opened. Then closed. Then the door itself swung open. "Come in, Brother. You look half drowned."

He stepped into the antechamber, dripping on the stone floor. "Do you have lodging?"

"Yes. And I think we might even be able to find you a clean habit." The Clare was of middle years, and her face bore the marks of somebody for whom a smile was the standard expression.

He instantly relaxed.

"I am Sister Mary Michael."

He used, for once, his actual friar name. "Brother Joseph." Not his birth name, of course. That he had all but forgotten, intentionally so. But also not his nickname, the one that referred to his girth. It was not appropriate here.

"Come to the guest common room. We will make a fire."

They would, of course, have a priest attached to them, but he like as not came only to say Mass on Sunday and High Holydays. Tuck had always suspected that some of the convents bent the rules on what women were permitted to do. At least with regards to confession amongst themselves. Still, he could offer his assistance...either in that or with some task that required a man's strength. Not that women could not do most things that were thought the province of men, but they were still smaller. Nothing would ever change that.

Mary Michael was as good as her word. She led him into a reasonably comfortable room with a fireplace...an actual fireplace...and called on a passing novice. The girl kept glancing at him with a mixture of nerves and something else.

Yes, female novices were as prone to temptation as male ones. Desperately so, if she found him at all attractive. He did not smile at her, which might be encouragement, but rather moved closer to the fire.

He doubted she had any choice about being here. Palmed off by a family with far too many daughters and far too little money for dowry. Marrying a daughter to God was a good way to dispose of her.

The heat began to flow into him. He already felt better. Mary Michael had returned. "So..."

"I was robbed on the road. I have no coins, and worse, no knife." That was always a disaster. A man...or a woman...without a belt knife was all but helpless.

"Somebody was desperate enough to rob a friar?"

It was a reasonable question. He lifted his hands. "You would think they would have waited for richer pickings, unless they thought I hid gold under my habit."

"Too many do. And it endangers those who do not." She settled back into her chair. "We can give you lodging, and we at least have cloth. One of my novices is deft with a needle, and even a friar should have a change of clothes. I will see what I can do about a knife."

"Thank you." With that small help, he would be fine.

"Too many, too, step outside the Church into the realm of politics."

She meant Abbott Moresford. He was sure of it. "Perhaps that is because too many do not wish to be in the Church in the first place."

Mary seemed to consider that for a long moment. "You may well be right. I admit I have two novices who...would be better suited to marriage and children. One of them loves children. I honestly am trying to..."

Tuck frowned. "Would her family be amenable to her being transferred to an order that works with foundlings?"

"Perhaps."

"It sounds as if she might be happier." And perform a valuable service while she was at it. Too many bastards were abandoned on the doorsteps of churches. There were several orders that devoted themselves to caring for them. The boys were prepared for apprenticeship or orders. The majority of the girls stayed within the orders, looking after the next generation of foundlings. Only a few left to wed or seek apprenticeships in those guilds which took women.

"It's a good idea."

"No house is ever made happy if there is even one person under its roof who would rather not be there." And with so many not having the choice, it was no wonder at all that the houses were either unhappy...or turned into something they should not have been. Something inappropriate. Something... Tuck's thoughts tailed off. He was glad to be a friar and responsible only for his own conduct.

Inwardly he laughed. His own conduct. Drinking, enjoying the table too much, chasing around with outlaws and rescuing witches. He had enough to answer for without worrying about the deeds of his brothers. Well, if he was damned, at least he had had some fun on the way there.

Lords who flogged friars aside. "Which reminds me. There is a lord south and west of here who has become convinced all friars are spies for the outlaws."

Mary rolled her eyes. "I heard the story that a couple of them used friar's robes to get into the city unnoticed. But..."

"If you could warn anyone else who shows up to avoid his holdings. I barely got out of there."

"So, it was he who robbed you, not some outlaw."

Tuck colored. "Yes, it was." Robbery it had been. "He did say he would kill me if he saw me again."

"Well, I think we can deal with him," Mary said, practically. "Next time the bishop is in town, I will give it a quiet mention...and he will find *all* of the church avoiding his holdings."

She seemed confident the bishop would listen to her, and Tuck grinned. Official excommunication might be hard to manage, but the unofficial kind worked almost as well. Especially on somebody like that. "Until he apologizes, of course."

"Of course."

Tuck grinned at her again. "Thanks. I don't exactly have the ears of bishops myself."

"He's my brother."

"Oh." Tuck shook his head. Two children given to the church. Unless, of course, they were children of the wrong side of the blanket, that probably meant a large family.

He suspected the wrong side of the blanket. Many bishops were bastards of noble, or even royal, birth. And for female bastards to be hidden away in convents, where their offspring could not later show up as threats...

Tuck was not of such birth, but he had known those who were. Well, it was not his problem, right now. For right now, he had a warm cell to sleep in and good breakfast to look forward to.

IN THE MORNING, he left. They had managed to find a friar's habit that fit him with minimal alteration, ably done by a novice of about sixteen. Of course, he had made sure she saw none of his body. No need to tempt the girl. She was nervous enough around him, anyway.

Outside, it was no longer raining, or even threatening to rain. The sun was rising behind Castle Rock. He headed for the first place he could think of to find gossip.

He headed for the Pilgrim. It had, of course, not changed since last year. In fact, he thought he saw some of the same clientele. Fortunately, they did not recognize him. Likely, they did not look past habit and tonsure...the latter also ably redone by the Clares. It had needed it rather badly...and it was a hard thing to do yourself.

The inn was open for breakfast, although he had already eaten. Instead of going in, however, he leaned against the outer wall.

"Are you heading on pilgrimage?" a female voice asked.

He turned, and shook his head to the goodwife. "No."

She pulled out a coin. "Then you are hoping for alms." She added, with amusement that reminded him of Clorinda, "To spend on ale."

"Perhaps." He took the coin, slipped it into his belt pouch, and offered a quiet prayer in return. She smiled, bobbed her head, and headed on her business.

Part of him had always felt a bit guilty about accepting alms. After all, he was not completely devoid of the ability to earn what he needed. Perhaps that was why the outlaws had felt so good to be with.

They had expected him to pull his weight, and he had. Of course, part of his weight had been in prayers and masses, but that was only reasonable.

He had prayed for her, that made the exchange somewhat even. Perhaps she had a reason...no, he knew she had a reason, for her belly had been swelling slightly beneath her dress. Her first, likely, based off of her age. A frightening time for any young woman, for too many did die in the throes of producing offspring.

He prayed for her more sincerely as he walked away from the inn. Loitering there now would have seemed strange, but her coin would, eventually, buy him lunch.

The streets were starting to become crowded. The sun was still bright, although no doubt it would cloud in by the afternoon. There were places, places he had visited, where the weather stayed the same all day. He was not sure how people handled that. Here, it might rain hard in the morning, then the water would depart to leave such a clear and crisp afternoon as anyone might love.

He would never leave England again, he had long since vowed. No more long sea voyages, either. No more worrying about bandits on the highway and pirates on the ocean. Well, bandits, maybe.

No more wondering about the Saracen, with their curved swords and veiled women. Their highest ranking men had harems, multiple wives and concubines under one roof. Women who never set foot outdoors, or almost never. If they did, they were so deeply veiled one could see only their eyes. Far more covered than any goodwife.

He shook his head, the memories of that distant land abruptly quite strong. The desert. The cats, with larger ears and slightly larger eyes than any farm tabby. A different breed of cats as the Saracens rode a different breed of horses. What horses they had! Even Tuck, who knew little of equines, knew there was something truly special about those desert bred beasts. He had asked one of the Saracens once, alone and unarmed and not a threat. He had told the friar that God had given horses the power of flight without wings.

He had not, however, had a good explanation for their tradition that mares were the best riding horses, swifter and with more endurance than stallions or geldings.

On the subject of horses, a farmer's cart came down the road, drawn by a shaggy black pony. The beast turned its head and attempted to snatch an apple from one of the stalls.

Tuck laughed a bit as the farmer yanked the reins and forced its attention back on the road. The pony actually sighed resignedly.

"Stupid beast," the farmer said, but not without affection.

"Beasts know only what they need and want, not the laws of men," Tuck could not help but point out.

"Well, this one should know that if he wants an apple I'll get him one. Now he won't get one."

Which did seem fair justice for the attempt at theft. As if understanding his owner's words, the pony sighed again, then padded onwards. Tuck stepped close to the wall to give the cart, full of wool, space to pass.

The exchange, though, had brought him down to earth. Or rather, back to England's green land, from his mind's wandering to the East.

There were, it was rumored, lands far further east, though. From which silk came, that fabric so rare, so expensive, so desirable. As if the pony's hunger had reminded him, Tuck bought an apple, turned around...

...and came face to face with Alan. To his credit, the outlaw kept most of the surprise of recognition off his face. "Brother."

"Old friend," Tuck said, not using the man's name.

"We were worried about you."

"A friar wanders. This one might, though, be quite willing to wander back."

Hubert studied him for a moment. "Robin was not pleased that you left without a word."

"If he doesn't want me to return, I won't." He kept his voice down. It was, in any case, up to the leader who was with him and who was against him. "But..."

Alan reached for Tuck's arm, gripped it for a moment. "Come on. He won't do worse than toss you out. Although I'm sure he'll want your reasons."

"He'll have them." In private, though. It was bad enough to express his doubts, his fears, to the outlaw leader. He certainly was not voicing them to the entire band.

What if everything he believed in was wrong? Or could he simply accept, as Robin did, her as the Virgin Mary and not think past that? Robin was not a stupid man, but he was also not an educated man in the way any man of the cloth was.

Or was he? Tuck did not know for sure. Robin said but little of his family or birth, and it could well be better than he admitted to.

Friars were not really supposed to question, but Tuck knew his Latin, had read his Bible. He had found contradictions in the Word of God. Contradictions preachers glossed over, did not reveal to their flocks.

What if it was all wrong? Or what if it was just a little bit wrong. What if the Word of God had...drifted...as any other story did? If what He had said had been passed through a few hands to many and become a story in which Little John, say, was a true giant, not just an extremely large man.

In some ways, that idea comforted him. "So...where are we going?"

THEY HIT THE ROAD QUICKLY. Tuck did not know Alan well, and the reason was obvious to anyone who knew the man. To know somebody well required talking to them.

For Alan to string more than two words together was rare and required a good reason. The sentence inviting Tuck to return was the longest he had ever heard from him. Therefore, they did not, no, know each other well. Alan had never allowed it.

The silence, however, was broken by squabbling birds and chittering squirrels, all dancing through the branches above. There was a saying that a squirrel could run from York to London, and never set foot on the ground. With the way farmers were clearing the greenwood, Tuck wondered if that was true any longer.

There were more and more farmers. Well, it was not his problem. The world would not change that much, surely, before Christ's return.

Unless that was a lie too. He corralled his thoughts. To believe that any part of the Bible was a lie was heresy. Of course, one did have to accept that certain things should not be taken too literally.

The laws of Leviticus, for example, had been negated by the New Testament.

Of course, who the heck really loved their neighbor these days? Or rather, loved them by the true definition...in which one's neighbor was everyone.

Alan took him down a narrow path, then across a stream, then up the other side, and into a clearing. Familiar smells overtook him.

"Tuck?" That was Robin's voice.

"I..." He had nothing to say, he realized, to the friend he had so betrayed. Nothing at all to say to him. His voice faded out, not responding to his thoughts.

"For Mary's sake, man. Where have you been?"

"I needed space. Needed time." He wasn't going to reveal his doubts. Not with the entire camp staring at him. He saw no sign of Richard, but did see two boys, one no more than twelve, whom he did not recognize.

"Richard is gone."

That hit him in a wave. Not that the old druid would have sought Last Rites, but at the same time. At the same time. "I'm back. But only if you want me to be."

"You should not have left."

He knew that. He knew it in his heart and soul. But he had. "I had to. Look. What happened to Richard?"

Robin turned along the edge of the clearing, beckoning him to follow. "Simple old age, as far as we can tell. He just did not wake up one morning."

"That beats most alternatives." Tuck's training wanted to say that Richard was in hell. His personality, his mind, wanted to say that could not have truly been allowed to happen to so good a man. It was a quite disturbing thought, really. More than he would and could have imagined before now. He did not want to consign Richard, even mentally, to the fires of hell.

"Indeed. But he was asking after you, only a couple of days before."

Tuck frowned. "I..." A pause. "The Blue Lady."

"Mary."

"Are you sure of that?" He turned his head towards the slender

young man. In some ways, Robin was prettier than Clorinda. Had that
been how his unnatural desires had started? Those who felt them often
went for pretty boys.

"Yes." Robin turned to face him. "But you are not. Clorinda thinks
she is Aine."

"I do not know. I only know that she got me out of prison, and..."
Tuck tailed off. His strength, in its entirety, had faded. He was not sure
what to believe any more. "My faith has been weakened."

"Or tested." Robin shook his head. "I respect Clorinda. But I do not
believe she is...can be...correct. Even if the old gods exist, they cannot
touch those who have been washed in the blood of Christ."

"The friar takes lesson from the outlaw." Tuck allowed amusement into his voice. It *was* amusing, if one did not take it too seriously. If one allowed understanding of the fact that this time he
needed it.

"Better than from the bishop in his sumptuous robes."

"Point. Although I did find...there is *one* good person of the church
in Nottingham." He laughed. "The abbess of the poor Clares."

Robin laughed. "Of course there is. The one with no temporal
power. So. What happened?"

"I intended to go to Glastonbury. I thought I might regain some
strength there, but I did not go far." He related the story of the friar-
hating lord carefully. He knew how to give a spy's account, and thus
he did.

Robin listened, silent, the only sound other than Tuck's voice being
that of an argument between two squirrels. Finally, he spoke, "Something needs to be done about this man."

THE TENSION HAD ALREADY FADED. It was Clorinda who made the first
overtures, sitting next to him at breakfast. They talked long about
Richard.

Tuck could not...he could feel his faith shattering, breaking,
spreading into tiny pieces. What Robin had said had helped a little.
Yet, only a little. He could not reconcile his beliefs with Richard's...basi-

cally decent nature. Sure, he had been obnoxious, but that was a crime worthy only of a stay in Purgatory. Not Hell.

He could not imagine Clorinda suffering such a fate either, for all that she insisted the Blue Lady was Aine and made libation to the old gods.

He could not...deal with the fact that people so close to him were damned by God. Thus, he walked away. Not far. He did not intend to leave again.

He simply did not know what to do. For the first time in his life, he wished he had been born a woman. No, not quite. He wished he had chosen a contemplative, cloistered order, where he would never be exposed to the tests and temptations of the world. Where he would spend his time in silence and in prayer.

Yet, he had chosen this, out of the limited array made available to him. He could not go back and have his life again.

He could not even go back and undo the time they had ambushed him, stolen his ale and asked him to do last rites. He should have left as soon as he had completed them.

Now. Now he was halfway to taking off his habit. The Church would do it for him if they found out he was even contemplating that they were wrong. No. He knew what his old novice master would have done...locked him in a cell for a few days. But he had tried that. Being alone with his thoughts did not help.

Perhaps if he went to the nearest village and listened to Mass it might help. Perhaps the sonorous rhythms of a ritual that went back to Rome could guide him. Or perhaps it was time to take the bull by the horns.

Perhaps it was time to face her. He frowned, shaking his head. And if she was not the Virgin? If she was not... Robin believed she was, believed it with the simplicity of one who did not know his Latin.

Because it made the most sense to him.

Tuck did still wonder if she was not merely some dignitary of the Sidhe. Finally, he spoke to the air. "Who are you?"

He got no answer.

"Look. You're driving me crazy."

The only answer was ringing laughter, he turned his head. The pixie was back, flickering into his vision, and then out again. Well, of course she would think it was funny. Perhaps this was all some game of the fae.

Perhaps the fae wanted this part of the woods protected, somehow. Perhaps one of their great gates was here, and the Wild Hunt sometimes rode through it.

Their existence, he could not doubt. Either the fae were real or he was insane. No man wants to admit to being insane.

He sat down on a log, staring into the trees. The pixie was gone. "Is that the only answer I am going to get?"

There was silence. "Are you trying to test me?" Was this entire thing a test of his faith? Or a test, perhaps, of his priorities.

The air seemed to shimmer blue for a moment. She was there...he could feel her. Who did his instincts, his heart say she was?

No answer. Perhaps he was simply out of tune. Perhaps he truly had lost his connection to God somewhere in that sandy desert, somewhere in that so-called Holy Land. He let out his breath. "I get it. I need to work things out for myself."

A hint of dark hair, and then she was gone. He did not move. He felt that moving was somehow unwise.

He stayed put. Then he heard the horsemen. He reached for the staff he had spent two hours cutting that morning but did not move.

The camp should be well enough hidden. They rode on by...if they saw the friar by the stream, they ignored him. Gisbourne's men, wearing his colors and well mounted. He wished the man would go back to the Holy Land. Back to the struggle for land and power that now embroiled it.

But he suspected that all or most of those who had gone there would come back, their tails between their legs, as whipped curs. The Saracens knew the land, knew its people, had the crusaders seriously over-horsed.

He made his way back to camp slowly. Robin was counting heads. Nobody had been taken, at least. They had that much.

"We'll get those guys," Robin murmured.

"Or perhaps," Tuck suggested, "it would be better to be ghosts. To vanish from their sight."

He knew this time he was right. Robin was ordering the men to strike camp. They would move from this place. A wise course of action, Tuck knew. Those riders might have found nothing this time, but they would be back.

As he moved to strike a tent, he realized that the Blue Lady had saved him yet again.

14

---

*W*hat did she want?

If she was Mary...and he recalled that the name of the good abbess was 'Mary Michael'...then perhaps she really was just testing his faith. It had, after all, been weakened lately.

Then again, was it God Tuck had a problem with, or his followers? He moved along the trail with John at his side.

"We are glad to have you back, Brother."

That surprised Tuck. He had not thought John noticed him enough to care. He had seldom pulled the friar into the banter. "I probably should not have run off."

"Friars are like birds."

Tuck laughed, not because he was insulted, but because John was absolutely right. They were heading for a small village Robin knew. One likely to be sympathetic. One where they could buy certain supplies.

Arrowheads, for the most part. It was simply not possible to move a forge with them, so they had to rely on blacksmiths who either knew and did not care or pretended not to know. John could, of course, carry almost as many as a horse could.

Tuck wanted to ask the man where he was from, how he had ended up in this situation, but he knew he would be lucky to get more than a grunt from him. That was about all anyone ever got out of him, when personal questions were asked.

Perhaps he was hiding something. Perhaps, likely even, he had truly committed some crime that deserved being made an outlaw. He was not a gentle man, but rather a controlled one.

Tuck thought it quite likely he had killed somebody, although also quite likely that he had not intended to do so. He did not seem the type, for sure, to commit actual murder, but a killing in the heat of blood was possible. He had never given confession. Perhaps he did not quite trust Tuck. Tuck thought that there was one man John trusted... For all Tuck knew he was another heretic or follower of the old gods. They certainly seemed common around here. Regardless, Tuck suspected John would take at least some of his secrets to the grave...and the rest would not pass beyond Robin.

Well. Tuck did not feel unsafe with him. Quite the opposite, in fact. Not entirely comfortable, no, but safe. He knew that no matter what, this man would, if he needed to, defend him with his life. And vice versa. At the thought, he tightened his grip on his staff for a moment.

At least he had one again. He had felt surprisingly naked while unarmed. He wondered if a knight became as fond of his sword. Some seemed to be fonder. Of course, poor people did not wield swords, and thus, the blade was the man's status as well as his weapon. Yeomen used staff and bow, sometimes knife.

"Is that it?" he inquired, as they hit a dirt road.

John nodded. "Yes."

Tuck shook his head. "No more than that?" he teased.

"Is more needed?"

Tuck wished he was going on this errand with Will. Much better company. Well, nothing he could do about it. John knew the people here, and thus, John had to go. Robin did not normally send men out alone. Alan being in Nottingham on his own had been a surprise...and, it seemed, against orders.

Of course, Tuck had always wandered off on his own, but sometimes, that was for the best. A friar alone drew far less suspicion than one accompanied by, say, a man with legs like tree trunks. John was right. Friars *were* much like birds.

A goodwife rushed towards them as they came down the road. "Please. We need your help."

Tuck shifted both hands to his staff, although he saw no immediate likelihood of combat. He glanced around.

"What with?" John asked, sparing no extra words.

"Gisbourne's men. They took half of our men for the levy and there is no way we can make the harvest without them."

A problem that could, perhaps, be solved. But not by them. Tuck frowned. "The best half, knowing Gisbourne."

"Including the smith."

That was wrong. Smiths were supposed to be immune to levy, for no village could function without its blacksmith. True, the lord needed smiths, but he was not supposed to simply take them. He was supposed to hire away the best, of course.

John let out a short, sharp breath. His temper was rising, but with none there who deserved it, he settled for just banging the end of his staff on the ground. The goodwife flinched. "We need our smith."

"Unfortunately, we are only two, as you can see," Tuck said. "On our own, we can't steal him back from Gisbourne. It's going to take some planning."

And he could not do it himself. He glanced at John. Surely, the big outlaw had some ideas. He was not stupid, as some thought men of his size tended to be. He was, also, more often in the council of Robin than Tuck himself. He was frowning.

"Something has to be done about him," the goodwife murmured. "He needs..." She tailed off.

"Not much can be. The prince will not exceed his authority to remove a troublesome lord," Tuck grumbled. "And the king will not return from Palestine."

"Is that a prophecy, good friar?"

"A reasonable suspicion." Richard would use any excuse not to come back to what he called the 'wet armpit of Europe'. Or worse, when in his cups. It was an open secret amongst those who had met the man that he would rather have ruled France alone and forgotten England ever existed. This goodwife, of course, would not know such things. A girl of about six ran up behind her, clung to her and regarded the men.

The fear in her eyes said more about Gisbourne's behavior than her mother's words. Perhaps her father had been among those taken, or perhaps an older brother. And they would likely not return. If Gisbourne was levying so heavily, he intended to return to the Holy Land to stake a claim there.

Perhaps, Tuck thought, all of the absentees should lose their holdings. Including Richard Lionheart.

What to do about Gisbourne? That was the topic of discussion. Will, Clorinda and Robin were talking animatedly. John was listening nearby...whilst sharpening a knife.

Killing him had been brought up. Then, his young son would inherit...probably under the regency of the man's wife. Who, by all accounts, egged him on. On the other hand...what could be worse than Gisbourne?

Tuck thought of the lord in the lonely castle and shuddered. There was worse than Gisbourne. Rare, yes, but most definitely in existence. Well. It was not his problem. What was his problem was going to be keeping everyone's heads together if things went bad. He frowned, listening to the ebb and flow of conversation and the rhythmic sound of John's stropping.

For a moment, it all seemed unreal to him. Gisbourne had completely lost it. No. Gisbourne was simply a microcosm of what was going on.

The crusades had become more important to the upper classes than the health of their people, than the life of their peasants. The king never set foot in his kingdom. Outlaws showed more honor than knights.

The world was upside down. The world was no longer what it should be.

He could not escape the feeling that none of it was right. Monks had more wealth than yeomen.

Well, at least, he was not one of them. He could feel at least somewhat virtuous on the matter. He had kept two of his three vows, when most managed none. And what did he have to be obedient to?

He was not sure he even had God, anymore. "What can we do?" he murmured.

Clorinda turned to him. "We can rescue them."

"No, we can't. Gisbourne would burn the village to the ground if we did. He does not care anymore whether the next year brings him a good crop or not." Tuck wished his words were other than true, but they were not. They were words that flowed around him, bound him. Words he feared to speak, almost, as if to do so made them truer.

"The friar's right, curse it." That was John, raising his voice slightly over the sound of stropping. He too did not want to admit to the truths.

"The only person who can deal with Gisbourne now is the king. John does not have the authority and Richard will never return from Palestine."

The best thing that could happen to England was a proven report of Richard's death. Would be nice if a few of the lords went with him. "At least we can suspect Gisbourne will leave again for the Holy Land."

"In his absence, we can probably do something. His wife rules," Robin muses. "And she is a very typical woman, she rules, but she seldom leaves her solar, and the boy..."

"The boy is an echo of the father, but he is still a boy." Tuck frowned. He almost felt sorry for the child, and he definitely did for Gisbourne's daughter. Who would, no doubt, be married off at fourteen, and who cared if she was dead of her fourth child by eighteen?

"The boy will be no better than his father," Robin mused. "The wife is, after all, no better than the husband."

"He is still a boy." Harming Gisbourne's child, which Robin's words could be taken as promoting, was not a wise course of action. "Perhaps we can at least rescue the smith, though. But it would have to be done carefully."

Gisbourne would retaliate, against people who were already likely to go hungry come winter. Some would starve. And then the tax man would come and take a portion of what little they had for the knights.

Gisbourne's horses ate better than his peasants. Tuck found himself somewhat angry. He knew there were still good lords out there. He had seen prosperous country. The greenwood encroached, here, on land that was often not even worked. They lacked the men or they lacked the seed.

Either way, it had to stop, but he had no clue how to stop it. Short of the unimaginable, a revolt against the king. To what end? Would John be any better were his hands not tied by merely being Prince Regent?

Tuck thought he could hardly be any worse, but the only thing he could do was the unpleasant action of praying for a man's death. He was not comfortable with that. What man would be? He would not do it.

No. He would simply pray for what was best for England and leave the details to God.

15

_____

The men had not been taken to Castle Rock. There, no doubt, the sheriff still enjoyed his ale. Another man Tuck would have liked to see brought low. Not killed, no. Reduced to poverty would be far more in the way of justice. He recalled a particular verse. 'It is easier for a camel to pass through the eye of a needle than for a rich man to enter the kingdom of heaven'. Everyone said that was impossible.

Tuck had dared to ask the opinion of a Saracen. He had explained that there was a trail in Palestine that led through a hole in a rock. Said hole was called the 'Eye of the Needle'...and it was, indeed, hard to lead a camel through it...furthermore, the heavier the camel was burdened, the harder it became, until it became impossible.

It was amusing how an infidel such as that had led Tuck to understand the true meaning of the proverb. It was possible for an unburdened camel to pass through the eye of a needle...therefore a rich man must unburden himself before entering Heaven. Or perhaps any man, if the burden one spoke of was sins, not possessions.

Perhaps the burden was guilt. They moved towards the compound where the levy were training. Some of them were little more than striplings, Tuck noted from his vantage point. They trained with rough-cut staffs. As he watched, one boy went down. He picked himself up slowly and seemed a little dizzy.

A hazard of staff training. Naturally, one tried not to hit anyone's head during a spar, but it still happened. Tuck frowned a little. Another group were working with bows. This set seemed more competent. He wondered if Gisbourne's men had grouped them by training or skill.

There was no sign of the smith. They had to get him out of there, but at the same time, his return to his village had to be a closely guarded secret.

It had to seem, thus, as if they were after something else. The obvious target was the armory. In fact, stealing an entire bunch of arrowheads from Gisbourne rather appealed to Tuck.

He was becoming a thief at heart, he thought. But then, they were only robbing people who deserved it.

Gisbourne certainly deserved it, and he would love to rob the lord who had tried to flog him blind. It was, he realized, revenge, not crime. Of course, it was not the kind of revenge most considered honorable.

He waited. It seemed like a long time, and his thoughts went round and round and round. He had done more than enough to earn centuries in purgatory. He had...

He sensed her, then, she was there. Watching over them. Or perhaps she wanted the smith? The sense that it was him she wanted grew. But he was sworn to God. Unless, of course, she was... "Mary," he whispered.

It might have been an acknowledgment, a prayer, or a hope. Or perhaps it was all three at once. He was not sure. He no longer knew what to believe, what to claim he knew. He no longer had faith.

Then there was no more time for thought. The armory was not unguarded, he noticed as Robin led them through the trees. However, it was lightly guarded. Anyone on duty was working with the levy. Two men, and one of them snoring loudly. The other was swigging from a skin that Tuck suspected did not contain water.

The incompetence of the enemy is a gift. Neither the sleeper nor the drunk noticed Clorinda and Alan flanking them, the two as quiet as forest mice. Both went down to well-placed hits on the back of the head.

The question was, where was the smith? Tuck shook his head. They were moving into the building.

Which was when he saw it. Out of the corner of his eye, something snake-like. Or dragon-like. Or perhaps even Devil-like. It could have been something of the fay, but he thought not. It was something else. The hair on the back of his neck rose, and he could feel sweat starting on his shoulders.

Yet, he could not warn Robin. Any sound would alert the rest of the guards, and they would come running. He began to repeat a prayer, not even under his breath, but merely in his mind. Over and over again, seeking protection from whatever evil he had just sensed.

Either it had all been in his imagination, or it worked. He felt the clouds lift a little, and he saw no more sign of the creature.

Carefully, they were taking what they needed. Arrowheads. Clorinda, to Tuck's surprise, was wistfully eyeing the swords. She tested a couple for balance, then set them aside; too heavy, perhaps.

Then, it happened. He felt something, a nudge in the back of his mind, and he yelled, "Run!"

They did...right as the building caught fire. Possibly it was an accident. Possibly the guards had set it to smoke them out. Had they delayed a moment longer, they would all have been trapped in the flames.

As it was...

"Alan!" Clorinda yelled.

He was still inside. Tuck turned, but the fire had just claimed the door. There was no way of going back for him. No way of saving him, or even of recovering the body.

The guards were closing on them. Roughly, Tuck grabbed her shoulder. "Come on. We have to get out of here."

Counting the half-trained levy, they were grossly outnumbered. Their best hope was that they would not have to count those men and boys, who might well cheer on somebody attacking this place.

He thought of the dragon...he thought of how the clouds had lightened, then he thought of the fire. No, it had not been a dragon.

The guards had started it, and now they sent arrows after the fleeing outlaws. He heard a yelp as somebody was hit, but a quick glance showed they had not gone down. If they were lucky, it was a flesh wound.

Most of those shooting were about as accurate as children at a fair, attempting to win some prize from a makeshift range. Tuck got to the trees, out of breath.

He glanced at Clorinda.

"If you'd warned us sooner."

"I didn't know. But I think the Blue Lady warned me."

"Not in time. Not in sarding time." She spat it at him, although he could tell from the way her eyes avoided his that her anger was not aimed at him.

Stunned as much by the words that had crossed her lips than by her fury, he could only stand there for a moment. Then follow the others, his head bowed a little.

They fled into the night.

Robin sat by the fire. He was securing a stolen arrowhead to a shaft. "Fire. Who would have thought they would..."

Tuck shook his head. "It could have been a coincidental accident." Or it could have been something worse. Something nasty and dark.

Did he really believe in the Devil? He was, of course, supposed to. That was one of the rules of being a friar. You believed in the Devil, and you believed in your own power over him.

Tuck was not sure he had any power over the Devil. How could he? He was only one man of distinctly uncertain faith.

"Perhaps."

"It was their own building, and much of their gear would have been destroyed. I wouldn't imagine they set fire to it on purpose, and they weren't in a position that would..."

"You're right. They weren't smoking us out." Robin frowned. "I don't like this."

"Neither do I." Alan had not received Last Rites or even a proper burial. His soul would wander. Yet, there was nothing Tuck could do about that.

Nothing whatsoever. He felt utterly powerless, and still confused. The warning had come too late. Did that indicate the Blue Lady...well. She was not God. She was not omniscient. She could not reveal what she had not seen.

So, he spoke again, "I think there was a demon."

Robin's entire body tensed. "Where?"

"In the trees. Off to the side. I don't know." Tuck rubbed his temples. "It could have been a hallucination or something fay. I don't know." He had the kind of headache that could be temporarily driven aside by ale, but for which he knew no true cure.

He did not want to be here right now. He almost wished he had stayed in the Holy Land. Yet, he knew, there were demons there, too. Most of them in the guise of good Christian men.

Demons. Had unseen demons whispered in Crusader ears? If so, why had he seen that one, and not those? Unless, perhaps, it had wanted to be seen. Had intended to scare him a little.

He shook his head. "I'm starting to think I'm going completely off."

"You're not insane, Brother."

"Maybe we all are. Maybe the world is. You haven't seen all of it."

"I've seen enough," Robin said, grimly, picking up another arrow-head. "I've seen people starve to fund these blasted crusades. I've seen children go off on pilgrimage, never to return. I've seen Churchmen wear silk under their robes."

"I've seen entirely too much of that last." Tuck tugged at his own habit, plain and scratchy as it should be. "Silk under their robes and women under their desks."

Robin laughed. "Or, sometimes, boys under their desks."

"Altar boys," Tuck noted. "I've heard of that happening, too. All too often." And such boys, unlike the mistresses, were likely to be scarred by it. Physically and mentally and spiritually. Boys afraid to ever enter the confession booth.

Of course, that was one of the reasons there was a wall between priest and parishioner. To prevent untoward happenings. It did not entirely work, and some small churches had only a sliding screen.

"Sometimes. At least the women probably know what they're getting into."

Had Robin been one of those boys, and developed a taste for it? Or was there something deeper involved here.

"Women can do the strangest things. But when they need a man, why not take a wealthy one, even if he can't technically marry you?" And how many of them were married, illegally?

"Good point." Robin brushed back some stray hair. It did tend to fall over his face. He studied Tuck. "And what about you? What do you do about your needs and desires?"

"I don't know. I've never had a problem with celibacy."

"Perhaps you're one of the few men suited to it, then." Robin considered him. "Some people seem..."

"Some people don't have needs and desires. God made us, perhaps, to serve Him." Tuck considered it. "But most do, because God meant us to..." To multiply, but he realized he could not say that to one who loved another man, for it did imply what was between Robin and John was profane.

Tuck was no longer sure of that. He changed the subject.

"I'm going to do some kind of service for Hubert. We might not have a body, but we can do something." And then...what did they do then? Gisbourne had to be stopped, but Gisbourne was probably already preparing for departure in the yard of the Pilgrim. It would be easy enough to find out, of course, whether he had yet left.

Whether he had... Tuck shook his head. "It's unholy of me, but I rather hope the Saracens get him."

"Then we have to deal with his wife."

"True, but the prince *could* put somebody else in as regent."

"Yeah. The sheriff."

Robin was so likely to be right that Tuck let him have the last word. He stood and left, heading to the area he was using as a chapel of sorts. Most believed God could only be found in a church. Francis claimed that all creation was His temple.

Tuck had always thought that more likely. He murmured, as he walked, words he had not used in far longer than he should have. The words of the Prayer of St. Francis.

Words that helped pull him into the state he had had so much difficulty achieving of late. Not grace, not quite, but...focus. Yes. Focus was the word. His mind was on God, but the Blue Lady hovered at the edge of it, smiling slightly.

16

_____

The next day, he found Clorinda at her own prayers. He stayed back, not wanting to interrupt. She spoke softly in Norman...not some old tongue of this land. But then, she was Norman. Easy enough to forget...most of the outlaws were Saxon blonde, but some others were dark, too.

The English, a German knight had told him, are mutts. Perhaps he was right.

She finally stood up. Softly, "How long have you been there, Friar?"

"Not long. I didn't want to interrupt."

"You show almost too much respect."

"What's the alternative? You're hardly likely to do anything but walk away if I tell you you're wrong."

"Or do you show respect because you aren't sure?" She stood up, rising gracefully to her feet. Her eyes met his.

He shook his head, breaking the contact quickly.

"You aren't sure, not anymore. Come on. Let's go for a walk."

"Will won't think..."

"Will knows you're not my type." She did not touch him, but rather headed along a deer trail away from camp. She moved with quiet grace, and silent. Every time his own footsteps made a noise, he flinched from the contrast.

"I don't have a type."

"So, you really have been celibate your entire life?" She stopped where a tall rock thrust out from the trees.

It seemed, for a moment, to shimmer a little. A gate to Faerie? "Yes, I have."

"And not just, I suspect, because of your vows."

He considered that. "I joined the church so I would not be expected to marry." He took a deep breath. "So I would not have to force myself to join with a woman when I have never wanted to."

"No choices. No thought that people might have choices. Is that really what your God is all about?"

He hesitated. "I don't know anymore." An admission that came close to an admission of guilt. He did not know anymore. He did not know who he was. What he was. What he could do about who he was.

"Have I ever denied the existence of your God?" she asked, finally, not approaching the stone, but rather regarding it.

He placed it in his mind...the Hemlockstone. Associated with witches. Unsurprising, thus, that it would also be associated with the fay. It was carved by the wind, the trees drew back from it. More than anything else, it looked like a large, squat house, with brick walls and a dark roof...as if it was roofed not with thatch but lead. That was it, it looked like a lead roof. Like a church would have. "No. But the Bible tells us there is only one true God, that all others are shades or demons."

"Is that what you believe?" She tilted her head. "Is that why you think when you see a goddess, that it *has* to be your God's mother?"

"I have wondered if what men call gods are, in truth, the lords of the Fae."

"Not a bad thought. Not a bad way around your dilemma." She glanced at the stone again. "I believe the old gods are real, but that they no longer walk the Earth as they did. Your beliefs have pushed both them and the fae into small corners. Tight ones. Into spaces where they have little room. One day, they will push back."

"I don't like that thought."

She laughed a little. "Tuck, it would not destroy your God...but rather the bindings your Church places on the world."

Tuck thought for a long moment. He did not look at her but remained silent. Wind unleashed by the absence of trees flowed around him, causing his robe to pull around his legs. "Bindings..."

"Can you stand there and tell me you would have chosen the Church had you not been forced?"

He could not answer that straight away. He closed his eyes, heard the call of the birds. Somewhere, a fox yipped a warning. Perhaps there was some stray dog. Perhaps some stray human. Finally, "It beat all the possible alternatives."

She nodded. "But what would you have chosen? Were you truly free, what would you do?"

"I have no idea." It was the truth. These people were freer than most, but it was a freedom that had its own boundaries.

A freedom circumscribed by the laws they had broken, but a freedom nonetheless. "I have never known anyone who is truly free. The king is a slave to the kingdom, the serf to his land, the abbot to the Church. We just have to make the best of things within the boundaries placed around us."

He wished, for a moment, that were not the way of things, but it was, and nothing he could do or say would change it.

"What if we could build a world in which people were?"

"It wouldn't work, Clorinda." He turned towards the stone. "If everyone was free to do what he or she wanted, then the important stuff would never get done."

Who would sweep the streets if he could choose not to do so? No. You had to give people incentives, or simply force them to do as you desired. Hence the levy. "The system works. We just need to do something about the people abusing it."

"You're right. But I wish such a world could be."

"All you would give people would be the freedom to starve." He looked away from the stone, out into the surrounding forest.

"But still. Are you happy?"

"Sometimes. Sometimes not. Happier than many Churchmen, I

think. If they were happy, they would not break the rules, would not keep their mistresses and their wealth."

"Then perhaps we need fewer and better Churchmen."

"But what, then, do we do with those who have no other place?" Tuck frowned. "Why would you care about the quality of Churchmen?"

"Because..." Clorinda tailed off. "If we had fewer and better Church-men, we would not have those so afraid that they hide in the cloister and pull everyone else in after them. People could believe as they believed without threatening them."

He was not sure whether she had a point or not. "It is not just the Church that says you're wrong." He felt he could be frank with her.

"Believe I'm wrong all you like. You aren't waving a noose anywhere near my neck."

He laughed a bit at that. "And what if I try and convince you you're wrong?"

"You aren't entirely sure I am."

He refused to look at her. Or to say anything more.

Tuck walked into the village, staff held in one hand. He was alone...all the better to get information. But what he first noticed was the boy. Maybe fourteen, and you could count his ribs.

Most people were bad off, but not that bad off. Tuck had not seen anyone on the edge of starvation in a while. He changed course towards the youngster. He pulled a roll of bread, slightly stale, out of his pocket and offered it.

The boy's eyes widened, as if he had never known Christian charity. It was sadly probable that he had not. "I'm supposed to give *you* alms."

"Not when I have more than you do."

Since the levy had taken half of this village's men, they had been on the edge of starvation. The women, the remaining boys, had only managed about a third of the normal harvest. Tuck felt a smoldering anger within him.

Maybe Clorinda was right, and everything should be broken down and then built up again. Except how many more would be harmed if that happened?

He could see it almost as a vision of death, like some terrible plague spreading across Europe. There had been plagues in the past, there would be plagues again. Inviting one struck him as a bad idea.

Still. If somebody did not feed these people, they would start dying. They might already be, in some cases, too far gone. Then, Gisbourne would come and tax away the crops they had raised.

"I'm going to kill him," the boy said, almost as if voicing Tuck's thoughts.

"Gisbourne." A pause. "Don't try it. You don't have the strength or the skill. What good would you be dead?"

"I wouldn't be desperately hunting for food." The boy's eyes sought his.

He sought escape. He did not care if he lived or died. How did Tuck solve this?

Raiding Gisbourne's stores and bringing it to these people...but they had tried that, in a sense. It had availed nothing and got Hubert killed.

They could, of course, give them money, but who would they buy food from? Who had it to spare?

Tuck assigned himself a couple of Hail Marys for even considering praying for Gisbourne's death.

He wondered how many did. This boy did, he was sure of it. "What you can do is get food...even if you have to steal it."

"Or break the forest law," the boy said, softly.

It was likely he already had...and that, Tuck realized, was something they could do. Not steal food, no, but even a couple of deer casually left at the edge of the village might make the difference between survival and death. And perhaps a little...and yes. They would still be stealing, and likely hanged if caught, but Gisbourne had left them no choice. "Come with me," Tuck said.

He had to get more food into this young man's system. Hunger fed hatred. A full belly gave a man space to plan. Of course, Tuck did not plan on shooting a deer or a pheasant himself. He would likely miss badly enough to embarrass himself.

But there were other ways to get food from the greenwood, if you knew how. Acorns could be turned into flour, although it had to be done right. Done wrong, and you ended up only with poison.

What he was heading towards was not an oak tree. It was a bramble patch, and amongst the briars and thorns were fruit. He picked one, popped it in his mouth. "Nothing like fresh blackberries."

The boy grinned. "I missed this patch. Thank you."

He lifted a hand. "Don't take all the berries. If you don't leave some for the birds, there will be no more blackberries."

That piece of wisdom was, perhaps, an old wives tale, but he passed it on nonetheless. What if it was true? If it was true and people did not abide by it...the idea of there being no more blackberries scared him. "The greenwood is not inexhaustible," he continued.

The boy did take more than half of the berries, leaving those least accessible for the birds. His lips were already stained dark, and the rest Tuck held in his robes as a goodwife would in her apron. They could take them to the village.

A few blackberries were little help, but they were still received with surprise. One goodwife murmured, "He must be the one that walks with the outlaws."

Tuck flinched. Not because she was correct, but because that assumption was even being made. That only an outlaw would do them a good deed. "Is there no Christian charity left?"

The goodwife jumped. She had not expected to be overheard. "I have seen none." She was thin and worn...not quite as bad off as the boy, but certainly not healthy. "The only charity I have seen is that we're supposed to give."

Tuck shook his head, letting his skirts fall once the blackberries had been transferred to somebody's basket. "You need give none, and any churchman who tells you otherwise is a fool. Who is your priest?"

"What priest? He has two livings and ignores this one."

Tuck frowned even more. Not that he could blame the priest, for not wanting to move amongst such poor people. Yet, excommunication of the de facto kind was as bad as that which was declared by the

Pope. "If anyone wishes me to hear confession, I will. But I would rather offer food."

He had none...but he did get half the village forming a line to confess. To confess sins born of hunger. Theft. Coveting, not of material goods, but of food. He resolved that he would at least get them some. One girl confessed that she had sold her body for two loaves of bread.

He shuddered. At least she was probably too thin to have ended up with child of it. Then again, the child would no doubt be dumped on the church porch and be better off for it. One woman confessed considering selling her infant daughter.

The child might be better off for that, too. Far better to be a rich man's ward than a starving peasant. On the other hand, girls who were given up were equally likely to end up either nuns or prostitutes. For a boy, it would definitely be preferable.

He listened, he gave them the penances that would make them feel better about sins real and imagined. That was how things were.

That was how people were. Humans. They needed this. Perhaps some might be comfortable confessing only to God, but most needed a priest's ear. Absolution was about shedding guilt. In some cases, about realizing what one had done was not a sin after all.

Not a sin after all. He wished he dared confess his, but when it came to heresy or even the edge of heresy the seal of the confessional had been known not to hold. He would not betray another, but who could he trust not to betray him?

Who could he trust to listen as he told them of the Blue Lady? Nobody, was the answer. He did not wish to meet a heretic's purifying end.

When the last was done, one of them offered him stale bread and water. He would have waved it off, but he realized it would hurt what remained of their pride. For some of them, pride was all they had. He could not let them suffer.

He had to do something. But what? Gold from Robin's stores...but again, who had food to sell?

There would be revolt here, too. He doubted they would bow to the tax men when the time came, but would they have the strength to fight them off? Or would this place simply sprout gallows?

The boy was at his elbow. "Take me with you."

Tuck turned to him. "With you in what sense?"

"I'm a burden here. I have two brothers."

A familiar litany. "You would not survive in the greenwood. Seek the Church. Novices at least get fed."

The boy frowned. "I don't..."

Tuck looked at him. Softly and gently, he spoke again. "There are bad choices and worse choices. You won't live if you stay and you won't live if you follow me."

"Maybe there's things other than staying alive."

"You say that because you're too young to understand death." He knew he was right on that front. The boy had no doubt seen death, in this place. Yet, he likely did not understand it.

"Either take me with you or I'll follow on my own."

He was fierce, he was determined, and Tuck did not know what else to do. "Come, then."

The boy followed...he kept his pace slow out of respect for him. He wished, not for the first time in his life, that he could give him some of his own copious mass. Even half starving himself barely seemed to dent his bulk.

As they went, he stopped, pointing out different things that could be eaten. Even stinging nettle, which could bring out painful welts, was perfectly edible when cooked. Squirrels could be eaten, if you could bring one down with a stone from a sling, so could most of the birds.

There was a wealth of larder here, barred from them by the forest laws.

17

*T*uck left the boy in the care of a younger man named Much. They were close enough in age to relate to one another in a way he could not.

He felt old and tired, he sat by the fire, taking a large swig from a bottle of ale. He needed it, after the time he had had.

Robin sat down opposite. "How bad is it?"

"You saw that boy. He's not the worst of them. If we do not get those people food, then there will be no harvest, and Gisbourne's men..."

"Will take what little they have left. Or try to."

"They're all likely to die. It has to stop. I don't know how to stop it, but it has to stop."

Robin frowned. "Simply killing Gisbourne won't help. The woman and the kid will carry on in the same vein. If there are riots, it will not be their fault."

"It never is." Tuck let out a sigh. "I can't stand this anymore. Atrocities in the Holy Land were one thing, but it is as if the plague has returned with those who have come back. It is as if the Saracens have cursed us."

"Have they?"

"They consider such things as much of the Devil as we do. In fact, they even believe in the Devil." That had shocked Tuck. The Saracens believed Jesus was not the son of God, but they believed in the Devil. They insisted their Allah and the Christian God were the same. That Christians had simply mistaken a prophet and man of God for the Messiah.

Some Jews thought the same way. But Jews definitely did follow the same God, having once been his chosen people. Until they had turned away, not acknowledged the Messiah. Some people used that as a justification to ill-treat Jews. In any case, Jews were not permitted to own land, not trusted to farm it. Sometimes not trusted to be there, although they were needed...for usury was not a sin to them. Who would lend money without getting interest? The answer was no one. Thus, the Jew. He wondered if usury were a sin to Saracens. That he had never asked.

He did know they ate like the Jews did. No pork. His mouth watered at the thought of pork, and he was glad he had not been born a Jew. Even if they were better people than many would acknowledge. A Jew had saved him in the Holy Land, had offered him water when he needed it.

"I did not know that."

"They do not believe Jesus was the Messiah and they eat as Jews do, but they do believe in the Devil and they claim to believe in the same God. They are more like Jews, I think, than Christians. They follow a man whom they claim was a prophet akin to Moses."

Robin nods. "And, I hear, have the finest horses foaled."

"Of their kind. They are not much like our warhorses, more the size of a palfrey, but swift. They wear only light armor and fight much with the bow." Tuck let out a breath. "By some superstition, they ride only mares. They also ride camels..." He made a face.

"Camels?"

Tuck sketched the rough shape of one in the ground, glad to have a topic other than people starving to death. "Camels. Ugly, ill-tempered beasts, but they can do a full days work without water and on the barest provender for sometimes weeks on end."

Robin rocked back on his heels. "But I have allowed you to distract me from the problem."

"I don't see a solution. Until these people have either won the Holy Land or given up, they will keep bleeding the peasants dry." Tuck closed his eyes. "What do they care?"

"Then we have to teach them to care."

"I don't know how."

Robin stood up. "Neither do I, but I'll think about it."

Tuck drank more of his ale, watching the slender man go. He did not know, now, what effect Robin had had on him, any more than he knew the man's real name. It was sometimes as if he had always been here.

No, he knew. He had seen the atrocities in Palestine. Robin had opened his eyes to the ones that happened here.

What they needed was to bring everyone home. Let the Saracen have the desert. They did not need to reclaim the Holy Land...the Saracen would not harm true pilgrims who came with only the arms they needed for self-defense.

But no, they had to make a war of it. "What is it, that humans have to do the craziest things?"

For a moment, he almost thought the air answered, with a feeling of strength and sorrow. She was back, and she was with him for a moment. "What do you want from me?"

No answer. No answer in words, no sign of any fae thing. It was as if he was a madman, talking to that which existed only in his own head. Perhaps he was. Had others not seen her, he would have known himself to be insane.

As others had, he knew there was more to it than that. A small voice whispered in his mind. How many had seen God?

A very few, and most of those nuns in deep contemplation. For all that women were supposed to be the source of sin, they also often seemed the closest to God. Perhaps it was not as simple as all that.

Perhaps women were simply better able to concentrate, for women's tasks often required fine attention to detail.

He finished the ale, standing up to return the bottle to the stack of empties that could be washed out and refilled. Bottles were expensive. He felt far more in command of himself than he had been.

Yet, his mind and heart filled with the deepest of regrets.

THE ARROW FLEW straight and true. Precisely, it snapped the reins the outrider was holding, leaving both him and the horse intact.

The animal spooked, leapt forward, and dropped him into the dust. Tuck shifted his grip on his staff.

The carriage held one of Gisbourne's tax inspectors. They were determined to delay him reaching the village until the villagers were able to hide all of their food. It would appear to him that they had nothing.

Robbing him was almost an afterthought. With a roar, John launched himself from the side of the road, landing on the carriage board. The driver elected not to be on the carriage board anymore.

Tuck laughed a bit, heading down the slope with more caution himself. Cowardice, in this context, was a good thing. Clorinda had stopped the fleeing horse, holding it by what remained of the reins and stroking its neck. The carriage horses were rearing up, but not running...and after a moment, John had their reins too. "Easy," Tuck heard him say.

The other outriders whirled their mounts. One went down, a shot in the shoulder that might or might not prove fatal. The third spurred his mount towards Tuck. He stepped to one side and tripped the beast with his staff. It went down, but he heard no crack...after a moment, it picked itself up, shivering, without its rider. The man took a little longer to get up, then charged the friar again, on foot.

Tuck transformed his staff into a spinning wall of wood. Even a sword struggled against an oaken staff wielded well...the blade flew from the man's hands, barely nicking the staff. He brought it into the side of the man's head, and he went down.

The inspector was now on his feet next to the carriage, with his hands in the air. "Take whatever you want. Just don't kill me."

"I think we'll oblige on that," Robin said. "Tuck, watch him."

Tuck stepped forward to do just that, as the men moved to search the wagon. Not a brave man, the inspector was blubbering a little.

"So. Going to take what little people have away from them. Tell me, what will you do next year when they've all starved?" Tuck asked. He let his anger flow from him. This was a legitimate target to take it out on.

"You're the friar." Not a question.

"Famous, now, am I?" Tuck kept the staff in a blocking position. The man was watching it, warily.

"Somebody needs to take that habit off you."

All talk. All bluster.

"Oh, yes, perhaps they do, but at least I'm not hiding a woman under it."

The man shrugged. "Less harm than robbing innocent travelers."

"You're no more innocent than I am. A babe in arms, both of us." Robin, from the wagon, gave him a look.

Tuck subsided, leaving the sarcastic banter there in the road. Still, there were points being made, pricks through metaphorical chain mail. Which, he noted, the inspector did not wear. He should. He was likely to get shot by somebody.

An English woman was a better shot, common wisdom had it, than a French man. Perhaps, Tuck thought with amusement, that was the real reason the king did not want to come home. He did not want to admit he was a lousy shot.

He was, too. Good with a sword, passable with a lance, lousy with a bow. Proving the truth of it, perhaps.

He should abdicate, Tuck thought. But he was too proud to do so, too proud to admit he did not desire England's throne, whilst making it obvious to all and sundry.

Robin and the others finally finished their search. "We're letting you go...although we'll be taking these fine beasties."

They left him his carriage and the carriage horses, and the two wounded outriders. They took the outriders' horses. They could ride in the back of the carriage, after all.

Tuck led one of the mounts...the one that he had tripped. It already seemed to have forgiven him.

When the inspector arrived in such disarray, he would find nothing to record, nothing for the men to later come and take.

Well, perhaps they would leave out a little, a token, so it would not be as obvious that they were hiding something.

Tuck felt good about things. Perhaps he should not, for he was, after all, committing both sins and crimes. But he did, and he was unable to prevent himself from doing so.

They had to go along the road a little while, and when they reached the crossroads, they saw a rider coming from the south. The horse was lathered, and the pace hard enough to founder the poor animal. Its ears were pinned back, as if it knew it was likely to be ridden to death. The rider himself looked no better.

He did not even stop when he saw them, but rather kept running north towards York.

"What was that in aid of?" Robin asked.

"I don't know. Perhaps the king died in Palestine." From Tuck's tone, it was clear he thought that was good news.

"Like the prince is any better."

"The prince, at least, is here." Tuck left it at that, but he did wonder what errand caused a man to ride so hard, and not to even notice what might have been obviously a bunch of bandits leaving the road. Which they now did.

Of course, it was possible he had not even really noticed them. Tuck would not forget that wild eyed horse for a while.

He would have never treated his faithful old mule like that...and oddly enough, the outlaws had kept the animal for him. Then again, mules did not eat as much as horses.

"So, what shall we do with these beauties. Sell them back to Gisbourne for twice what they're worth?" somebody nearby asked.

Tuck could not help but laugh. Clorinda cut in, "I would not wish Gisbourne on a horse. No, I'll take them up to the horse market north of here. They'll fetch a decent price."

Giving them to the villagers was not mentioned. They would end up horse steaks if that happened. The money they fetched could be spent on a higher quantity of food at the market.

He should volunteer to go with her. Take the mule cart, buy as much food as they could carry, some for the outlaws. Some for those who needed it even more. They could not make bread in the green-wood, of course, unless it was acorn bread.

On the other hand, they were nowhere close to starving. They had not even had to tighten their belts much. Tuck almost wished he had had to do just that, his being already rather too long.

18

$\mathcal{T}$he great market north of Nottingham was called Goose Fair, given the primary goods on offer were herds of geese, driven into town by goose girls. They would finish their fattening in yards in the city and then be eaten on Christmas day. There were great flocks of them, and they reminded Tuck that winter approached again.

It was rather daring to sell the horses here, for they might well be recognized. Clorinda had done nothing to disguise them, both being plain bays with stars. Hiding the stars would make them look like shady horse dealers, and they were nondescript enough...he hoped. The mule was less nondescript, but *he* would be tethered at the edge of the fair.

Carnies sought to relieve men of their money with games of so-called chance. A group of children were competing in an archery competition, with small bows and less distance to the target. About a third of them were girls. He wondered how they would feel when told to set aside such things in favor of making cloth and babies. Of course, many women, even those who appeared goodwives, never did.

As he walked away from the cart, having paid another of the youngsters to watch it, he almost tripped over a stray goose. The bird was flapping its pinioned wings, desperately seeking an escape from its fate in the cookpot. He did not see the goose girl...nor was he about to attempt to grab it. It would peck him hard if he did, and nobody wanted to get pecked by a beak that size.

He let it run past him, and then glanced around. Games of chance and contests. A girl was rolling a hoop. A goodwife and her husband walked past arm in arm, greying but clearly as much in love as the first day they had found privacy behind a haystack.

It was a good place to get lost in the crowd, and Clorinda and Will were dealing with the horses, acting as husband and wife. Which they might as well be, lychgate wed or not. Tuck was free to explore, as long as nobody recognized him as 'that friar'.

Most people did not look past habit and tonsure. An open-air bar of sorts had been set up, with men already getting drunk despite the relatively early hour. A widow regaled them with tales no woman should have known, much less spoken. Raucous laughter echoed, and a teenaged girl fled with her face colored and her hands over her ears.

Tuck shook his head, and elected, for once, to avoid the siren call of ale. He dodged too a man trying to get him to play horseshoes for a bet. He was not very good at the game, and he suspected they had weighted the shoes somehow.

It was his general assumption that every sideshow here was a con of some kind. A man had a bear on a leash. He was not dancing with it right now but feeding it an apple. It opened a mouth from which the teeth had been pulled.

Poor creature, Tuck thought. Bears were not amongst those animals that had been given to man to use. Talking of which, a pair of house cats chased each other, hissing, through the fair. Likely they were feral, but who knew. He could not be sure whether they intended to fight or mate. Far more obvious in their intentions were the young couple trying to hide behind one of the wagons. They risked pregnancy and being hauled to the church by both sets of parents. Perhaps, though, that would not be the worst thing.

Tuck shook his head. At least they had some choice, likely withdrawn from... Tuck stopped, his eyes catching the flash of a noble lady's colors. Gisbourne's lady!

She walked through the fair surrounded by servants, stopping at a peddler's stall that claimed to have fine cloth. She sniffed at it, and shook her head.

Like as not it was fine linen, not the silk he claimed. A lady like that would know. Tuck held his breath for a moment, then released it. The Lady of Nottingham would not know him. The sheriff, now, he might have to worry about. All this lady saw was a friar. He stopped at a different stall, this one that of a peddler offering to sharpen knives for the goodwives. Being quite capable of sharpening his own, he looked at the handles the man was selling. None appealed. The lady was talked to a vendor of spiced sausage.

Now, that reminded Tuck that he was hungry. He did not tempt fate by approaching her, however, but headed further down the row of stalls, looking for food. His stomach was doing a fair imitation of those cats, all of a sudden.

He found bread and fruit for a reasonable price and kept moving, eating it. Another stray goose flapped into one of the stalls, knocking down the various items. "I think that goose won a prize," Tuck couldn't resist but call.

The stallholder laughed. "I think that goose won a place in the cookpot." It got away from him, though, scurrying down the lane.

Tuck wondered which of the goose girls had so little control over her stock. It was not unusual, of course. They were usually maidens, sometimes lads, of little real experience. Geese were supposedly easy to herd.

Supposedly. These were demonstrating the contrary quite nicely.

He found himself at the edge of an open area. Two young men raced their horses around it, the animals' hooves thundering in a reminder of the messenger. They still did not know what he carried that was of such urgency as to sacrifice a valuable animal on its altar. These horses, though, pulled up. They were sweating, but still prancing, apparently more ready to go again than their riders.

Tuck moved away, before he ended up the one trampled when one of them lost control of an excited mount. Racing was a natural thing for horses, as easy to them as walking, and they seemed to enjoy it. As much as one could tell what, if anything, an animal felt. Some argued it was nothing...no joy, no pain, no fear.

Tuck had observed enough animals to refuse to believe that. They knew pain and fear alright, so why not joy? Why not pleasure in running?

He remembered the wild eyes of the messenger's mount. That had been fear. Fear of being beaten if he stopped, fear of collapsing if he continued. That animal had known.

Yet, no news had come through any channels in which they had an ear. Perhaps it had been the private affairs of some lord.

Tuck thought of the lord in the lonely tower. They had thought of doing something about him, but Tuck thought Sister Michael's way better. Excommunication de facto. He would either come crawling back, or endure his isolation. Either way, likely, a good number of his men would leave him.

It was a worthy punishment, and one that well fit his crime. Talking of crimes, a boy scrumped an apple from a fruit stall, darting off into the crowd before the stallholder could finish 'Stop, thief!'

Nobody seemed to have the heart to go after him. Tuck finished his bread, shaking his head.

The fair was chaos...and then suddenly something in that chaos changed, shifted. It was, of course, the prosperous who were here. The poor had no money for such luxuries. Yet, even the prosperous could feel fear.

That was definitely fear flowing through the crowd like a wave. Perhaps the racers had lost control and somebody had been trampled after all.

No, it was something else. Had Will and Clorinda been recognized? The ripple of emotion and movement had not started near the horse trading pens. Nor did it seem to come from the flocks of geese that now squabbled.

No. It came from...this way. As if pushing against a tide, Tuck made his way towards whatever was causing such a disturbance. It might have been a fight. There were enough drunks there.

Then he saw it. From one of the trees at the edge of the fair somebody had hung an effigy. It was suspended from a gallows noose, and was a poor quality job, stuffing escaping in places.

But it wore the colors of Guy Gisborne.

PEOPLE HAD MOVED BACK from the effigy, as if it carried a poison with which they dared not risk being contaminated. Rightly so. Somebody would hang for this, and Tuck doubted the men would care if they got the right man.

Or kid. The amateurish effort, and the very style of it, struck him as something done by apprentices or novices. Apprentices, more likely. Or perhaps...no. He had left that boy in the greenwood. And he was more mature than most his age, aged by hardship and responsibility. Sometimes, Tuck thought, boys needed hardship.

The whisper that went through the crowd, though, had Robin's name in it. Tuck shook his head. Robin taking credit or blame for things he had not done was one thing, but this? This was unprofessional. However, he could not correct them without risking being the one hauled in. His friar's robes might or might not protect him.

"Is that supposed to be Guy Gisbourne?" came a voice from nearby.

"I think so." Tuck turned slightly, to see the man who had spoken. Norman, with an aquiline nose and dark, piercing eyes. He looked almost like the king, he thought, but smaller and thinner. It was not, of course. No noble or royal would be in a place like that without either an entourage or a far better disguise.

"Somebody needs to learn to draw, then."

Tuck was inclined to agree, but he shook his head. "Somebody is going to end up like that effigy."

"True." The man let out a breath. It was clear he wanted to say something else, but could not or dared not.

Tuck was out of words too. Any hint that he thought Gisbourne deserved this treatment would get him arrested. He suspected half the crowd would agree with him.

The mood was likely to go from tense to truly ugly any second. He started to disentangle himself, moving laterally through the crowd, keeping one eye on the dangling form. At least it was only an effigy...they had not grabbed one of Gisbourne's soldiers. For whom Tuck felt a certain sympathy. Even the ones who were not levied had little freedom to seek other employment. Of course, some of them seemed to enjoy the excesses.

He thought of the cowardly tax collector. Then the crowd surged. First towards the effigy, almost carrying him with them.

He used his staff to clear himself a bit of room, carefully. He did not want to hurt any of these people, but he was not about to allow them to trample him.

He had seen people die that way, and as the mood became uglier, he knew some would right now. Today.

People were going to die, and there was nothing he could do. Well, he could do one thing. He scooped up a small child in one arm, carrying her clear of the melee. There was no sign of her mother.

She was the only one he could help. The only one. He set her down at the edge of the riot, then looked back towards it. It had just become a roiling mass of people. At least few or none of them carried blades. Chances were there would be a lot of injuries, relatively few deaths.

The girl, Saxon blonde, looked up at him trustingly. Her mother was somewhere in that mess, he had no idea where. It was, at least, not spreading further. Sensible people had got out of the area.

Sensible people. Now there was something he was not, would not be for a long time coming. Had he ever been?

He thought not, with some amusement. Well. Not his problem. None of it was his problem, per se. Except the girl, now. Well. When things settled down, she would point out her relatives to him. He would get her home.

Then he would get out of there, find Will and Clorinda and leave.

The effigy had been torn down.

19

"Things are going to get worse," Robin said, quietly, glancing around at those who sat around the fire.

Not the entire band, of course. Tuck sat a little bit back, an empty ale bottle next to him. He would not drink any more. He needed every brain cell he had to be working properly.

If his brain had really been working properly for, now, almost two years. Had it really been that long?

"I agree," came Will's soft minstrel voice. "Tuck says your name was flowing through the crowd."

Tuck frowned. "I wanted to correct them. It was an amateurish display, all of it. It didn't even look like him."

He wondered at the man in the crowd. Had he been a poorly disguised Norman lord, distant kin to Richard? Or, no. It was possible he was kin, yes, but on the wrong side of the blanket, not even acknowledged. Kings acknowledged bastards born of women of rank, but not those fathered on serving maids.

Which happened all the time. Women threw themselves at men of great rank and power, they always had. Perhaps why bishops so easily found mistresses. "Not remotely."

"I didn't see it," Robin noted, "But I'll take your word for it. Who do you think did it?"

"It struck me as likely to be a bunch of kids. Apprentices from Nottingham, perhaps." Amateurish and childish.

Robin nodded. "But it struck a chord."

"It did. But who's fault is that?"

"Gisbourne's," Will cut in, almost amused. "I heard this song regarding him. My only regret is that I didn't write it."

Tuck could not help but laugh. "Did somebody write him into something scathing?"

"Oh yes. And bawdy, to boot. Implying that his wife has to seek her entertainment elsewhere."

Tuck winced. Impotence was a bad thing of which to accuse a man. And they were in mixed company, Clorinda...fletching arrows as she listened.

It seemed as if she could not involve herself in conversation without occupying her hands. But she laughed instead of blushing.

Tuck shook his head. "Clorinda, you are the furthest thing from a lady I have ever met."

"Why, thank you," she said, with wry humor she might well have somehow obtained from her husband.

Tuck shook his head again.

Robin grinned, but then wiped it from his face. "Let's focus on the matter at hand. What do we do about Gisbourne?"

"There's nothing we can do." Will's voice, quiet, reaching for his harp. "He will either return from Palestine or he will not. Only the king..."

"The king will never return," Tuck mused. "Honestly, he should be forced to abdicate."

Robin frowned. "That might be going too far."

"John's hands are tied, the country is going to rack and ruin, and Richard plays soldier in the Holy Land. What more reason would we need?" Will sounded angry, moving to Tuck's side literally as well as figuratively...of course, that might have been because Tuck had strategically positioned himself close to the ale cask.

"The removal of a king is a major matter." Robin glanced at Tuck.

Clorinda muttered something in French. Tuck thought he understood it. She was talking about breaking the system again.

"The system can be made to work again." Tuck spoke as much to Clorinda as to Robin. "But not as long as people like that hold power. Break it down and we'll have mob rule and chaos. Allow this to continue..."

"...and we'll have mob rule and chaos. You're right." Robin's shoulders slumped. "But so is Will. There is nothing we can do about Gisbourne. Anything we do is as likely to start more riots as anything else."

"More riots might not be a bad thing. It depends on the where and the what over." Tuck frowned. "And we don't need something else like the fair. Kids got killed." He thought of the little blonde girl he had saved.

He had saved one. Two or three others had gone down under the trampling feet and not risen again. "What can we do?" His voice sharpened.

He wanted to hit a few people over the head with his staff, but it would avail nothing. "This is almost enough to make *me* wish I had stayed in Palestine."

"You hate the place," Clorinda pointed out from behind her arrow.

"Well, true. I just can't stand to see this. All of it. Any of it." His pain was obvious. "I feel as if..."

"Well," she challenged. "If you were in charge, what would you do?"

"Reduce the tax and the levy so it reflected what people could pay, not what I wanted. That alone..." That alone might make enough of a difference that people could survive. "Sell jewelry before I took more from the peasants."

Clorinda laughed. "Have you ever owned a piece of jewelry other than that wooden cross of yours?"

Tuck shook his head. "No. What would I want with it?" He reached for the ale keg. "This, on the other hand, is my weakness."

"Uh-huh. You don't get any more without sharing."

Any hope of formal discussion faded at that point. The next day, Tuck took staff and robe and headed away from the camp.

He needed to think. He needed space...not to the point of leaving again, but simply that little bit of time on his own.

He contemplated the matter of Prince John. A man about whom Tuck knew little. A man doomed to play second fiddle to his less responsible brother.

Thinner than his brother and taller, he knew that much. Perhaps smarter, definitely less of a fighter. A better king? Clearly, for he was not the one deserting his responsibilities to hare off on Crusade. Would things be better if Coeur de Lion stayed home? Impossible to know or tell.

Prince John. Tuck thought of the lean man who so resembled the king and his brother. Wrong side of the blanket, surely.

Yet, even the son of a serving wench might know who his father was. Might have the ear of the royal family.

Might be able to get an audience for a poor friar who had information of vital concern to the prince.

He would not do it without talking to Robin. But if he could get in, if he could make John aware of what was going on, perhaps the Prince could do something. Not remove Gisbourne, no. But he might be able to put pressure on him. Scare him, even. He deserved to be scared. And humiliated some more, but they could manage that on their own.

Then again, were they in truth responsible for the riot? Had somebody found their own way to humiliate Gisbourne? Far better to do it in the flesh, of course, but he had left again for Palestine. It would be months, if not years, before he showed his face again. Perhaps they were responsible for that, too. It was entirely possible he had left because he was too embarrassed to remain.

Then again, a lord should not be embarrassed about being out-shot by a yeoman. Yeomen tended to be better at archery, for it was often the only weapon they knew. The weapon every man and, for that matter, many a woman, was expected to know. Only the fact that Tuck wore habit and tonsure exempted him from being bound to master it.

Fortunately. The village he approached was better off than the one they had been helping, but not by much. People were thin, but not starving, clothing threadbare, but not rags. If they had the right to choose whether the Crusades happened, he had no doubt what choice they would make.

He had no doubt that their voices would be raised in a no, and he could feel that no building. If something was not done, chances were they would take care of Gisbourne's family. Certainly there was ugliness in Nottingham.

That could not be allowed to happen. England would slowly fall into civil war if it did. And then when Richard did come back?

No. He would not. Sooner or later, John would have full power. What would he do with it? That they needed to know what kind of man he was was obvious.

Was he the weak intellectual most saw him as, a shadow of his brother? Or something more?

Tuck wandered towards the inn. It was a little early in the day to be drinking, so it would likely be quiet. In any case, he saw few men. Those not gone on Crusade or otherwise were presumably out in the fields. He saw children and women. Of course, most of the women were out in the fields as well. It was a rare farmer who did not need to use the labor of his wife and offspring in the summer and harvest...harvest took every set of hands you could get, down to those barely out of swaddling clothes. At this time of year, though, the men struggled to find work and the women turned to spinning and weaving.

He remembered in better times that monks would turn out of the abbey to help in the local harvest in exchange for their own bread. That villagers would assist the lay brothers. Now suspicion stood in the way of all of that.

You still helped your neighbors, but people did not trust the Church or their superiors. Perhaps some even went so far as to blame God for their hardships.

All it would take, Tuck thought, was for this unseasonably dry weather to last a little longer, and the countryside would go up like a tinder box. Possibly literally as well as metaphorically...fires happened after droughts.

People would realize they were not likely to have food for the winter...and they would know who to blame. God, yes. But also man. He felt, for a moment, a sense of the Blue Lady's presence.

If she had any ideas, he would appreciate knowing them, now. Other than praying for rain, which he would do anyway. Perhaps God would listen.

But God did not always change things. He sent hardship to test people. And sometimes, Tuck thought, even God could not or would not...likely would not...break his own laws.

He would not always change the weather, and Tuck wondered if that was not because of those laws. If perhaps a drought was sometimes needed for balance.

Some people would blame such things on Satan. He felt her hand on his shoulder. It was all he could do not to turn around.

Instead, he walked into the inn. "Got anything a hungry brother can have for lunch?"

"I'm afraid only stew."

"Stew's more than good enough, and bread, if you have it." He rummaged in his purse.

The tavern keeper, a broad woman, waved him off. "I don't expect money from friars."

"I have it, you need it." It was clear, though, that she was not going to be moved.

"Where are you heading, Brother?"

"Nottingham, for now." It was almost winter. Cold rain was threatening from the sky.

"Not a bad place to winter."

Tuck shook his head. "No. I don't think I'll winter around here." Winter in the greenwood was unpleasant, but his alternative was to winter at an abbey, and he would rather the company of outlaws and heretics.

What did that say about him? No, it said something about the Church.

"You want ale with the stew, or just smallbeer?"

"Ale."

She slid stew and ale and bread over to him. He took them to a table and sat down, just as the rain started. He could hear it pattering onto the thatch and the street outside.

He had not quite realized he was heading to Nottingham until he said it. He should, perhaps, not go alone, but who could he take with him on this kind of mission?

Nobody was the honest answer. It was nobody's place to go with him. He would be better on his own. Unless he got caught, and then...they would not know where he was.

Or would they? He felt watched over. Safe. Protected. He knew he should not rely on her, and yet he did.

Robin's way was the only way, now, he could deal with her. She had to be Mary. He could not accept her as anyone else.

Yet he had doubt.

The stew was not very good. Little meat in it, and what there was was rabbit. Including the bits of the rabbit one only put in stew, although that had never bothered him. It was the vague lack of seasoning that did.

Ah, yes. They were short on salt. That was it. Of course, salt could be quite expensive. But rosemary? They should have more rosemary...that stuff would grow best when you did not wish it to grow.

Or, of course, the tavern keeper was just a better brewer than a cook. He sipped the ale.

No. She was not a better brewer. He ate and drank nonetheless. He was not about to waste food unless it was literally inedible. Then he left as quickly as he could.

For Nottingham.

IT FELT ALMOST as if he was being guided or drawn there. Of course, he knew who he was looking for. That was a rational thought. To find the thin man. The man who looked like the king.

But where? He had not traveled with the entourage of a nobleman, so perhaps was not staying in the castle.

Perhaps he was no longer here. He could have returned to London before the winter set in. That was even more logical. Nottingham was not a place somebody from court...if he was from court...would long choose to remain. The sheriff was in charge, most of the time, and he had a major aversion to spending Gisbourne's money. Which, Tuck supposed, was better than wasting it.

That or Gisbourne was demanding every penny be sent to him. Or spent on arms and men. And ale for the men.

Ale. Tuck was determined that before the day was out he was going to have drunk something better than the swill in the village.

Then he saw the girl. A wisp of a thing she was, but she closely resembled, too, the man who looked like the king. And based off of age...his daughter? She was well dressed, although not in the garb of a noble lady. More that of a merchant's daughter, or a Jew's.

Not a Jew, though, not with those features. Pure Norman, that girl, or close. It sometimes seemed to Tuck as if, except for the hated Jews, England melted everyone together, slowly drifting them towards some middle ground. Well, and the Moors, some of whom were darker than the brown of Tuck's robes.

He shook his head. Then, subtly, he followed the girl.

She did not go far. She vanished into a townhouse, her skirts the last thing he saw. Barely of marriageable age, that one, not quite ripe. Some said marriage at fourteen was fine, some thought sixteen better.

Most peasant girls could not afford to wed until eighteen or nineteen, unless bound to an older man.

The townhouse was, like her, dressed like a rich merchant. A storefront occupied the lowest story, the family would live above. Right now, it was closed and boarded, but the sign indicated the merchant traded in spices.

Wealthy, then, and perhaps one of the few men made wealthier by the Crusades, for the Crusaders returned with such from exotic lands. On the other hand, fewer of the Saracen caravans moved. The most valued spices were those that came from fabled India, where it was rumored men rode upon behemoths.

He could not imagine how a man would control something many times the size of a horse. Or perhaps they followed their masters out of love? Ha. Hardly likely.

A spice merchant, then, was the man he sought. A friar would have little business with such except for one thing. One thing for which his friendship with Mary Michael might help. Clares, after all, seldom left their cloister except to die. For a friar to pick up something for their kitchen, or incense for their prayers, 'while I was going that way' would be reasonable. He trusted her.

She thought no better of those who abused their power and position than he did. This man...likely knew nothing at court. Perhaps Tuck was wrong, and he did not know who he was, although could he not? With the royal features stamped across his face? He did not envy him. It was far easier to be of common and unknown birth.

Finally, he walked up to the door and knocked.

It opened, the girl standing inside.

"When will you be open?"

She hesitated. "Tomorrow, when my father returns."

"Thank you." He did not want to push it, but this trapped him in Nottingham another day. "Do you know if he has or will have incense?"

"We have it. But I'd get into trouble if I sold it to you. He doesn't..." She tailed off.

He didn't trust her, and she had almost blurted that. Of course, she was very young. Younger than the fourteen he had guessed. More like twelve. She would be pretty, one day. Of course, she would not have her pick of suitors, not with the wealth her father displayed. Her husband was possibly already chosen. "I won't get you into trouble." Of course, it would look strange if he came back tomorrow, when there might be other spice vendors.

Unless, of course, he told them he had not been able to find any. They did not communicate that much or that swiftly as to catch him in such a lie. He assigned himself three Hail Marys in advance and left. But when he looked back, the girl was standing in the doorway. It was as if she had been left there alone, with no human company.

20

---

*H*e slept the night in the Poor Clares guest house, although he did not impinge on them for food. A cell cost them nothing, but he could afford to eat at the Pilgrim. Could and did.

In the middle of the night, he heard hoof beats. Frantic ones, and in some number, as if a small band of cavalry rode through Nottingham's streets. Thus awakened, he found it hard to return to sleep. He lay there, reaching for the wooden beads of his rosary. Sometimes, he had found, counting the beads helped him achieve rest. Not their intended use, but perhaps a worthy one.

It did not help. He lay on his back, staring at the ceiling. The feeling which came over him was peaceful but carried him no closer to repose.

It seemed, then, as if the walls of the cell faded away. He closed his eyes, opened them, saw the same featureless grey. Perhaps he slept after all, and this was a dream. As he had that thought, the grey faded back into green.

He stood, it seemed, on a hilltop. A high one, and it was winter. Snow had settled on the ground. Tough hill sheep grazed nearby, their heads in hillocks of grass. He did not, however, feel any cold.

"Where am I?"

At first, there was no answer, then he saw footsteps in the snow.

Women's sized, and the feet bare, not even wearing the sandals of a nun. Lacking any other thought as to what to do, he followed them.

The sky was almost pure white, threatening more snow. A cold breeze blew, but he only knew it was cold rather than experiencing any chill.

There was a cairn, and the footsteps ended at it, as if the woman had vanished within. Or perhaps, fairy or angel, taken wing. His mind did not question.

It was, after all, obviously a dream. The cairn was made not of grey stones, but black ones. He followed the travelers tradition, grubbing around in the snow until he found a stone and then placing it on the cairn. Thus, it would remain for future travelers, marking the trail. The stone he placed on the cairn was white, and then it faded to black.

What could that mean? That his contribution would blend into the rest? That who he was would be forgotten? Or... He did not know.

The wind stopped. The moor vanished, faded away, the baaing of the sheep appearing further and further distant and then gone. There was only the black cairn.

He frowned. Black was generally bad. Black was also the color of the black friars, a different order.

Then, abruptly, he was back on the hard cot, in the guest cell. He felt as rested as if he had, indeed, slept.

THE DREAM, however, stayed with him. Its details did not fade, as dreams are prone to do, leaving only the faint knowledge that one had, indeed, dreamed.

No. It clung to him, and he found himself looking for stones, black or white. The only ones he saw were mud colored.

A white stone on a cairn, turning black. Good intentions turning to bad. He could think of no logical explanation other than that.

It was a warning. It was a warning not to approach the spice merchant. Instead, therefore, he found a quiet place to watch the man's return. Two wagons, one driven by a rough laborer, a man with a red face, blonde hair and Saxon features. Too red, that face. The consumption of much ale lay behind it. Or perhaps whiskey, that harsh drink favored by the Scots. Tuck would not touch that stuff, fearing he might learn to like it too well. But yes. He thought that was a face that came of whiskey, shaded to the color of drink.

The spice merchant. Now Tuck studied him, he did not much resemble Coeur de Lion. His was, rather, the generic face of Norman nobility and royalty, the aquiline features so many at court boasted. His daughter came out to greet him, the two embraced for a moment.

Why did he feel that it was dangerous to approach, even to merely talk? He did not feel there could be any danger, not in his rational mind.

Building a black cairn. A cairn was a marker for those who were lost. It could also be a gathering point. Finally, it could be a grave.

A grave. That was the thought. Contributing to a death, of a person, of a concept, of a relationship.

He knew he must not talk to the spice merchant. That if he did, people would die. That the message came, not from God, but from the Blue Lady.

She cared, he thought, about England. Possibly about him. Or she intended to use him. To what end?

If he let her do so, he might be sacrificing his soul. He had a need to know why, to know what she sought.

He turned to walk away, heading for the market square. There, those merchants who were transient or could not afford store fronts were setting up shop.

His entire reason for coming here had been negated now. He at least had to have something to take back to the band. Perhaps he could purchase something useful. Weapons would be too suspicious.

Ale might work, but they had plenty. He moved through the stalls, thus, with the air of one who did not know what he wanted.

"Good brother."

He turned. There was a man selling relics. Inwardly, Tuck rolled his eyes. There was easily enough wood of the true cross floating around to build a man of war. Maybe more than one. He did not like relic sellers. At all. This one was a hunchback, which did not help. The unfortunate individual squinted up at Tuck.

"What is it?"

"Just a moment of your time."

"I'm not buying." He hated to be so firm, although having said that, why would the relic seller target him instead of the wealthy in the crowd? There were certainly enough of those.

The relic seller shook his head. "I'm not selling...to you." He gave Tuck a conspiratorial wink.

Tuck sighed. "What do you want?" He glanced around. A few heads were turning at the scene.

Softly, he lowered his voice, "I'm looking for the friar who walks with outlaws."

"And what do you have to say to that one?"

"Richard is in a Saracen jail."

"If that was the case, half of England..." Tuck tailed off. No. John might well sit on the news. Especially if he did not have money for the king's ransom. Which was entirely likely.

Tuck hoped, though, that it was not true. For all his dislike of Richard, he wished jail on nobody. Even if it tended to make for good time to contemplate.

If Richard did not return... Then John would be king, for Richard and his wife had no children. There was even a rumor around the court that there could be no children, for that would require consummation of the marriage. Tuck had even heard that Richard preferred boys.

No proof of that...and he no longer cared about such things, sins as they were.

But the relic seller was gone.

If Richard was in prison, then John would be obligated by duty, if not brotherly love, to raise the ransom. Where would it come from? The people already had nothing left. The treasury was empty.

Which meant, that Gisbourne and his ilk would squeeze the peasantry further. That would trigger the revolt they feared.

The relic seller either thought they wanted the revolt or thought warning would help prevent it.

Who was the spice merchant? Naturally, Richard had illegitimate siblings. One was in the church. The other had been ennobled. Neither, thus, was the spice merchant.

Tuck shook his head. The Blue Lady had warned him away from the man. Why she would do so, he did not know and was not sure he cared to know.

He might even fear to know. He had barely escaped torture more than once, and he was not a brave man when it came to such things. A clean fight, not a problem. As long as he had his staff and the space to swing it.

Was that relic seller going around...yes. He saw the man approach a different friar and shook his head. "That one's going to be decorating a gallows."

"Is he speaking sedition?" A voice from nearby, not a familiar one. One of the guardsmen.

"He's speaking trouble and crazy rumors."

"Outlaws again?"

Tuck shook his head. "He's spreading some rumor about the king being killed or imprisoned in the Holy Land. Like I said. Trouble."

He felt somewhat guilty...the guards would likely take this out of the relic seller's hide, but on the other hand...

What if the rumor was true? What if it was? Either Richard would be ransomed or not. He was not sure that the best thing for the country was not for him to be executed by the Saracens. He would not, though, wish that fate on him. A man who lived by the sword would die by the sword, yes, often enough. Yet...

Tuck shook his head a little.

"I heard that one too. Doubt its true. But it could be harmful."

"Put the guy's head in the stream for a few minutes and he'll stop spreading it," Tuck suggested. He wasn't suggesting killing the guy. Just cooling him off.

The guardsman laughed. "Oh, he'll stop spreading it. Besides. I don't think he has a peddler's license."

The momentary camaraderie was surprising and almost bother-some. Tuck knew this man worked for Gisbourne and was loyal to him. Yet, he was still a decent man. He could tell. "I doubt it. And we'd be doing the goodwives a favor convincing him to go peddle elsewhere."

It was often women who fell for such things, both more devout and more naive than men. With exceptions.

He did not think Mary Michael, for all that she had likely not left the cloister since her first blood, was naive.

Naivete was not circumstances, he sometimes thought, but a kind of willful ignorance. Women, perhaps, cultivated it so their men would not feel threatened by them. On the other hand, he knew plenty of willfully ignorant men, too.

"Likely. I'd doubt he has anything..."

"Pigs' bones," Tuck pointed out, referring to a common scam. It was, at least, less harmful than robbing a graveyard to get actual human remains. Which he had seen happen much in the Holy Land. They could legitimately say the bones were of 'saints from the Holy Land'...when like as not they were those of Saracens. But still, that too was a form of willful ignorance. The very naming of that land as Holy.

Christ might have lived there, but did that really hallow it more than any other place? Tuck thought not. Holiness, he thought, had to come from people, not place.

The guard was laughing. "Take care, Brother." And he was heading off in the direction in which the relic seller had left.

21

"The king imprisoned?" Robin let out a short, sharp breath, lifting one foot onto a rock to tighten the laces of his boots.

"That is the rumor." Tuck frowned. "However, I wouldn't exactly refer to the man I heard it from as reliable. I think he may be a trifle insane."

"If Richard is imprisoned, then John will pay his ransom. I can't imagine him not doing so."

"There's little love lost between them."

"Brothers are still brothers." A brief cloud passed over the outlaw's face. Tuck wondered if he had a brother.

Who that brother was, what had happened to him. He thought of his own siblings...two brothers, four sisters. All healthy and happy last he talked to them, but with that last being a good while ago.

Well, that was not his problem right now. "They are. But John does not have the ransom, nobody does."

A ransom for a king would be substantial, and the Saracens would treat him well, but hold him until it was paid. It was well within their customs. They would also likely attempt to convert him to their alien faith.

Tuck laughed inwardly. A cannier man might fake conversion to gain release, knowing that no oaths made under duress were true and binding. Richard Lionheart was not a canny man. He was, in truth, a rather simple and straightforward fellow.

"No. So, how will he gain it?"

"Put the squeeze on the Jews," Tuck said, instantly. That was a grand old tradition, right there. The crown needed money, the Jews would be forced to lend it on pain of expulsion or worse. Everyone assumed all Jews were rich.

"Yes. He will, won't he." Robin seemed thoughtful. "But I do not like the idea of stealing ransom money. I have nothing against Richard."

"I do. He needs to come home. Of course, he can't do so if he's in a Saracen jail. But all this assumes the rumor is true."

"The sheriff would know."

"We could bribe his servants," Tuck mused. A good servant was invisible. Which tended to mean their masters forgot they were there, did not think about what they might see or hear. He knew of nobles who would casually undress in front of a manservant or maid as if they were alone...not realizing how much they gossiped about their mistress' blemishes.

Well, any woman who had been married a while had those. Pregnancies took their toll. And Tuck, no prize himself, shook his head a little. "I suspect they have heard something that would tell us the truth. But what about this relic seller?"

"You set the guard on him."

"I did, but they won't do more than fine him and maybe have him cool his heels for a night in jail. He was not speaking treason, after all. Just...rumor." And if he had the sense not to mention he was trying to get that rumor to the outlaws.

Maybe he thought they would take him in if he led them to a share of the ransom money.

"Other possibility would be to talk to the Jews. If John puts the squeeze on them..."

Tuck nodded. "Might I suggest we do both?" He glanced up at the sky. It was threatening rain.

"Will you talk to the Jews?"

It would seem a strange request, except that the Jews he had met had shown a strange respect for wandering friars. Apparently, they were the closest to their own rabbis, as they called them. Not priests. Jews did not have priests.

Jews, Tuck thought, were mighty strange creatures. They were damned, of course, for denying the divinity of Christ...who had been a Jew. Some would damn them further, for being responsible for His death.

Tuck did not agree. God had chosen freely to send his Son into a situation in which he was likely to be killed, in fact intending for him to die. One did not damn a sword for the intentions of the wielder. Yet, they would cling to their alien faith through all persecution. For which he admired them.

"I will."

He knew where to find the Jews of Nottingham, such as they were. He wondered how long it would be before they were thrown out of the country again.

No, he knew exactly how long it would be. It would be when the loan John was about to take out to ransom his brother came due. That was how powerful men treated Jews. Used them and abandoned them. They were not worthy of anything more. Just a useful tool.

He thought of the spice merchant.

He sensed no warning now. Had the Blue Lady intended only to ensure he was in the market place to see the relic seller?

No. He had been warned. He was sure of it. One of these days, he was going to demand a long talk with her.

He was going to *ask* her who she was and not take any kind of answer but one that felt like the truth. Except if all he had to rely on was how it felt, then... "I'll go tomorrow."

Robin nodded. "I'll send Reginald with you as far as the city."

Reginald was the boy. A good choice to sneak into the castle kitchens and get the gossip. He could probably even get in legitimately, accepting a copper or two to run some errands. Common boys were almost as invisible as servants. "Okay."

～

THE NEXT DAY, though, dawned dreary.

"This is unpleasant," Reginald complained as they headed towards the city.

Tuck nodded, glancing up at the raindrops. "It is. Although I've been out in worse."

"True. It's only raining half-heartedly."

"Let's hope it stays that way. I don't feel like arriving in Nottingham looking like the rabbit that fell in the mill race."

Reginald laughed, cheered by the image as Tuck had hoped. "Your ears aren't long enough, unless you borrow a set off that mule of yours."

Tuck joined in. "He's using the only one he has...wait, no. He's not using them, or he'd hear me calling him."

Reginald's laughter, ironically, came close to a bray. "Well, what do you expect from a mule? They're not horses."

"Smarter," Tuck noted.

"I think I'd rather have a beast that isn't smarter than I am."

Nottingham lay before them, the castle looming on the rock. "So. You know what you have to do, right?"

"Easy enough."

"Don't get caught. I don't think we'd get you out as easily as we did Clorinda." They would be more alert, now, to such invasions of the castle, small as they were. More alert... Tuck shook his head.

"I won't."

"They all say that."

Tuck's task was safer, but more annoying. Not that he had problems with Jews, but they tended to have a suspicious nature. Of course, this was likely caused by the way they were treated, and then became another cause for it. He shook his head.

Jews. Well. They were not his problem...he was certainly not of the school who thought they should all be expelled or converted.

They would not dare refuse to loan money to the crown, and the crown would not pay them back, either principle or interest.

He left Reginald at the gate, watching the boy whistle his way into the city. It was amazing how much larger he was now...not only had he recovered his weight, but Tuck swore he had grown two inches. Yet, what life and future did he have? Already an outlaw at that age...but then, he would likely change enough in appearance to return to the world as an adult.

And he was not starving any more. A fair trade, Tuck supposed.

Nottingham did not truly have a Jewish quarter, like the cities of the old eastern Empire so often did. Jews, though, clustered together. It had to do with, he had been told by one, needing a certain number of adult males to found a synagogue. Which, he supposed, made sense. There was no sense building a church to stand empty...here or in the Holy Land. Some of the Crusaders had built churches, but not congregations.

Cart before the horse, that. Thus, the Jews occupied one particular street, which Tuck headed towards, tapping his staff against the ground as if tired enough to need it for support. A good way not to appear a threat, that.

A good way not...well. He was not a threat, not to them, not to anyone. He was not here to get into a fight, drunken or otherwise.

Then he saw him. The spice merchant, on the other side of the street. That sense of warning came again.

Was the man a spy for the crown? For the sheriff? There was nothing about him...Tuck did not sense the evil he had felt from the tower lord.

No, this man was not evil. He was dangerous, but not of his own volition. That was the sense he got.

That this man would betray them without ever intending to. He kept moving, head down. For once he was glad that the first signs of rain were forming. It might drive the man indoors.

No. The man was following him. Then he called. "Brother."

Tuck turned. Their eyes met again. Be careful, that sense told him. He could, for a moment, almost smell roses.

He wished he could reassure her. "Yes, good sir?"

The man approached. "Would you please pray for my daughter?"

"Of course." If that was all it was. Perhaps it was the girl who was the danger, not her father. Perhaps the girl was *in* danger. "Is she in some kind of trouble?"

"She claims to be in love with a most unsuitable man."

"Ah. I hear teenage girls do such things. Hopefully she will grow out of it."

He made a rueful face. "Hopefully she will, as the man concerned is married, among other things."

Tuck winced. For a girl to end up a mistress at such a young age would taint her for any good marriage, unless the man was of great rank. "I will pray for her."

The man studied him for a long moment. "Good. Thank you." He let out a breath. "I think God sends children to try us. Of course, you would not know."

"No." Although there was, these days, no of course about it." Tuck let out his own breath. He could not see how this conversation could be dangerous.

"Thank you." the man repeated, then as the rain increased, he fled towards a nearby tavern.

Tuck kept going. The daughter was in trouble, and that was what the warning was about. It was, thus, trouble that might spread.

He did not like the thought or sound of that. Trouble spreading was not something he wanted to even think about. Especially not trouble involving a pretty girl. Robin might be immune to their charms, but he was less sure about some of the others.

Well. He would pray for her, that being all he could do about the situation right now. She was just some confused kid, he knew. In love, or thinking she was, and not yet accepting of the fact that she would not be permitted to be.

Of the fact that her life would be ruled by circumstance, not her own will or choices. Such was the way life worked.

He reached Jew Street not long after. The houses here all had store fronts. Only a couple were money changers. One traded in fine fabrics, another had dedicated his business to both selling and buying jewelry.

Typical Jewish occupations. But then, what else could they do? They were not permitted to own land. Likely they did not even own these houses, just to make sure they could be thrown out when needed. One of these buildings presumably contained their synagogue.

A young woman, her hair covered, came out of one of them. She was not dark, like the women of the Holy Land, but was of the fair kind of Jew...the strands that showed beneath the scarf were red, not brown or black.

"Lady," he called.

She turned. She was about eighteen, and he saw the gentle curve of pregnancy beneath her dress.

"I would speak with your rabbi." The rabbi would know everything in the community. Would understand, too, why the brother had come. The Jewish priests, such as they were, wed and have children.

"Try the house with the red door," she said softly, before turning towards one of the other houses. She would not, of course, go to the market on her own. A young and beautiful Jewish woman would be a target for all kinds of mischief.

An older woman came out of that house, and the two set off down the street together. Hopefully, they would be enough protection, each for the other. When people encountered Jews, all bets were off.

He went to the red door and knocked on it. A boy answered. "Young man. I am looking for the rabbi."

The boy looked him up and down with more suspicion than the young woman had had. "You are not here to convert anyone?"

"No. I promise." Jews converted, sometimes. It was rare.

Saracens who converted to Christianity would be killed if found. They believed apostasy to be the worst of all crimes.

The boy nodded. Then he called something in the rather gutteral tongue of the Jews, into the house.

Tuck heard a response, then the boy switched back to English. "Come on in."

He noticed the sign of a Jew's house above the door...a small metal cylinder. He had never worked out what its significance was.

Perhaps he should ask, while he was here. It would demonstrate, after all, a certain respect for their beliefs. He intended to treat them with respect. It would cost him nothing and possibly gain much in the long term.

Inside, the house seemed normal. An older man, a little overweight, came down the stairs. "I am Levi."

"Can we speak in private?"

Levi nodded, moving into a back room. On the way, he poked his head into what was obviously the kitchen, calling something in his own language. "My wife will bring us wine and bread, if you wish."

Tuck was not about to turn it down. The room he was taken into looked like any room in any house. The only exception was a large bound book...a book! Tuck had never seen a book, of any kind, in a private home before. He stepped over towards it. "You have a book."

"It is the Talmud. Our scripture."

Tuck felt embarrassment. Of course, a rabbi, responsible for teaching scripture, would have a copy. Books were expensive, but it was likely that the entire community here had come together to make sure they had one. He did not touch it, but moved to sit down.

"So. Not often does a man of Christian cloth come here."

"There is a troubling rumor."

"Are they talking about throwing us out again?" The rabbi made a rueful face. "They tolerate us as long as we are useful, eliminate us as soon as we are not."

"There is a rumor that the king has been taken prisoner in the Holy Land."

"Indeed?"

"John's chances of being able to ransom his brother are slim."

"So, of course, he will come to us for a loan. Which he will not repay."

"I don't see how he can. There is no wealth anywhere that I can find." Tuck rested his hands on the cloth of his habit. "Those once wealthy have little, those once poor have nothing."

The rabbi nodded. "I can't confirm your rumor. Nor can I deny it. But I have heard that John has been calling the goldsmiths and other London Jews to court. Which..."

"...is evidence that he is going to ask for a loan, be it to ransom Richard or just to keep the treasury afloat." Tuck frowned.

None of this could continue. Something would break. And the relic seller had attempted, he realized, to nominate Robin for the role of leader of the revolt.

That there would be a revolt was now inevitable. The only question was how large it would be and how quickly it would be quelled.

"I am thinking it might be time to leave England," the rabbi mused.

"Where else is better? I have traveled to the Holy Land and back, taking a different route. I have not seen true prosperity." Tuck frowned. "Of course, there may be pockets of it."

"And few places even tolerate my kind." The rabbi studied him. "You show respect. That's unusual."

"I see no reason not to. I might disagree with you, but that does not mean that I am going to treat you like dirt."

"Most people do."

Tuck nodded. "I'm not most people. I actually keep my vows. Mostly."

Mostly. He could hardly call what he did obedient.

22

$\mathcal{W}$inter settled over the land. People were starving. Tuck was very much aware of both of these things.

Richard had, the rumor mill said, been ransomed, but he still refused to return to England. Instead he demanded more men.

There were none left to send. The harvest had been brought in mostly by women and boys...if any more men were sent to the Holy Land, it would not be brought in at all. Not that there were not plenty of adult men left.

They were simply the ones canny enough to not be present when the tax men showed. The men on levy were supposed to be returning, but few had. Many, of course, lay under alien sand.

Tuck, for his part, sat under a very English tree. The broad oak, one of the largest he had ever seen, kept the rain off almost as well as a tent would have. Despite that, his clothes were wet and he was thoroughly miserable. A huge part of his misery came from the cold he had caught somewhere or other. His head felt like a small army of smiths was hammering away in there.

Clorinda approached. There was no swing to her walk, she sat down much as a man would, and offered him a cup of tea. "Here."

He took it. It smelled bitter. "Is this your grandmother's cold remedy?"

"Yes."

"Not sure the cold isn't better." He drank it anyway, wincing at the taste. If it helped the symptoms, it would be worth it. If it did not, he would just refuse the next cup.

She laughed a little. "I wonder if humans will ever invent medicines that don't taste foul?"

"No. We won't. Healers will always make sure they do to encourage us to get better."

She laughed again. "Point taken. Although I would also note...somebody brought in some chickens. Enough to make soup for everyone."

Now there was a traditional remedy...for both the cold and the weather. "Mmm. I could use me some of that right now. Or some weather magic, if such a thing existed."

Clorinda shook her head. "We need the rain for next year's crops."

He knew she was right. "Still..." He glanced out at the sodden forest. "I would like it to stop some time. The way things are going, we may be looking up the measurements for an ark." He also know he was exaggerating.

"Maybe if you wore some decent boots," she mused.

He wriggled his toes. "No. Water settles in boots. It runs right out of sandals." He knew friars who did switch to boots in winter. He was pretty sure it did not help.

"So...you seem a lot happier."

He furrowed his brow. "I'm trying to be. I'm still having issues. Just..."

"How about just trusting that the powers who rule the world know what they're doing?"

"When I don't even know which are real and which are not..." Tuck glanced at the grey sky. "I should be defrocked."

She laughed. "You loyally serve your God, you mostly keep your vows, you help people who need it the most. I think that would be more important than a few doubts now and then."

They weren't a few doubts. "I just want spring to come." He needed something to do.

"I don't."

He looked at her askance.

"I fear what will come with the spring. With everything that's going on. Robin thinks there will be a revolt, the only question is when."

"Before the end of the winter, if its going to happen this year. When the food runs out."

Clorinda frowned. "I would think when spring brightens..."

Tuck shook his head. "I would think soon. We have food, out here in the wood...most of it stolen from the crown, but we have it. They don't."

She let her shoulders slump. "Then I am even more worried. What can we do about it?"

"Nothing." That was the bitter truth, that what was going to happen would happen regardless of any efforts against it. Would be civil war. Would be... "People are going to die. All we can do is damage control."

"We could try and get food to some of the worst off before it happened."

"We'd have to steal it." Tuck laughed. "But then, what are we if not thieves?"

"I have an idea." She stood, gracefully, and vanished through the trees.

CLORINDA'S IDEA materialized the next day, refined, no doubt, by Robin and John. Tuck followed them along the path in the chill rain.

Of course, Clorinda had volunteered him. Of course. There were plenty...then again, he thought, he would be no less miserable sitting under a tree than on the move. It was still raining, making him think of ark measurements again. The path was made of mud and leaves and the occasional log. His feet sank into it so hard he was worried he might lose his sandals and have to finish this expedition barefoot.

He wanted spring. That was one of the few good things about the

Holy Land. It got wetter than this, at a certain season, but never this cold.

Or maybe that was a fair trade.

Gisbourne did not keep most of his stores in Nottingham itself. He kept them in granges throughout the land. The bread here was for the training levy and for the castle. There was also ale.

Of course, they had no means to carry enough bread for a village. Yet. The men began to fan out as they approached, but it was Tuck and Reginald who moved through the center of it. Reginald, of course, wore rags. Tuck wore his oldest habit, one that had several holes in it. They looked quite convincing as desperate beggars, traveling together, no doubt, for protection. Although better fed than he had been, Reginald was still skinny. It was likely he would always be skinny, that that was the way he was made.

The guards eyed the beggars.

"Can you spare alms?" Tuck asked, making his voice a wheedle. He never actually begged for alms, but he knew how to do it. You just had to put that very slight hint of desperation without actually whining.

"Go. Get out of here."

"Nothing for a poor brother and a young man who has no parents to return to?"

The guard aimed a kick at him. Tuck intentionally found it hard to move his corpulent self out of the way. "You obviously don't need any extra food and the boy should be working the land."

They did not actually need to get inside, of course. Just hold the attention of the guards as long as possible. "The boy is an orphan from Nottingham. He has no land...he has no family...he has nothing. I am taking him to one of our novice cloisters."

A good lie. It might even work. It was certainly holding their attention. "Eh. If all the lads go into the church, who will get us our food?"

If all the lads go into the levy...but Tuck did not voice that. "Got to have food to get it," he did say.

The guard grumbled. "Well, we're not allowed to give anything to beggars or friars. Move along."

Not allowed to give alms to the Church? Tuck let both his eyebrows shoot up. "I hope you tithe appropriately, then." The veiled threat in there...not that most of the people he knew tithed...would be understood. One tithed to the Church or one did not get the remission of one's sins. The only people exempt were those for whom tithing would result in unbearable hardship.

Of course, most of the people Tuck knew had no money and not enough food for themselves.

"Move along."

The guard did not notice Clorinda coming up behind him. Another of the men, one Tuck did not know well, dealt with the second guard. Tuck winced a little as they fell to the ground. Had they committed any sin other than working for a bad master?

He murmured something as they headed into the grange. Oxen were stabled on one side, a cart conveniently stood in the yard.

"Good," Robin said, coming in behind them. "Food and the means to transport it."

Tuck moved to check on the oxen. He would rather have found horses. Oxen were stupid. Horses always seemed much more willing to be in partnership with man. Mules, of course, were different again.

He wished he'd been able to bring his mule. But he harnessed the oxen quickly, getting the beasts out into the yard with only slight difficulty and putting them to the yoke. Of course, oxen were stronger than horses.

They would be able to fill the cart much more. They had to hurry. There would be a shift change sooner or later, and that was assuming there were no guards asleep somewhere. Tuck was sure they were, and his best hope was that they had drunk too much ale to be awake.

How was this place so lightly guarded? That worried him...with the traps that had happened in the past. They piled bread and sacks of fruit onto the wagon.

Worried him. He moved over to Robin. "This is too easy."

"I agree."

"We should make sure that the food is not poisoned."

"You have a nasty mind, Brother."

"Maybe I do, but I cannot help but think there is a trap here, and we have not yet found it." Gisbourne was the one with the nasty mind, the one who set the traps.

"More likely an ambush once we're out and slowed down by the wagon." Robin frowned. "But we can check."

There was no ambush, and that only made Tuck, walking next to the cart, more certain there was some other trick.

23

*C*lorinda was frowning, examining the loaf of bread. "Moldy. They did not leave poisoned food for us..."

"...just useless food," Robin finished.

Some people thought moldy bread might cause St. Vitus' Dance, Tuck mused. It seemed unlikely, though. Who knew what made a man sick? Only God, Tuck knew.

Anything else would be tampering in His domain. Tuck shook his head. "Of course. Not a trap, just a statement that it could have been a trap."

"It's not all unusable. But we'll have to go through it. The fruit is fine."

Robin nodded, wearily. "It is better than nothing. It is better than starvation."

Unspoken was the fact that moldy bread was better than no bread at all. Better, but hardly desirable. Tuck turned away, headed over to where the oxen had been tethered. They were too fine as work beasts to kill and eat, but they might well have no choice but to do so. Food was more important than anything right now.

He rubbed one of them on the snout, but being a mere ox, it did not respond with affection. He abandoned it, thus, for his mule.

If things got worse, somebody might try and take the mule to eat it. Nobody among them, but the villagers could no longer be trusted with animals.

Of course, perhaps they should hide the oxen. What would the farmers use to plow? The animals were as vital as the people, and keeping some of them intact...

He patted the mule again. The creature rewarded him by gnawing on the sleeve of his habit. "Quit that."

It gave him a woebegone look, the clear expression of an animal who was not happy at all about being told to stop what it was doing.

He shook his head and could not resist scratching the base of its scruffy mane, it's tonsure having been as messy as his of late. John had proven to be a fair hand at maintaining it, thankfully. Glancing over, he saw that Clorinda and Robin were still talking.

About the useless food. Well, maybe the pigs could eat it. Of course, the pigs would always survive. Pigs always did. They could eat anything, even more than humans, and seemed to store it all so easily.

Eh. They would have pork, but a man who ate only red meat became sick. It imbalanced the humors. A man needed a diet that held everything within it.

Bread was important. Bread... The temptation to raid Gisbourne's own granary in Nottingham itself next was strong. Except that they would likely be expected.

Probably, they would be killed if they tried that, and that would avail people nothing. He shook his head. "I envy you," he told the mule. "You don't have to think about anything but the next blade of grass."

Of course, there was still plenty of that. For now. Not so much grain, though. The mule searched him with its lips, hoping that he had something edible concealed in the folds of his robes.

"I don't have anything."

It gave him another of those looks. He glanced over again. He felt left out, but he also felt that he could not join in. Should not. There was no way for him to be involved.

He did not have the knowledge. He did not belong here, yet he did.

Inexorably. There was no escape from the belonging, from the effect being with these people had on him.

He felt more at home here than he ever had, but he also felt he could not be truly one of them. Not now and not ever.

He wished he had taken a different path. Never become a friar. Then he remembered that he had hated all other options worse.

Hated them. He thought of Clorinda. What options had she had? Perhaps she had a point, a small one. No.

Society was as it was. He stood up and walked back to the fire.

THE VILLAGE WAS IN FLAMES. From the top of the hill, Tuck could only watch.

He had no intention of going down there. He was not a coward, no, but what could he do for them?

They protested. Now Gisbourne's men burned them out. They were making more outlaws as he watched. Practically breeding them.

"Whether you're right or wrong, Clorinda, I fear what you seek is about to happen."

"If it does, it will be their own fault." He had not realized she was next to him.

"Well. What can we do?" Nothing was the answer. Nothing at all.

"Help them as best we can." Clorinda sighed. "Get the king back."

"I think we would be better off if John was king, to be honest." And seditious. But then, he had committed enough of that to be defrocked then handed over to the civil authorities. More than enough.

"Perhaps so. And Richard is unlikely to leave an heir."

That was probably correct, even if the rumors about him preferring boys were untrue. He was not with his wife enough to sire children. Tuck shook his head. "I agree. I feel sorry for his wife."

"At least she will not be worn out bearing too many children and weaning them too quickly so she can have the next one." Clorinda snorted at him.

Tuck rolled his eyes at her. Not that she was wrong.

"Still. She probably does...well, actually, I doubt she gets too lonely."

Tuck snorted. "We need to focus on the task at hand."

"I was trying to distract you?"

By implying the queen had a paramour. It was likely true. Women had to be discreet, but some certainly did stray. "I want to kill them all." He forced his mind back. Forced his focus back.

All he found there, though, was anger. He assigned himself several Hail Marys as penance for the words.

"So do I, but it wouldn't avail anything. What would is finding shelter for those people."

They were being herded out onto the road. "Shelter." Tuck let his breath out. "What shelter? Its winter. They're going to die out here."

"Not if we find a place to take them in."

"Who would dare?" Tuck glanced at Clorinda. "You aren't usually the hopeful one."

He knew that the other outlaws were hidden. If Robin shot one arrow into the sky, they would kill the guards. Robin, too, held off, afraid that it would do more damage than it would prevent.

This would certainly be the last straw for the tense countryside when word of it spread. If they had arrived ten minutes sooner...

Robin had something planned. Tuck knew that. Yet, he was still unsure of whether the outlaw could salvage anything from this.

Then he saw the figure approaching. "Great. What's he doing?"

"I don't know, but..." Clorinda started to move forwards. Tuck did not follow her. Stealth was not and never would be his strong suit.

She vanished in the undergrowth amazingly quickly. The green dyed clothes she wore blended in, but there was more to it than that. He could not even hear her.

She was gone...and he knew she was going to back up Robin. He now stood before the gate, bow in hand.

He was going to get himself killed. That galvanized Tuck into action...he followed as best he could, wishing he was smaller. Wishing he was quieter. Wishing he had changed from his habit into Lincoln green.

He still could not bring himself to do that, as if wearing the clothes of a layman would sacrifice what remained of his integrity as a brother. Perhaps it would.

Robin spoke, but Tuck could not hear what he said. Three bows were lowered on him.

More bows than that were aimed at the men, unseen, but nobody yet fired.

They trusted their leader, and even Clorinda... Tuck stopped. Breathing. Trust Robin. Trust him even when he did crazy things. Like shoot the arrow shaft. Not a sight he would ever forget.

He would not forget this one either. Robin was...scolding them. That, Tuck could tell for sure, although not one word in ten reached his ears.

Scolding them as if he were their mother. Or their Mother Superior, Tuck thought wryly. Yes, definitely an abbess scolding a novice.

The thought actually caused him to smile. Then the three bows lifted higher...

...and all three men fell dead in an instant. One of the arrows did seem to come from somewhere nearby. Clorinda.

Robin lifted his hand. "I warned you."

That part Tuck did hear.

The captain turned. "He has men hidden in the woods. Find them."

The survivors seemed somewhat reluctant to bend themselves to that task.

"Find them, I said!"

Nobody else fired. Tuck considered what best he could do. Staying put seemed smart. Yet, he found himself drawn inexorably towards the scene, felt the feminine presence.

Robin was about to need him. For what, he was not sure. But he was about to need him.

That was when the guards charged the slender outlaw. Robin flicked his bow over, using it as a staff. It would undoubtedly ruin the string, but string could be replaced.

Tuck covered the last bit of space in moments, and then let out a war cry, swinging his staff towards the nearest of the guards.

They were not expecting him. Not at all, he realized after a moment. The guard went down like a fallen tree, another turned towards him.

That one lost his sword, the weapon flying to land point down in the ground, the hilt moving from side to side, humming for a moment before it settled. He backed away, rummaging for a knife in his belt.

Tuck hit him in the solar plexus, and he went flying, landing on his butt. He did not get back up.

"I didn't need your help."

"Says who?" Tuck called to Robin cheerfully. "We have them outnumbered now."

He was ashamed of himself for enjoying the fight, but it was really...easier and more enjoyable than most battles. These people were supposed to be professionals.

Robin's legend would spread...but so would that of the Friar. Tuck brought the third guard down by thrusting his staff between the man's legs and jerking it sideways. He went literally head over heels.

"So we do!" Robin laughed. "I vote we take what we can and go."

It wasn't much...but Tuck relieved one of the guards of a very nice ring, slipping it onto his own finger. It even fit. Not that he would keep it, of course, but it was the easiest way to carry it.

So he kept telling himself. The villagers were getting their small, poor possessions and their beasts. When the guards woke up, it would be to an empty village and their own dead. Nothing else was left behind.

They could not stay. They had to abandon what remained of their homes and furniture, for Gisbourne would only send more men next time. What the fire had spared would be, thus abandoned. Why would he care? They were used up, their land was close on used up.

Some farmers were starting to make inroads, clearing the royal forest. Illegal or not, it was a possible way to survive. They hunted every way to survive they could find.

The law did not matter anymore. Tuck had the sad feeling that one day the greenwood would be gone.

No, not gone, but reduced to pockets and fragments. People had too many children, having so many to ensure one survived. Peasants had fewer, but they still had too many, and there were always more people.

Was that so bad? Man had dominion, Tuck reminded himself. But dominion had to come with its flip side, respect.

Francis respected the world with all that was in him. Brown friars were supposed to do that. Tuck had never been quite sure how. How did he respect a sparrow? He elected for mostly leaving them alone.

Of course, he did treat his mule well...even when the animal did not reciprocate. Mules respected nobody except themselves.

They were back in the woods, now, faded out. The villagers had scattered, with a place arranged to come back together. Tuck knew the place. An old village, abandoned after some plague. It would become a home again, until Gisbourne found it.

They might, though, get in one harvest without being taxed. Clorinda had a point. Maybe taxation was bad, but if the lords did not take tax, how would they protect the peasants? The problem was not that the lords took tax, it was that they were not using it in the right way. Taking too much. Funneling everything into the thrice-damned Crusades.

It was all about that.

24

"No," Will said. "Hold your staff higher."

Tuck turned to watch, and saw Will cheerfully beating up Reginald in the name of teaching. They were using willow staffs, not oak staffs, so that the blows would bruise instead of breaking. Willow was also lighter.

Which was good and bad. Reginald was having issues getting the willow staff high enough. He had recovered from lack of food, but would always be small. That much was obvious.

A small man had to use other tactics, Tuck mused. He'd be better off working more with the bow.

Or with the sword, but few here knew how to use one. Tuck tapped his own staff, but then he watched for now. Not bad, for a small guy. He did still need to build muscle, though.

Tuck frowned a little bit. He glanced around. They were better fed than the villagers, but not much. Hardship did not hit a fat man as swiftly as others.

They would have to go gather more food. Where from? They would have to move camp...they had left barely enough blackberries for the birds within an hour's walk. Clorinda had gathered elderberries and was doing something arcane with them. They were too bitter to be edible. He thought she might be making wine. Or something.

He wouldn't mind some wine but he wanted to watch Reginald train more. Under other circumstances, what would have become of the boy? Something better than this, something with more of a future. He doubted a royal pardon would ever be forthcoming, and short of that, none of these men could ever again live under a settled roof.

He finally tore himself away, walking to the edge of camp. He sensed her presence suddenly, abruptly, flowing around him. "What do you want?"

The Blue Lady did not respond. It was simply the sense that she was there, watching.

Supporting. "You should tell me who you are." Then he wouldn't be afraid, or would he? Would he rather be able to fool himself into thinking she was no spiritual threat or know that she was?

Or know that she was not?

No answer.

"You really don't like telling anyone anything, do you?" He tried not to sound amused, but it came through. She was almost like a recalcitrant child. Or like somebody who enjoyed leading people up the garden path.

He hoped that she was not that last. It would bother him to know he was being used by a spiritual entity that might well be leading him to hell.

Bother? Now there was an understatement. "Yes. I'm scared of you."

He saw her, then. She stood with one hand on a tree. A garland of flowers was twined into her raven black hair. Her blue gown almost touched the ground; he could see the toes of one bare foot. She seemed no more than sixteen, all of a sudden.

How old had Mary been when she married Joseph? Little older than that, likely. Or maybe a little older...perhaps Joseph had been forced to wait for his bride until his shop was established.

Perhaps... Tuck shook his head. He wanted to believe that was who she was.

"All truths lead to the truth, Tuck." Her voice was rich and warm.

"That's not good enough," he responded. "Why won't you tell me who you are?"

"Because I am who you need me to be."

That implied a heresy more profound than any he had even imagined. All gods being the same god? That was a ridiculous idea. The Saracens might claim to serve the same God he did, but they saw Him so differently.

So differently. Did Clorinda even see the same woman? And what...if the Saracens did serve the same God, but saw Him differently...

"You begin to understand." And she was gone.

Tuck shook his head. "I think I prefer the company of my mule."

TUCK DODGED to the side with the agility of a far smaller man. The stall overturned, spilling bread rolls and butter pats out into the aisle of the marketplace.

The man who had overturned it was advancing on a guardsman. "No. I will not give you anything." The poor owner was...trying to hide behind Tuck. Given there was plenty of space back there, the friar did not entirely blame him.

Plenty of space, but he did not need a hanger on. Not that he could get rid of him. Or blame the poor man for acting as he was.

This was not the only altercation. Gisbourne's men were attempting to raid the Nottingham market. They were taking whatever they wanted and not leaving payment.

The people were exploding. Tuck could have predicted this, could have warned them had they listened to him.

He wished himself safe in the greenwood. The stallholder elected to run.

Tuck did not. One did not run from a riot, he had noticed. It tended to get you chased down. To get you hurt. He rested his staff across his hands and waited.

The guard looked at him once, decided he was not a target worth messing with, drew his sword and turned towards the big man.

"You going to bring in the harvest yourself after you've killed everyone? Oh wait. What harvest...there was nobody to plant it."

He was exaggerating, but not by much. As little food as there had been last year, there was likely to be less this. Less seed, fewer hands for the planting.

The guard ran the man through. Tuck tried to react, but he was not close enough.

"You want to be next, friar?"

"Not particularly." He kept his staff ready, sure and certain he could take the guy down if he needed to. "I was trying not to be used as a human wall here."

The guard laughed, wiping his sword off on the dead man's tunic. "Go. Get out of here before you get hurt."

Tuck made as if to take his advice, moving away from the area. He did not, however, plan on going far. The riot was getting worse, growing as isolated incidents became less so. He could hear a woman's high screams, screams of utter loss. A child had been injured or killed; he was certain of it. Or possibly her husband.

There was going to be nothing left of England at this rate. Nothing but darkness and chill. Nothing but pain.

No. They would put everything back together. He wished the news had been of Richard's death. Raising the ransom had likely took whatever John had left, plus a large loan from the Jews of London and York.

"It's time for them to come home!" A woman's voice. A goodwife by her dress, but she stood on one of the tables in the alehouse, which creaked under her. The wind threatened to give the men around her a view of things only her husband should see. "All the men should come home, harvest the crops. Forget the Holy Land!"

Tuck edged closer. Would the guards dare to shoot a woman? If they did, then they would not get out of here alive. He was sure of it. That was probably what went through their mind.

"We will not pay any more ridiculous taxes. We will not give you any more of our sons to fight Saracens and bleed out in the desert sand."

Most of the desert was rock. He was not about to destroy her image, though. Whoever she was, she knew how to speak. He sometimes wondered if they should not let nuns give sermons. She proved a woman was capable of it.

"We want a king who stays in the country, who stirs only to visit his nobles. One who does his duty."

Good luck on that, he thought. Kings were notoriously lazy creatures who tended to enjoy the perks of the crown more than fulfill its duties.

John, Tuck mused, was less so than most. Richard, of course, simply had his priorities wrong.

"Richard should abdicate!" That was the sudden cry, and it startled Tuck, for it seemed for a moment to have come out of his own thoughts, out of his own mind.

Richard should abdicate. He could not even disagree. He could not... Well. That was the way of things. The king could not be forced out.

"Richard should be dealt with!" That was an uglier mood, flowing through the crowd. It did not get too far, but the word that was unspoken was an ugly one.

Assassination. It would not be hard. Some melee in the Holy Land, who would even know that the blade that took the king's life was not a Saracen's curved scimitar.

But to hear it being openly espoused was disturbing. Tuck could not even blame the guard who loosed an arrow into the crowd.

People charged him. Tuck was forced, in the process of avoiding being trampled, to knock a couple of them aside with his staff, scowling as he stalked towards the woman. "Was this what you were trying to start?"

She jumped down off the table before she became a target. "What do we have that makes it worth not starting trouble?"

He did not have a good answer for her other than, "Our lives."

"Not for much longer, the way things are going."

"For what its worth, I agree. Richard should either come home or abdicate in favor of John. But he will come home on his shield."

"And some, I think, would encourage that. I don't. Let him crusade... But not with our money and not with my sons."

"Crusaders are supposed to be volunteers." Tuck suspected victims of levy had been taken, but...

"They did volunteer. But they are wide-eyed boys, who will volunteer for anything and never count the cost."

She was right. Tuck flinched a little. Reginald might have volunteered. Reginald might still...it was one sure way to obtain the pardon that would allow him to return to settled life. A king would not dare refuse pardon to a pilgrim, of any kind.

"You know similar."

"I think all boys are like that. Some never become men. Some girls never become women, for that matter."

It was not limited to the male gender, by any stretch. The refusal to grow up, the refusal to set aside the attitudes of childhood was a human thing, Tuck thought.

"Sometimes, it's good to be like a child."

"Sometimes," Tuck agreed. "But we should get out of here." The riot had roared away from them. "Before the guards spot you."

She picked up her skirts, nodded once, and ran. Tuck suspected she was a widow. No husband to keep her in order. No husband to help her think things through, either, although women were sometimes better at that than men.

Tuck just walked away.

"Halt, Brother."

Tuck stopped, turning to face the guardsman. He said nothing.

"Who was that woman?"

"A rabble rouser. I don't know. I've never seen her before." His answers were completely truthful. He did not know who she was, and he would certainly not help them find her to execute her. That would be the inevitable result of her being discovered by them. They would hang her for sedition without even thinking about it.

Without, certainly, considering there might be some truth in her words. One did not speak so about one's ordained king...in public anyway.

Tuck had heard far worse things said about Richard over a cup of ale in a quiet back room. You could get away with a lot if they thought you drunk.

The guard shook his head. "You swear that you do not know her?"

"I swear." He could do so in a clear conscience. He wished he knew her, but he did not. He wished she was...no, not a man. Younger and fitter. No.

They did not need somebody that stupid.

"Avoid her. She's going to be fitted for a noose and I'd hate to see her drag others with her."

"I fear it is too late for that."

Tuck glanced over...the riot was starting to head back this way. "If you'll excuse me."

The guard made no attempt to prevent Tuck's escape from the scene.

he river that flowed through Nottingham was large enough for boats to come up it, although the rapids south of the city were a problem. The ambitious spoke of building some kind of canal to bypass them.

Perhaps one day that would be done. One day a long time in the future. It did seem that people made their slight improvements. Better millstones.

Of course, one took one's flour to the mill and paid the mill tax. Tuck wondered how many old-fashioned querns had been sneaked out of storage. And, idly, whether they could get their hands on one. A quern was inefficient, but it did not make bad bread, in the end.

The mill tax. The levy. All the ways in which the lords took what the peasants had made and built to pay for the protection they were supposed to provide.

There would be more riots. And before too long a lord would die at the hands of his people. What would John do about it? Tuck stared across the river and wondered.

A grey heron rose up from the bank, spreading its great wings. There was a heronry not far away from there, the birds were a common sight. Some people liked to chase them off, for they ate a lot of fish. Of course, one had to be careful. Their beaks were long enough to possibly kill a man.

Tuck shuddered a bit at that thought. What a way to go...killed by a bird. Almost funny, in a dark way. The heron, of course, was nowhere near him.

Something darted through the water itself. Probably an otter. They ate a lot of fish too, and men liked to set hounds on them. He hoped it would get clear.

He hoped... Even the animals were suffering a little from the depredations the countryside was currently experiencing. Only a little and not as much as the humans and their livestock.

But he felt a certain peace come over him. He found himself able to pray for the first time in what felt like a good part of a lifespan. Perhaps it had been years, for that matter. No, not years, not solidly.

He felt the presence of God in that place, not far from the city. He wanted to ask Him why He was letting this happen, but he knew the answer.

Humans had free will. That had to include the ability to make mistakes. To fall into temptation...otherwise there would be no virtue in living a good life. There was nothing to reward if there was not the choice to sin.

To sin. Tuck looked out across the river. He had done plenty of that, but he felt himself still to be on the right side. As stupid and dangerous as it was.

It was not man's place to judge, he told himself. A piece of scripture ignored entirely too often. People enjoyed judging. They liked to compare themselves to their neighbors, to say they had better clothes, a better house, a better garden.

It was human nature to judge. Or, Tuck supposed, that would never have had to be said in the first place. Human nature to fight, to struggle to be at the top of the hierarchy.

Human nature had all kinds of problems attached to it, but Tuck just shook his head. "I need guidance," he asked the air. "What can I do to help prevent what is happening from becoming worse, from turning into something terrible?"

He did not, of course, expect an answer in words. Answers to such questions never came in words.

They came in knowing or signs, in clues for which way a man should follow.

Tuck no longer knew what he knew. Not anymore, but at least he felt calm. He felt as if his mind and emotions were, once more, under his own control.

He felt like a man again. That was what mattered. A man, a friar... He was still a friar. Likely he would not be if his order ever found out what he was up to.

Why not? Because he had taken a vow of obedience, and if they said he was no longer a friar...he would add that sin to the rest. He still thought of himself as a servant of God. And, perhaps, of Mary.

Mary. The Blue Lady had implied all gods were one god. Why did that idea scare him so much?

Because it made Clorinda right. Because it meant that the order of man as ordained by God was meaningless. Thoughtless. Without truth. It meant that kings might not have Divine Right, because what the Saracens and Jews said was as valid as what the Pope voiced from his pulpit in Rome.

It meant the Old Gods were not just real, but valid and powerful. That, Tuck realized, was what he was so afraid of.

He was afraid that They would rise up, take over. Invalidate everything he knew, everything he had learned, everything he was. Make him not just no longer a friar, but no longer a person.

Okay. That was silly. Yet, it was what he felt. It was the root of why he had run from the Blue Lady. If all gods were real, then part of what he believed, an important part, was no more than falsehood. If all gods were real, then...

Then there was no reason to obey the Church. He had given his life to the three vows, and if this was true, he had done so for nothing.

Nothing? The otter dove through the water again, dangerously close. It was safe from Tuck, as he did not have a dog. Perhaps it was smart enough to realize that.

Nothing. He had walked most of the way to the Holy Land, as much on foot as he could. He had ridden ships. He had seen the desert.

He had not entered Jerusalem, but he had glimpsed her before he turned back, knowing what would come.

He had lived in the greenwood and in the tents of kings, in the castles of the nobles and in a farmers' hay loft.

Nothing? All of that was worthwhile, all of that was worth considering and remembering. He had had a life he preferred to that of a husband and farmer.

So, no. He had not wasted it, even if it got him no closer to God. Or, perhaps more accurately, even if the husband and farmer could be as close through a different understanding.

He turned from the river and walked towards Nottingham town.

THE CAMP WAS SUBDUED when Tuck finally returned to it. Nobody seemed to have much to say, and it was cold winter that closed in on them. The air was chill, and hoarfrost was already settling on tents and branches.

Tuck put the mood down to the weather and settled down near his tent. Hopefully somebody would have some interest in conversation. When winter settled in, there was little else for a man to do but talk. Well, and other things...there was a reason most babies were born in the fall, after all.

He was relieved to hear Will's harp, the minstrel testing the strings and their key, adjusting the tuning. Then he began to sing, softly.

A love story. Tuck glanced around and saw Clorinda looking up. As usual, she had her hands busy with some work, but the smile she gave the singer said it all.

The song continued, and then segued into a cheerful harvest song. The minstrel knew exactly how to cheer everyone up, Tuck thought wryly. Exactly how. And that was a good thing. They needed him.

They needed Clorinda, who made the best arrows. Reginald, who was good at sneaking into places. John's strength. Much was the best shot, after Robin himself.

What did they need Tuck for? It had been, to start with, as a minister. Now, he was less sure. He had been drawn into their world, their life. He could never escape.

Yet, he lived. He lived and was free. As free as a man could be. The king in his castle, no more free than the peasant in the fields.

As if reading his mind, Will moved into a ballad on that very subject. He gave it a sarcastic edge, though, that was no doubt Clorinda's influence.

All men could be equal, she had told them. Yet, that was not how...surely society could not be run that way? Surely humanity had to be ordered and striated for civilization to survive.

Each man in his place, each woman also. That was the way of things.

Then they heard hoof beats. Lots of them.

"We may be discovered."

Tuck rose to his feet, moving to his tent. He grabbed what he most needed. If all else failed, he could set the mule free. The beast would likely find him again. It was affectionate, in its own way. As much as, sometimes, it acted as if it hated him.

Well. That was not his problem. The tent was knocked down, kicked down.

"Leave the tents," Robin said. "Either they have found us, and already know we are here, or they have not. We can make more."

Tuck nodded and made his way to where the mule was tied, next to the two oxen they still had.

Reginald was behind him. He took the halters of the oxen.

"Let them go if they interfere with your escape," Tuck told him, reaching for his mule's halter.

The beast had his long ears both swiveled towards the approaching riders. No doubt he knew exactly how many horses were approaching. He was not happy about it.

He started to lead Brownie away, but he was ready to release his lead rein and chase him away, turn it into a red herring.

They would not hurt him. At worst, they would catch him and put him in their own stables. He was an ugly beast, but it was a strong and healthy one that would work for them.

So he felt no qualms about leaving Brownie behind. He could always steal him back later.

The horsemen swept into the hollow. He heard them waste precious time checking the tents...but there was nobody there.

"Fan out!" he heard.

He kept moving, quickly, keeping the mule between himself and them. They might see only the animal. Of course, they would still chase the beast, even if they thought he was on is own.

And here they came. He released the mule, slapping him on the rump, and then dived into the nearest cover.

Too late, he realized the nearest cover was composed mostly of stinging nettles. Fortunately, not many of the little pricks could reach bare skin as opposed to habit, but he had to *stay* there.

They were chasing the mule. "Stop. Its a loose beast. They must have let it free in hopes we would follow it. They went this way."

Tuck waited. And waited. He then saw his opportunity. Most of them rushed into the trees on foot, having secured their horses. One had lingered, apparently unsure the mule had really been alone.

He rose out of the vegetation like an avenging angel, pretty much staff first. The solid oak connected with the side of the man's head and he went down without even crying out.

Good. Solid. Tuck checked for a pulse...alive, but he would not be waking up any time soon. Rather than finish him in cold blood, he moved quietly towards their horses.

They had tied them to trees by the bridle reins. Poor horsemanship, and they deserved what happened next.

Tuck untied every single one of them and sent them scurrying after the mule. It would hopefully take them hours to catch them when they got back.

They would know it was enemy action but have no way of tracing who did it.

Then he moved after them. Which was easy. They crashed through the woods as he had once done, clearly having no practice moving quietly through the undergrowth.

Fools, he thought. And then realized that even if they captured anyone...

Except they were not here to capture. He knew that...they would have brought a wagon if so. They intended to kill anyone they came across, possibly asking questions later. If they happened to take out some innocent swineherd, so be it.

He was too far behind them to be of much help. He heard one surprised cry and saw a body fall. An arrow from good cover, no doubt.

Why was he even worried about these clowns? Because even incompetent people could get lucky. If they got lucky, then they would...

Then, just in time perhaps, it occurred to him. He moved to the side, vanishing into the trees. He had learned how to do that. Now he was not in the path of their retreat if they gave up and tried to go back to their horses.

And there they came, running from the outlaws. Tuck managed not to laugh at the thought of what they would find when they got to the clearing.

26

*R*obin led the way into York, Tuck three steps behind him.
They were further north than they normally went. York had something Nottingham lacked. Solid outer walls. From the look of them, they had been started in the Roman period and finished more recently, set upon banks. Gateguards waved them through without hesitation.

Tuck wore his habit, Robin was dressed as a peasant, carrying a staff that was, in reality, an unstrung bow. Nothing to see here.

"Why are we here?"

Robin just smiled. "Because the city fathers of York are nothing like Guy of Gisbourne. Watch. Learn."

He got like that sometimes. Tuck actually rolled his eyes. "Mary," he muttered.

Robin laughed a bit. "Exactly."

Tuck hoped he would hush. The city fathers might be decent people, but York had an archbishop. Not a place to even hint at heresy. Tuck stepped to one side to avoid slop being emptied from an upper story.

York was larger than Nottingham and more prosperous. That was a low bar, right now, but at least people here were not starving and their clothes not rags. Even the dogs seemed sleeker. One of them turned to pad after them.

"Robin, you have a new follower."

Robin turned. The dog was no more than a puppy and gave him a puppy's look. "He claims his owner does not feed him."

As, if anything, the beast was fat, Tuck laughed. "I think he just wants to be scratched behind the ears."

Puppies. Of course, the puppy reminded him distinctly of young Reginald. Some humans were very much like dogs in their blind loyalty to master or cause.

A young voice called something and the puppy, with one wistful look at Robin, turned and padded away. Its tail, though, was still wagging.

"That dog is better off than many humans."

"Happier, certainly. But then, dogs are always happy. You can beat a dog, and five minutes later it will be happy." Tuck mused on that. Some humans were like dogs in that manner, too. You could abuse them, physically or verbally, and it would be over and done with and forgotten.

And other humans. Clorinda, for example. She was most definitely a cat, sensual and belonging only to herself. Robin...also a cat. No. A wolf. Robin was a wolf. Wolfshead. Maybe there was something to that particular euphemism.

Tuck himself...a cat. Definitely a cat. Most of the people here, though, seemed to be dogs.

Robin headed for the unfinished Cathedral, a skeleton of stone bones reaching for the sky. Tuck wondered what dedication they planned for it. What monks or nuns would sing God's praises within the building and any cloister attached to it.

It did not matter. That, at least, he could feel and agree with. Order did not matter. Maybe heresy, to a point, did not either. There were Christians in Egypt who claimed they and only they knew the true word and life of Christ. Maybe they were right and everyone else was wrong.

Maybe they were wrong and everyone else was right. But everyone could not be right. Or could they?

All gods are one God. He shook his head. A Jew, wearing his skull-cap, moved past them on some business.

All gods are one God. The Saracens thought only their God was real, and yet showed more tolerance than Christendom. What did that teach him?

Robin had quickened his pace.

"Where are we going?"

"The gallows."

Great. Was Robin planning a jail break? Tuck did not know if any of the others were within York's walls. They likely were. He tended to tell his men only what they needed to know and have a narrow idea of what that was.

What did Tuck need to know? He was not sure at all. All he knew was that he had just stepped in a pool of horse urine. He shook it off his foot and continued. Nothing to be done about such things, after all.

Still, York was relatively clean. The streets were well cobbled. This had been a rich city and retained some of it even now. It had been a Roman city, which Nottingham had not. Perhaps that was the secret. Its age. Its...strength. Oh yes, there was a strength to this city.

There was a crowd starting to gather. How had Robin known, three days ago, that there would be an execution today?

Simple, Tuck thought. York always did all of its executions on the same day of each month. Some cities did that. Stored up the criminals and then made a big deal of it.

Tuck did not ask Robin anything more. He trusted him.

Robin glanced at him. "Work the crowd. Ask for alms. Act normal."

He didn't give him a cue for no longer acting normal. From which Tuck gleaned that it would likely be extremely obvious.

Robin usually managed to be just that. He moved away from the man, producing his begging bowl. Crowds gathered for executions were always good for alms. Perhaps it was an expiation thing, of the guilt they took on themselves by even being here. By watching men die for entertainment.

They were not starting with an execution, though. As Tuck glanced over at the gallows dais he saw a flogging frame being set up.

He shuddered a little but kept moving. "Alms for the poor. Alms for the poor." He phrased it like that, implying he would give the money to somebody who needed it more.

He fully intended to do so. Oh yes, he would give these alms to somebody who needed them, yes. Anything he got.

A few small coins dropped into the bowl, but most people's eyes were not even on him, or even close to him. They were on the flogging frame.

The boy who was being flogged was no more than fourteen. Broken apprenticeship, perhaps. Who knew? He already had welts on him, that looked to be from a belt or similar. He already...

Tuck shuddered. The poor kid...he was thin, too. Yet the crowd's mood was shifting, the peculiar elevation of institutional violence.

He wanted out of here. Better yet, he wanted to see an arrow fly, cut the boy down from the frame. But there was no move yet.

They could not save everyone. They could not help everyone. They could not...they had to focus on what they could do. The boy was a casualty in a war nobody really grasped was happening.

Clorinda grasped it, but her solution was to start a different one. Tuck frowned. His breath was let out quite sharply. It fogged in the air. When had it gotten so cold? Maybe some of the cold was inside him, not in the air that flowed around.

The boy got off lightly. Five lashes, counted easily, then he was cut down and helped away. He would live, but he would hate. Tuck could almost feel it. He had already hated, and he was seeing hate's reward...but what was the alternative?

That brief preamble over, the gallows were being checked. The hangman was checking the drop, carefully. Taking pride in his work.

Pride for a hangman was a swift death. The prisoner was being led out. It was, Tuck noted, a woman. She wore no hood as yet...but also no covering on her head. Her hair fell in stringy rat-tails.

A witch, perhaps? It was odd how only women were ever hanged as witches. Men always seemed to escape their fate, somehow...to the point where 'witch' was considered a female term.

Clorinda said it simply meant 'wise one'.

He was pushed towards the dais. He did not resist the crowd as they surged forward. It sometimes seemed that the hanging of a woman got more excitement than the death of a man.

She was not young, her hair streaked with grey. He could hear the guards say, "Don't let her say anything."

She broke free of them. "I will say what I want to say. I say this. That if our men don't return, there will be nothing for them to return to."

The guards grabbed her.

"Elizabeth Brewster. Guilty of speaking sedition and of witchcraft."

Tuck wondered if they had tossed in 'witchcraft' just because it could never be proven or disproven. It was always a good charge to add to make sure you could get away with killing somebody.

Was she the one they were supposed...and then the arrows flew. Whether she was or not, Robin had signaled his move.

Tuck was almost at the foot of the platform. He pulled himself onto it and his staff after, once the initial volley had landed. "Tuck. The cells behind the gallows."

So, it was not her, but they had decided not to allow anyone to die today. That voice was John's...he too had made his way to the front, better with staff than with bow.

Tuck cleared himself a path through the remaining guards, making his way into the cell. A blade caught in his sleeve and, from the sharp pain that followed, his arm. A flesh wound. He carried on, dropping down the far side of the dais.

The final holding cells were a temporary structure. He knocked out one last guard and simply started to open all the cells. He truly did not care if he let out a murderer or three. They all seemed very thin. Who had the food to give to prisoners condemned to death? If they starved before their hanging date, so be it. None were women except for the first one, but one was a greybeard...old enough, easily, to be Tuck's father.

What on earth had he done to be in a death cell? Tuck did not know and might never find out, but there was a vague similarity between him and an outlaw he did not know well, a man named Alan. Some relative, perhaps.

There were two rough looking outlaw types as well, and one more young man who simply looked at Tuck, then at his own hands. "Come on. We're getting out of here." He offered the man his hand.

"I..."

"Don't give me any deserve it crap. We're leaving."

The crowd, denied one form of entertainment, seemed remarkably content to accept another. Robin had come visible at one end of the dais...and as Tuck watched, he shot the noose from the gallows.

That might have elicited a boo or a rush. The mood of the country was such that he gained a cheer.

Somehow, in all of this, the hangman was just standing there. Tuck almost felt sorry for him. Almost. But then, had he really chosen that profession? Hangmen tended to be orphans, apprenticed young. Never allowed to build the kinds of connections that might lead them to be sympathetic to their victims.

Tuck decided he could feel sorry for him. But they were fading away in all directions. The two criminals and the boy faded with them. He was not sure where the witch had gone.

She would not have been unwelcome, but she seemed to have made her own escape.

Tuck only hoped that the two men who looked like murderers would not prove to be liabilities.

∾

By the time the outlaws reached Nottingham again, the story had gone ahead of them. It had grown, as all stories grew.

Tuck sat in the tavern, trying not to laugh. According to the man expounding right now, for example, Little John was at least ten feet tall and used an entire, full grown tree as his staff.

He began to realize that their legend might even outlive them. It might even join with the stories of King Arthur. Become something that was part of England.

Was that what the Blue Lady wanted? To create a legend? To create something oppressed people could believe in?

Clorinda thought they should fight. She thought all of the peasants should fight. Take over where the lords were letting them down.

Tuck thought...oh, he knew what he thought they should do.

"And then there was the friar. He pointed at the cell doors and they opened."

Now that was almost too much. Tuck was being called a witch! Well, not exactly, for there was nothing negative about the man's speech. "Now, that is a little much to swallow. Magic?"

"God is with them. God has abandoned the kings and lords."

Tuck digested that. "If He has, it is only because some of them have abandoned Him."

"You would know that, Brother, I suppose. What do you think of this friar?"

"I think you are exaggerating your entire story." Tuck grinned. "But then, that makes it a better story."

Not that the truth was not a good story. Not that the truth was not, in some ways, the stranger story.

The stranger laughed. "Of course it does. More ale!"

The serving wench came over, refilled everyone's tankards including Tuck's. The stranger put his hand on her butt as she left. She didn't object, but rather grinned over her shoulder at him.

Well, serving wenches could get away with being like that. They could even, sometimes, get away with taking a man upstairs for a few coins. Heck, the largest brothels in London paid rent to the Church.

Sure, people disapproved, but it was normal. Men had needs. Most men, anyway. "Ten feet tall?"

The man laughed. "He sure looked it to the person who told me."

Of course, nobody was that tall. Except possibly the legendary Goliath, and Tuck rather suspected that man's height had also been exaggerated in the retelling. Most likely he had simply been a very big man. Like John. Probably the same size. "A new Goliath, eh?"

"Yes, except this one seems to be working with David, not against him."

Tuck laughed. It was a great image...and one he definitely planned on sharing with Robin. "I heard there was a beautiful woman."

"Yes," the man agreed. "A truly lovely maiden, who fought as well as any man. I can only suppose she was the outlaw's lover."

Not quite right, but Tuck did not correct him. "And what else did you hear?"

"That they robbed the crowd blind before the attack and gave the money to those who needed it more."

Which was not exactly true. But it was true in the general, if not the specific. Tuck shook his head. "I'd bet they counted themselves in those who needed it more."

"Oh, probably. But it makes a better story."

It would become a minstrel's tale. Tuck wondered if any of their names would be right. Maybe Will could take care of that.

But, he also suspected that Clorinda would be the outlaw's lover. "Between you and me," Tuck whispered, starting to stand, "the only woman the outlaw loves is the Virgin." And then he left, before the man could realize who he was.

It was a dramatic gesture he quickly regretted. He had left almost an entire tankard of ale behind to make it.

Well, that was his own problem. But he had corrected one small detail...and he did not realize exactly how that part of the legend might spread.

Outside, he left the small village quickly. He could only get away with so much of that, and only get away with it at all because few looked past habit and tonsure to the face that belonged with them. Even if they did, they saw the friar...and Tuck wondered if his name would survive.

How had he ever got into this situation anyway? In his mind he heard feminine laughter. The Blue Lady.

She was laughing at him. He scowled. "Hey."

No. She was not laughing at him, she was laughing at the story. At the legend. At the image of John being ten feet tall.

Tuck grinned at that realization and set his feet back towards the Greenwood.

27

*H*e did not get that far. Soldiers came from a side road, blocking his path. "Brother."

He sighed, showing them one empty hand, then freeing the other by leaning his staff against his shoulder. It was a classic gesture. It meant 'I might be armed, but I won't use it on you'. Not that he wouldn't if he had to.

If he had to. There were four of them, and well armed and armored. He was not sure he could defeat them. So, he stayed casual.

"What's your name, Brother?"

"Tuck."

"That's not a name."

Tuck grinned. "It's the one everyone knows me by." He paused. "Brother Joseph Francis."

"Why Tuck?"

Tuck slapped his belly. "Tuck in. It's been with me since I was a novice," he admitted.

"So. What do you know about outlaws?"

"That they get kind of annoying when I'm traveling alone." He tugged at his habit. "But they realize I have nothing worth stealing."

"Unless, of course, you stole it yourself."

Tuck remembered the unnamed lord in his tower. He wondered if the man was even still alive. He had not had much in the way of stores of food. "Why would I do that? Vow of poverty."

"Pheh. Like any abbot alive keeps that vow."

"I'm not an abbot. As long as I have food in my belly, a place to lay my head and a tankard of ale, I'm happy." Keeping as close to the truth as possible was, he knew, the best way to lie.

"Oh, let him go," one of the others said.

"What if he's the one who freed two murderers up in York? If he is, he's responsible for anyone else they kill."

Tuck managed to keep from flinching. The guard had spoken his own worst fears on the matter.

Not much he could do about that. "I'm not."

"But you know about it."

Tuck laughed. "Only the tavern tales...in which one of the outlaws was ten feet tall and another opened jail cell locks with a gesture."

The guard laughed. "I didn't hear that version. I heard the outlaw leader was a beautiful woman."

"See. Its impossible not to have heard about it." Tuck grinned. "I'm just a friar, you know. A little embarrassed by the entire thing, to be honest."

"I'd bet you are. The man's a disgrace to his order and should be defrocked."

"For that, somebody would have to find him." Tuck shrugged. "Short of arresting every friar in Nottingham..."

"We've considered that, but the Church would be on us like..."

Tuck shrugged again. "Am I free to go?"

They did not want to let him go. That much was clear. Perhaps he should vary things up by sometimes going abroad in normal clothing...except that he had worn his friar's robes for so long he would feel naked. Not himself. Empty.

Of course, he felt that a lot lately. But they were starting to move back. "Thank you."

Then he heard the rider behind him. "That's the one! The outlaw friar!"

Tuck turned. "What makes you think that?" But his heart sank. The man had been in the group of people in the inn.

He should have left the road sooner.

It was the second time he had been arrested under this suspicion. The difference was...this time they actually knew it was him. Or thought they did.

He wondered if he could change his appearance once he got out. That he would escape, he did not question. Robin would get him out.

Or, he would make the best of what he could do from inside. They had put him in a cell not so very different from the one he sometimes borrowed in the guest house of the Clares. Except for the fact that he was locked in, he could have imagined himself there.

He lay on his back on the bunk...which was harder than that one, without even a small reed mattress.

He thought of the Blue Lady. He thought of her before God, which showed how far he had fallen. Or risen. He was not entirely sure which, not at that point. He was not sure, anymore, who he was. What he was.

A friar. He told himself that no matter what happened, he was still a friar. Even if they defrocked him, he was one in his heart.

They undoubtedly would. Probably they were finding somebody willing to do it now. He stared at the ceiling. "I messed up," he murmured.

No. Her presence seemed to say that no, it was not his fault.

"It is this time." He could not hear anything except his own voice. It was too late in the year for any birdsong to filter in through the small hole they were providing him for a window. Too late in the year for squirrels to be up and about, but they would not be here anyway.

He was not in the castle. The cell he was in was in a levy station, and he suspected it was normally used as a punishment cell for recalcitrant recruits. Probably fairly often. It smelled a little...a faint smell of stale urine. They had provided him with a chamber pot, but that smell indicated not every prisoner had used it. Or been given one.

It was a possible weapon. He examined it for a moment. It was heavy enough to hit a guard over the head with...but almost too heavy to lift.

No doubt they thought he would not be able to do so. He could do it, but he was not sure it was the best way. Apparently, the outlaw friar was not a serious threat, in their minds. Perhaps they saw only his girth, not his strength. It would not be the first time. He laughed inwardly and sat back down on the bunk.

Okay. How did he get out? He could not assume they would find where he was and spring him. It was likely they would, but he could not rely on it. If he could rescue himself first and save them the trouble, it would be infinitely preferable.

How did he get out? There were no true windows in the cell, just light and air holes set high on the wall. The walls were stone. The sick prisoner gambit? That one was so old it never worked.

He could try singing like a canary and spinning them an entire bunch of lies. That at least might buy him some time. If he could...

A hole in the door opened. "Friar?"

It was one of the guards. He got up and went over. The man handed him a plate of bread and a tankard of smallbeer through the hole.

At least they wanted to keep him in a reasonably healthy state. For questioning, but they might have let him starve or poisoned him.

It might still be poison. He did not consume it straight away, but set it down.

They did not have to open the door until they intended to move him. However, he could get some human contact. Maybe...just maybe he could subvert a guard or two. The man who had come with the food, though, had already gone.

It was several more hours before he was disturbed again. When he was, the door opened. He tensed but did not attack. It was a priest.

"So. We are in a lot of trouble." The door closed behind him...and locked.

"You're taking a risk being alone with a man who's supposed to be desperate."

The priest laughed. "You're unarmed. Unless you plan on hitting me over the head with the chamberpot."

He walked over and sat down next to Tuck on the bunk. "The Church wants you turned over to them for trial. The sheriff wants you in the castle."

"And you?"

"Supposedly, I'm here to get the truth out of you. They figured you would talk to a fellow man of the cloth faster than to one of them."

There was something familiar about him, but Tuck could not place the man. "Supposedly."

"Either you are not the outlaw friar and know nothing, or you are and won't talk to anyone. Short of torture, and if they do that, the Church will be angry."

Unless, of course, the Church did it. If they found out he had been flirting with heresy and blasphemy, they would. Without hesitation. "And if I say they have the wrong man?"

"Do they?"

He turned toward the other. Then, softly, "Brother Hereward?"

"Indeed. You didn't recognize me?"

"It's been a while." And he avoided, thus, answering the other's question.

"A while, and the country in turmoil. If I can get you out, will you come to London with me?"

"What could we do there?" Tuck kept his voice very quiet. He did not know what the guards might be able to hear.

"I was hoping you would be able to answer that question."

28

*H*ereward visited him several times more. They talked...and Hereward spun lies to his jailers. Lies intended to ensure they would think Tuck an unfortunate innocent. Maybe a little mad. Being a little mad was not a bad thing in this day and age.

A lot of people were. Still, it did not get him out of the cell. It bought time, though. Time before he would be handed over to the Church.

He doubted even the sheriff could avoid doing that, in the end. But he would likely face severe question when and if he was.

Could he keep her secret? He felt almost as if she had sent Hereward. Or God had. Or perhaps Clorinda was right, perhaps there was really no separation between the two. Perhaps both were equally divine, both aspects of the other, both parts of one whole.

Heresy. No. Blasphemy. Even thinking it meant he should cast aside robe and tonsure. Worse. He would burn if the Church found out about these ideas.

Ideas they needed to stop. Ideas that might undermine their power and wealth. Ideas Francis, Tuck began to suspect, had fully understood.

He murmured the Prayer of St. Francis under his breath. He was not just praying it but appreciating it. Enjoying and contemplating every word. The man had had as much of a way with words as Will. Directed in another way, of course, but most definitely there.

The door opened. Two priests. Hereward was one of them. The other had a hooded cloak over his priestly robes, his face hidden.

"Come. We have been authorized to take you to receive mass in the chapel." An honor, Tuck thought. It could also be something else.

The sheriff might have decided to get rid of the problem, Tuck knew, by arranging for him to be killed while trying to escape. He followed the two out. The guards looped rope around his wrists, tight enough for him not to have much chance if he did try to run.

He could not get out of this without help. There was the faint smell of blood from somewhere nearby. It might have been an animal, or somebody injured during a spar, but there was something about it that made him shudder.

Perhaps it was simply their situation. Him, the two priests, four guards surrounding the group.

Then there were three guards. An arrow in the throat of one, and he saw the feathering on it. Lincoln green.

Robin! He turned, but Hereward grabbed his arm. Then cut the bonds with a knife as the other guards fell. "Let's go."

Hereward had just sacrificed everything for him. The thought caused his breath to catch in his throat.

Then the other priest, who had not spoken, threw back his hood. It was Much. The man grinned at him, then produced a long knife from under his robes as they ran for the gate.

Nobody on the other side fired. A few arrows did streak across the courtyard, but they were aimed at nothing in particular. Covering fire.

They reached the gates and were outside.

Outside...and there was a small army there. At its head rode the sheriff.

"Ah. Good. Our bait brought the entire herd."

Tuck's heart went cold in his chest. There were enough men here...and where had he found them...to take the entire band. If they did not vanish quickly.

He was about to be killed. He knew that for sure and certain. So was Hereward...and that was his fault. His entire life did not so much flash before his eyes as fall around him like leaves.

It was over.

THE SHERIFF HAD his blade lowered more or less to Tuck's eyes. He was on horseback and that might well be as low as he could reach.

The friar stood there. He knew he could not escape, he could not move fast enough. He had no staff.

Then Robin, stepping out of the trees. "Let the rest go and I will come with you willingly."

He no longer, in this moment, looked like a boy.

"So they can break you out later? I don't think so." The sheriff looked down at him.

He had his bow, but no arrow nocked. He could still use it as a weapon easily enough. The look on his face was a little grimmer than his usual air of merry amusement.

Tuck let out the breath he did not realize he had been holding. His hands were free. Did he really need a weapon?

He was the hostage here. If he could pull back, Robin certainly could, and they could run. Except that these were not levy troops.

These were hard bitten soldiers with exceptional gear. Mercenaries. The sheriff was hiring mercenaries. With whose coin? Tuck wondered, bitterly.

It felt as if the world was about to end. The sheriff was a large target, but if he went down, then Tuck, Hereward and Much would all die very quickly. There were simply too many of these men to take down in one volley.

Too many. Perhaps that could be used against them.

"So, you want to make a fight of it? How many of these men are you prepared to sacrifice, Sheriff? What about your own life?"

The sheriff dismounted, dropping his blade to Tuck's throat. "I think that unless your men shoot me in the eye, your beloved Brother will die with me."

Tuck almost wished they would do it. It would not take long and then he would have no fears or worries for anything except the state of his soul.

Some of them might indeed be able to kill the sheriff before he could move, but none seemed willing to take the risk.

Tuck knew what they should do. Fade back into the trees, leave him to them. He also knew they would not.

Robin stood there. For a moment, he seemed no more than a boy again. A slender, almost feminine figure. The charisma that caused men and women to fight and die for him had faded. It had become nothing more than prettiness.

Then...there was a sound from the hay barn. A sound Tuck knew. Sometimes, if one tossed fire into a hay barn, it would cause a massive explosion.

A moment later, he felt it. The sheriff's horse spooked, tore the reins from the man's hands and bolted into the woods. The shockwave was not enough to knock Tuck over, but it staggered him a little. Anyone closer to the explosion would not be hearing anything for a while.

Somebody had shot a fire arrow into the barn, perhaps intending to cause a distraction. They had got more than they bargained for. Tuck was honestly trying not to laugh at this point. But what he actually had to do was run.

Quickly. Hereward was just behind him. Then the priest was no longer behind him. Tuck did not look back, but the soft sigh he had heard said it all. Somebody had shot the man in the back, and they had done a good job of it.

Hereward was dead or dying, and it was his fault.

29

"*I* promised him I would go to London."

Robin nodded to Tuck. "And a promise must be kept. Perhaps we should all go to London."

"The prince will not listen to a raggedy bunch of outlaws," Tuck mused. "It's a shame nobody here is of noble blood."

"Tuck, I would say half this island has noble blood...if you look hard enough." Robin's eyes had brightened a little.

Tuck knew that look and was unsurprised when Robin got up a bare moment later and slipped away. He had had an idea. An idea that might well lead to something. But he did not discuss it with Tuck.

Wise, that. Tuck had learned to be a better fighter and picked up the basics of tactics, but strategy remained beyond him. Likely, he thought, he had the wrong kind of mind for it. God gave people different abilities so that they might complement one another.

He had been taught that the nobility had different abilities from the peasants. Now he was not so sure. In some cases, yes...Jews, for example, seemed to be born with a greater ability than the common man to handle numbers, but less awareness of the land. Because, perhaps, it was not their land, from which they had been exiled. Perhaps those people, who sought to return to their homeland, chose not to allow themselves to love places of exile. Or perhaps the law that prevented them from owning land forced them to it. Perhaps it was simply that they spent more time cultivating the skill.

People were all different. That much Tuck knew. Those differences were both important and not in the grand scheme of things. If people were born with different abilities and skills, then that had to come from God.

Tuck turned towards the fire. It had been reduced to dying embers. London. It had been three years since he had last been there. He doubted the place had changed much.

London was the city of all cities. The Romans, it was rumored, had made it the capital of Britain. A port, with ships coming up the Thames. Ships from France and Belgium and Germany.

Everything was tied together. The farmer was needed and the merchant, and the long distance trade brought other things together. For a moment, Tuck envisioned humanity as a vast, interconnected web, its nodes individuals, cities, nations.

He felt as if he had fallen through the net. No. The net had been torn, the countryside still seethed on the edge of revolt. Rumor had it there had been revolts further south, closer to London. In the land through which he had to travel to try and finish Hereward's mission for him.

To talk to Prince John. To show the man what was happening. What could he do? He was only prince regent, and no major decisions could be made without the absent king. Maybe that was what needed to be changed.

Richard would probably not return. Sooner or later, Richard would die and remove himself from the equation by that means. That was the way of things. John and his children would be the line that continued, and poor Berengaria, alone.

Tuck shook his head. It was not his problem, except that it was his problem. Any other man who abandoned his wife and lands to go on Crusade would...probably be removed by the crown. Could a king be removed? God had placed him on the throne.

Or had He? Perhaps all of it was a sign that Richard and John had somehow been switched, born in the wrong order. Could God make mistakes?

The heretical thought that maybe God had nothing to do with it did cross his mind, but it was dismissed.

The fire burned lower. London. The white tower. The streets. Far too many people crowded into far too little space. That was what London was to him. People went there to seek their fortunes, and most ended up dead in gutters. Young women ran away from home and landed up in the bishop's brothels.

London was, Tuck realized, the second to last place he wanted to go. Yet, he had promised, and it had not been, truly, a promise made under duress. It had been a contract, a deal between the two men.

It had been, to an extent, a choice made out of his fondness for the other man. A fondness he had all but forgotten, but which had sprung back up full grown the second he had realized who it was. A friendship that had lain dormant.

Yet there were other friendships, too, and Robin seemed bent on risking half the band in London. Clorinda...Clorinda should not go to London.

THEY TRAVELED OPENLY down the street. Tuck rode his mule, a pair of hose under his robes so as to prevent anyone from seeing anything they should not. The animal, who much preferred pulling a cart, kept flicking a long ear back at him in an irritated manner.

Brownie would have to put up with it. Clorinda rode in the carriage, awkward in the clothes of a lady. Robin was in there with her.

He was going to claim to be minor Saxon nobility, a Lord Robert Locksley, and Clorinda his wife. Will seemed entirely at ease with the arrangement. Of course, from what Tuck knew, Clorinda's questionable virtue was completely safe with Robin, of all people. The rest of the band were outriders, or with the baggage train.

Tuck had positioned himself at the rear. He, of course, was Locksley's confessor. Which was the one thing anyone was saying about this that actually came close to the truth.

People did not keep the sort of records that would have revealed such a deception. Eventually, the prince might find out there was no Robert Locksley. But it would likely be long after they had left. Especially with Robin claiming to be a Saxon noble...many of whom had been stripped of their lands and had only their titles, if that. The Conqueror had given many estates to his followers, using any excuse to claim disloyalty on the part of their previous owners. It was an old ill, but not so old that some did not resent it.

It was still the best way to gain entrance to the palace. Possibly even an audience. If the prince was doing his job, he would hear a grievance brought by a nobleman.

Then, perhaps, they could tell him what was really going on. They might even be able to do so without breaking their cover.

The mule's gait was rough. Tuck almost thought he should have walked...but he was so pleased he had been able to find the animal after having to let him go, that he did not want to leave him behind.

It was spring now, the winter having faded away, but the showers of April kept threatening from otherwise clear skies. A jay scolded them from the trees, perhaps worried they might disturb what remained of her winter stash of acorns. Then a second one joined in, from further down the road.

Tuck had observed jays carefully burying acorns. And not recovering all the ones they had buried. The ones they lost, perhaps, would grow into oak trees. The greenwood was a web, and breaking any piece of it could be disastrous. He worried a little about the increased clearing. Would that break some strand they had not perceived? Yet, people had to eat. The greenwood produced food, but not as much as carefully rotated fields.

As long as there were people to harvest and people to plant, that was.

They had traveled far south from Nottingham, now, but they saw only a slight increase in prosperity. The buildings were a slightly different style and there seemed to be more stone churches. More steeples. Steeples were an expensive proposition, and Tuck doubted any villages were building them at the moment. Still, they were also landmarks. It would be far harder to get lost in a country where every church had a steeple.

Not that that would happen. Some communities preferred flat towers. Felt steeples were an ugly extravagance. Tuck had realized long ago that churches were not built for God. They were built for man. God did not really care where you were when you prayed, but being in a church helped one to concentrate. Besides, the churches provided space for preachers to give their sermons and the mass.

They rode into a village. The small convoy stopped, but Tuck, at the back, could not well hear the conversation. Will was the lead outrider, his silver tongue placed where it could do the most good.

The one Tuck felt sorry for was Clorinda. Robin could come out and ride a spare horse, but the woman was trapped in the carriage. If she rode as an outrider, her sex might be betrayed, and that would cause drama they did not need.

Clorinda in skirts was a sight Tuck had thought he might never see. The words being exchanged had become somewhat sharp and also somewhat uncertain. Eventually, the man stepped aside and let them pass, but he looked daggers at the outriders, only softening his gaze a little at Tuck. Of course, he saw them as nobles. As the cause of all ills. And a Churchman...but he had softened his gaze. Perhaps because Tuck wore no jewels and was not in the wagon with the lady, but with the baggage train. He was not putting on airs, in other words. He smiled at the man, knowing that would disarm hatred faster than any other gesture.

"Two more days to London," Robin commented as they dismounted in the inn courtyard. Tuck caught the look Clorinda gave him. She was not happy about this, even understanding the necessity.

"Would your lady appreciate the assistance of my daughter?" came a voice.

The innkeeper was a man, a stout one. His offer was in no way unusual, and it might be suspicious to refuse, but the hairs rose on the back of Tuck's neck. He caught Clorinda's gaze. She simply nodded to him.

Of course, if the girl's intent was robbery, then she would get a very nasty surprise. Tuck could think of four places Clorinda could hide weapons in that gown, and was sure she had used them all, plus a few that had not occurred to him.

He elected not to worry about her. It was also likely that the 'maid' would try to pocket a jewel or two...and she probably needed them more than they did.

Inside, the place was almost too clean. A hunchback cleared one of the tables as they entered, favoring Tuck with a glance surprisingly cheerful for one with such an affliction. Well, maybe he was not doing so badly. He was, after all, here, not a beggar in a city, starving on handouts. Tuck's opinion of the innkeeper revised upwards slightly.

Perhaps it was only the girl who was bothering him. Bothering him, however, she was. He could not escape the feeling that she was the kind of trouble they could not afford.

He sniffed at both ale and stew before sampling them, thus. The ale was mediocre, the stew was excellent. Usually, the average inn, these things were the other way around. In fact, the ale seemed a little stale. Perhaps they did not brew their own...a stupid decision for any tavern.

Perhaps their brewster was sick and off her stroke. Either way, he was not tempted to get more. He was, in fact, not even tempted to finish the tankard he had.

"You too?" John asked as he sat down. Clorinda was noticeable by her absence. So was Robin. Perhaps he had noticed something odd about the maid as well and was staying close.

Tuck tapped the tankard. "I think their brewster must be sick."

"No. I think its a bad batch of hops. They're probably just trying to get rid of it."

He might be right there. Tuck let out a breath. "For some reason, I'm not comfortable here."

"I'm not comfortable anywhere." John sat back a little, causing the chair to creak under his weight.

Tuck wondered if he was talking literally or metaphorically. It was, in either case, more than he normally got out of the big man. He swallowed some more of his stew. "I don't know. Something is a little wrong here."

"The hunchback?"

Tuck shook his head. "Probably an honest man, possibly pathetically grateful to have a job and a place at all. His kind so seldom do."

There was a tendency to believe that hunchbacks were a judgment of Satan on the parents, especially the mother. Other deformities were often viewed the same way. Tuck knew that sometimes such children did not survive...and it was not always because their deformities killed them. Blindness, he thought, would be the worst. A hunchback, at least, could do useful work. What was there for a man who could not see?

"Probably. He gives me the creeps, though."

Tuck lowered his voice. "The one that bothers me is the girl."

"Think she might decide to lift a couple of our lady's jewels?"

"Yes, actually." Tuck shrugs. "But I trust the lady to be careful. You never can be too careful."

"And I notice Lord Robert is not here. Defending her virtue, no doubt." No irony in the man's tone, but a twinkle in his eyes.

Well, Clorinda's virtue was questionable only because she and her husband had never stepped inside a church. There was no hint of infidelity between the two. Tuck glanced around for Will. He had positioned himself close to the stairs and was looking more bodyguard than minstrel. He trusted Robin, but perhaps he, too, had noticed something about the girl.

Or perhaps Robin had asked him to do it. Tuck turned back to John. "Watching like a hawk, knowing him. He doesn't like to let his wife out of his sight."

John laughed. "Maybe he's afraid she'll start looking at other men."

"No," Tuck deadpanned, every bit the retainer taking amusement at the expense of his lord. "He's afraid he will start looking at other women if he doesn't remind himself constantly why he puts up with her tongue."

John laughed louder. His atypical verboseness was clearly, to Tuck, a role he was playing, but to outsiders...

Clorinda, of course, did not often use her tongue that way, but the persona she had put on for their journey was rather acidic. The laughter had attracted some attention, but after a moment, the two were dismissed.

Normal behavior for travelers journeying with their boss...even for a friar who was presumably the confessor.

"I can see why he puts up with it."

Tuck thought that good acting, given he had never caught John glancing at a woman in any sexual manner. "Even I can, although her tongue would not be worth breaking my vows for."

"Sometimes I think nothing would get you out of that habit. No pretty barmaids, no serving wenches, no handsome lads. Lady Godiva could ride past in all her glory..."

"John!" Tuck feigned being utterly scandalized. "You know..." And then he shrugged. "You know nothing and nobody is going to get out of my habit.

The big man laughed again and clapped the friar so firmly on the back he stumbled.

"Just because I'm about the only friar in the country with no mistress tucked away under his habit." Tuck added. Which wasn't true, but close.

"You could fit one in there, too." John made a great show of looking Tuck up and down.

"If she was reasonably small." The joke, of course, also referred to certain sexual practices generally engaged in only by prostitutes who did not want to risk pregnancy.

"I know, I know. God fulfills all of your needs. For me, I wouldn't mind getting my hands on that girl, if it wasn't for the fact that some-body would shoot the hat off my head." John was not about to publicly admit to his preferences. Tuck could say he was firm in his vows and not have anyone suspect a thing. John...

"Watch out. You know what tavern girls are like. She'll take you for a hefty fee then raid your pouch to boot." Tuck grinned at his friend.

"I know. I know. I'll wait until we get to London and go to the bish-op's brothels."

Tuck knew he would do no such thing. Well, maybe. Some of them probably...no. John was not like that. He did not go after random boys. He was dedicated to the man he loved.

Tuck rather thought that made it alright.

30

*L*ondon sat beneath a veil of fog. Nottingham often looked much the same...a wide river valley that trapped the stuff. London, however, was larger. It had walls, but the city had long ago spilled beyond them. The bad part of town, the very worst neighborhoods, was south of the river. Approaching from the north, London radiated prosperity. Church towers and steeples poked out from the mass of houses.

"Not so bad, is it?" John again, pulling back to ride next to Tuck.

"You haven't seen Southwark," Tuck complained. "Or, more to the point, smelled it. Or Fleet Street." Which had a stream down the middle that tended to be used as men always used streams in cities.

John wrinkled his nose. "Can it be worse than standing outside the tanning caves?"

Tuck had been *in* Nottingham's tanning caves. "Yes," he said, without hesitation.

"Well, it still doesn't look bad from here."

"It's probably no worse than York, really." The wind changed, and a faint whiff of city did, indeed, hit Tuck's nostrils. From here, though, it really was 'not that bad'. He had certainly smelled worse in his time.

They were cresting the ridge north of the city and seeing it from a distance. In truth they were a good three hours ride from the northern gates.

The greenwood here had been reduced to patches, open country being the rule. Cattle and sheep grazed in some parts. Strips of cropland glinted in others. Much of it, though, lay fallow, and Tuck noticed the cattle and sheep looked thin. An emaciated horse lifted its head weakly as they passed.

No. People were no better off here than further north. He felt almost guilty...and he would not be surprised if they were attacked. They had had to deal with the maid who had, indeed, tried to take Clorinda's jewels. She had been switched by the innkeeper, but Tuck doubted it would have any real, long-term effect. It never did, on that kind. Who knew, anyway, how desperate she was.

Then they encountered the ox wagon. The road was better than most places, but a stream had changed course to run across it. The wagon was stuck firmly, the oxen pulling and the driver knee deep in the mud, trying to help them by pushing it out. He was having about as much success in the matter as one would expect. Almost none.

John slipped past to ride to the front. He looked big enough to pick up the wagon, oxen and all. Tuck pushed his mule afterwards, squeezing through the narrow gap between their own carriage and baggage cart and the side of the road. It was not a large enough space, really, for the mule to fit through. He made it, though.

Several of the men had dismounted and were joining the unfortunate farmer in the mud. Then John pushed past all of them, cracking his knuckles. He looked almost amused as he claimed a prime spot at the wagon's rear. Then he set his hands against it and pushed.

It did not move right away. It was, after all, very thoroughly stuck indeed. It did, however, move. Slowly, wheels spinning in the mud, and then finding purchase on the other side. Tuck smiled a bit. John was increasing the legend a little, although whether it would ever be connected to the outlaws, he would never know.

He climbed out of the mire. "We should be careful. We don't want to be the next people to get stuck."

Will backed the carriage up, then took it at a run once the farmer was clear. The tactic worked. For his part, Tuck let the mule pick his

way around the edge. Mules were smarter than horses and they generally knew exactly how to avoid getting stuck in a quagmire.

The farmer had thanked them, but not really moved on. There was
no way of getting past his heavy wagon on this road. Occasionally, he
glanced back. Perhaps he was amazed that they had demanded
nothing for their assistance. Amazed they hadn't screamed at him.

"We should have been nastier," Tuck murmured to John. "He'll
never believe we're really noble retainers."

John laughed quietly. "Oh, he will. I made sure to be just the right
amount of condescending."

Whilst demonstrating that he could have picked the guy up and
planted him in the quagmire head first.

At least that seemed to be the last bad patch of road, and as the sun
began to set, they finally reached the gates of London.

LONDON. The streets were not paved with gold, but neatly cobbled. The
city was an assault on the senses. John and Much had to ride slightly
ahead to clear the way for the carriage, for the road was full of people,
and the farmer's cart did not provide enough assistance. People just
filled the street again behind it, a flowing tide.

Tuck saw goodwives in bright scarves, apprentices in various quali-
ties of clothing and an old Jew slipping quickly through the streets. He
did not linger. Three nuns emerged from one building, carrying
baskets, their heads bowed. Spice shopping for the convent, perhaps.

Either way, they did not linger, except to glare at an apprentice who
made an obscene gesture in their direction.

Tuck could not help but smile. Boys would do things like that, and
boys would...always be in trouble for it. It was the nature of boys. He
had gotten yelled at by nuns a few times as a boy himself.

Then they were past them, and the road split. Fortunately, the slow
ox wagon went a different way, towards the produce market that Tuck
knew was only a short distance away. "Brother!" John called. "The best
inn?"

He turned, then adjusted the mule's pace to match John's horse.

"The best inn, in my mind, would be the Golden Rooster. It's not much further."

"Thank you."

There was nothing all that strange about asking a friar where the best inn was. Friars knew all the best inns and taverns, on the whole. The only thing not worth asking them about was brothels...and even then, Tuck knew a few who could properly advise. He shook his head, amused.

Then he went back to watching the crowd. A merchant cursed as a woman threw slop from an upper window, narrowly missing him. Tuck shook his head. She should have been more careful, but the language that burst from the man's lips...

A Moor strode up the street in the other direction, vanishing into the same spice store the nuns had come out of. Men traveled, sometimes very far from their lands of birth. Tuck was a good way from his, but nothing like that. Yet, he had been as far. Or, perhaps, he had been born here, the result of trading that happened in bedrooms and tents, or the child of...perhaps even the child of the spice merchant.

A pair of guards or soldiers, of armed men, followed the Moor at a discreet distance. Tuck somehow felt they had not been hired by the object of their surveillance. Not everyone trusted Moors, although he had found them as honest as any man.

The sign of the Golden Rooster was slung across the street, ropes secured to the buildings on either side. It glinted with cheap gilt paint.

"Here?"

Tuck nodded. "They have private rooms and they even have baths." A rare luxury that. "The lady will be quite comfortable."

And hopefully not have to threaten to kill her maid this time. That had been an embarrassing moment, perhaps even a dangerous one. They could easily have been revealed as...something.

They turned into the inn yard, and two stableboys rushed out. One of them hesitated, looking at Tuck's mule.

"He doesn't bite," Tuck assured as he dismounted, careful not to land on anything unpleasant in the yard. "Although if you have food anywhere, he'll eat right through your clothing to get at it."

The boy actually laughed. "Sorry. The last mule we had stepped on my foot. Deliberately. Twice."

"He won't do that either. I could always put him away myself."

Seeing a potential tip vanish, the boy shook his head. "We'll manage." The older one, though, signaled him over to take care of the carriage horses first.

Tuck had not been in this inn in some time. To his relief, it seemed to have changed but little. They had added more cobbles to the inn-yard and replaced worn ones, a sign that they were prosperous. The only smell was of the stables.

Eventually, he surrendered his mule, and went into the common room. John was negotiating rates for all of them, haggling a little.

Tuck knew it would be a bench in the common room for him, and thus ignored the conversation. Instead, he took in the room. It was busy, of course, mostly with locals here for ale and talk. An animated argument was going on at one table, and he could not help but turn towards it.

"Then, the woman slapped him right on the cheek and informed him 'My eyes are up here'. She hit him so hard he fell back on his chair."

"Uppity woman."

"Nah. He deserved it. You know, the man's a total ass. I don't know how his wife tolerates it."

"Because she's a good one."

Tuck sighed. He didn't think a good wife was a woman who toler-ated her husband's peccadilloes. No, a good wife would tell her man what she thought of him if he tried anything like that. It was, though, entirely none of his business.

Besides, Will was flagging him down. He'd claimed the largest table in the place, chasing off a boy not much more than an apprentice. Tuck sat down next to him.

"What's going on over there?"

"Argument about whether it's reasonable for a woman to hit a guy who deserves it."

Will laughed. "Did you catch what he deserved it for?"

"Something about where her eyes were."

Will laughed louder. "Then I'd say he deserved it. But you know what some men are like."

"I do." Some men only wanted to know about one kind of woman. The kind who walked three steps behind them with her head bowed. Like the Saracen women. They did that when they left the women's quarters at all. Three steps behind a male escort, only their eyes visible in the mass of cloth that covered them.

Tuck thought that Clorinda would kill as many of them as possible if she was forced into such a situation. The Saracen princes, some of them, had harems of fifty, sixty, a hundred women. Most of whom were probably ignored and forgotten. No man could handle that many wives. And one of the desert nomads had told him that the Prophet actually forbade a man from taking more than four women, and that only if he could afford to keep them properly.

Like powerful people everywhere, the princes ignored the rules. That was life, Tuck thought. The poor would be ground down by rules, the wealthy would ignore them. The good decent folk in the middle...would manage as best they could.

Will broke into his thoughts. "But here comes something to cheer us all up."

That something was a pitcher of ale. Tuck poured himself a tankard, then took a big swig. His eyebrows shot upwards. "Whewf. I remembered the ale here being good, but their brewmaster has excelled herself!"

Will took a sip of his, then grinned at the friar. "Now I know why you wanted to come here."

"Is there a better reason?" Tuck slowed down, savoring every taste of the brew.

"Perhaps not. As long as the lady finds her bed comfortable, or you know who will be sliced up by that tongue of hers."

Tuck shrugged. "For this ale, it would be worth it. But unless things have changed since my memory, I think she'll find it satisfactory. As much as she's found anything on this trip."

"That's the truth of it. I'm pretty sure she would much rather have stayed home." Will sounded distinctly thoughtful. "So would I."

Tuck was pretty sure that he was not acting. Not this time.

he White Tower loomed over the river. Tuck stood looking at it, from a good distance, of course. The place held no pleasant connotations. There was something about it that gave a vibe of...maybe it was the ravens.

For some reason, ravens liked to hang out there. Perhaps it had been their place before the humans had come here.

Superstitious people held that the ravens were tied to the luck of the crown. That bad things would happen if they ever left. Tuck saw them just as huge black birds. Birds that would no doubt hang around by the gallows and claim what they could. The fact that they were so dark of feather did not help.

Yet...there was something about their flight that, perhaps, made him understand the edges of how people felt about them. They did have a certain stark beauty to them, the beauty of death itself.

He wondered if he would be fortunate enough to survive much longer. The chances were John would have them all arrested. London jails were not a place one wanted to end up. Worse yet were the dungeons in the White Tower itself, or so rumor had it.

London was not a place Tuck wanted to spend a lot of time in, free or jailed. As he turned to walk back down Tower Hill, he saw an odd juxtaposition of prosperity and poverty. The former rode on the back of the latter. Beggars were common, many of them blind or otherwise mutilated. Many, perhaps, had returned from the Holy Land with such injuries, then been promptly cast aside by those who had so used them. Not all, though, were men. Most...for women in such dire straits always had the option of the bishop's brothels, as did a certain kind of man.

Morality tended to vanish when one was starving. Which was why Tuck walked with his hands on his staff and his eyes alert. These people would slit his purse given a quarter of a chance, and his throat for not much more. Anyone who was not themselves in rags showed the same wariness. He saw no women alone, and only one accompanied by what appeared to be a bodyguard. Some merchant's wife, no doubt.

The liberty of London sometimes seemed to equate to the liberty to cause trouble.

The city, though, flowed around him. It was more dangerous than the greenwood and less attractive, but it had its own energy. The energy that came from all of these people.

Tuck wondered how large, for a moment, a city might grow. This was probably about the limit. The stripped countryside outside could produce little more food for these people, and there was little space to grow it within the walls. He did hear, through the other noise, the occasional sounds of chickens. Those did not need much space...and no doubt other yards had cages of rabbits, too, which betrayed their presence with no sound.

The shout caused him to turn. "Thief!"

A ragged boy was running through the crowd with a purse that clearly did not belong to him. Tuck was in no position to stop the lad and might not have if he had been. The kid clearly needed the money more than the fat, well-clad merchant pursuing him. Judging by the reactions of others, Tuck was not the only one who felt that way.

"Third time this month old Weaver there has been robbed," a feminine voice muttered.

It was the fact that it came from a woman that caused Tuck to turn. She wore the garb of a guildswoman, of one of those rare females who held rank and status of her own right. Not a brewmaster, either. A dyer, he guessed, from the bright and exceptionally beautiful colors she wore.

He could not resist answering. "Indeed. Maybe he should carry less money with him."

If he'd been robbed more than once, then he might have a reputation for carrying a fat purse...a foolish thing in most cities, let alone in London.

"Man will never learn." The Weaver...no doubt job title, not name, was now stalking along the street, but the thief was long gone.

Tuck detached himself and headed up the street, amused by the brief diversion.

Tomorrow they would try and get an audience. With somebody. Likely not the prince himself, but they might get to somebody who could, at least, listen to them. Just a little.

He shook his head, and wondered if wandering past the actual palace of St. James might not be a good idea. There was no telling, of course, if the prince was in residence. He was not the king, he did not warrant the royal flag. It might be interesting, though, to know if he thought he could anyway.

Instead, he made his way back towards the tavern, only to run into Much coming out of it.

"Tuck. Thank God."

"What happened?"

"Reginald got himself arrested."

IF ANYONE WAS GOING to end up in a London jail cell, Tuck thought sadly, it was Reginald. The boy was good, but he was reckless. "What did he do? Flirt with the wrong girl?"

"Insulted a man's clothes...and the man turned out to be a Guildmaster."

Tuck sighed. "Can we bail him out?" Likely the Guildmaster would take some small recompense in return for pretending it hadn't happened.

"Likely. But we need to do so without it being associated with us. Or let him stew until after the meeting."

"I'm inclined," Tuck commented as they went back into the inn. "To leave him there for a couple of days. Might get some restraint into the lad."

But he had chosen the wrong time to do something embarrassing. "Likely," Will mused, "The Guildmaster will get hold of him, make him do a couple of days of menial labor, let him go. He's too old to be bound into apprenticeship."

Which commonly happened to troublesome boys with no family. Might be the best thing for them, but they did rather need Reginald back. He was trouble, but he had his uses. "You know what. Let me handle it."

"We need you for the meeting."

"Then we let him stew." Or escape. Hopefully if he did give his jailers the slip, he'd know better than to come back here.

Tuck thought that if he did he would likely get lost, anyway. London was a complicated enough place if you had been there before.

"Okay. Well. In that case, Robin wants you upstairs."

Tuck went up the back stairs of the inn. One of its few private rooms had been rented to Robin and Clorinda. The latter sat there in her nightdress. She seemed remarkably unconcerned to be seen by the two men in a state most would consider to be half naked. Maybe three quarters.

Well, she knew by now that neither was interested in her.

"I'm going to switch that lad when we find him," Robin grumbled.

"I'll hold him for you," Tuck offered, his tone wry. "But the meeting?"

"Our cover is that we need money. Assistance. Once we're in there, we tell the full story, slightly edited."

Tuck nodded. "You want me there."

"Having a Churchman there, even if he's only a friar, would definitely help. It might make us look less like ragged Saxons and more like legitimate nobles."

"Clorinda's clearly not a ragged Saxon." Tuck flickered her a grin.

She laughed. "Ragged Normans aren't much better."

"But you and I are, as are most of our retainers. If asked, Clorinda was the fourth of four daughters. I was the best match her family could find for her and the convent turned her down."

Clorinda grinned mischievously. "Convents. Plural. They were willing to sell me to the highest bidder."

Given how she'd acted in public on the trip, it was entirely feasible. She had channeled her irritation at having to act like a normal woman into a very convincing performance as a spoiled noblewoman with a sharp tongue.

Tuck grinned. "Be careful, or we might just do that. You'd be worth a lot to a Saracen prince."

"Is it true that some of them have as many as fifty wives?"

"Well. Women. Wives and concubines. Their religion speaks against it, but when have the powerful listened to that?"

Clorinda grinned. "I bet the women have a lot more power than their men realize."

She might well be right, Tuck thought. Or she might be thinking wistfully. But then, a palace full of fifty women... "They keep them locked up like treasure. The only men allowed near them other than their husbands have been cut."

Robin flinched, as any man would, at any reference to eunuchs. Some men even flinched at gelding horses and oxen.

Tuck shrugged. "Some eunuchs are born that way, some are cut, some make themselves that way with vows."

Some women would have been embarrassed by that. Chlorina merely smiled, "And we know which kind you are," she teased. Then, she got back to business. "We get as close to the prince as we can. We make sure that somebody close to him knows just how bad things are."

"I still don't know what he can do." Tuck sat down, heavily.

"He can't do as much as if he was the king. But he can do something." Robin reached up and ran a hand through his blond hair. "He can, at the very least, censure Gisbourne and his ilk."

"Who will ignore it. Look. I'm only here because I made a promise to a dead man." Which was binding, for Hereward could not release him from it. "The rest of you didn't have to come and I honestly..."

There was a loud thud. It sounded like it came from outside in the street. Tuck moved to the small window.

A wagon had overturned. Fortunately, it was empty, but it rather neatly blocked the street outside. The oxen struggled to free themselves, breaking the traces and, being oxen, walking away from it. They seemed to be looking for grass between the cobblestones. Horses would have run.

"Just an accident," Tuck commented, turning back to the others.

Robin, though, was on his feet, tense. He looked out of place in his current garb, it being far higher quality than the normal green clothing he wore. And his hands twitched for a bow.

"Somebody overturned an ox cart outside."

Tuck turned back to the window. "Oh. Hell." He assigned himself a good dozen Hail Marys for the swear word, but it was warranted.

The wagon now blocked one end of the street. Riders the other. "Gisbourne."

"Here?"

"Here."

Robin went over to Clorinda's luggage, pulled a bowstring out from it and began the process of converting his 'staff.' "We do not attack. We make no move until they do. They may not know for sure it is us. Let Will try and talk us out of it."

Will and the others were still downstairs. "Failing that," Tuck noted, "there's a back door."

Unspoken was the likelihood that Reginald was indirectly responsible for this. The boy might well have been recognized.

Clorinda started to pull on day clothes.

"You going to be able to fight like that?" Tuck asked.

"You fight in a skirt all the time."

"It's a habit!"

"And you should consider getting out of it occasionally."

Tuck found his grin expanding to almost touch his ears. "No thanks. But where did I put my staff?"

"Behind you," Clorinda pointed out, reaching to pick up a bow and then moving towards the window.

Tuck rolled his eyes and picked it up. He still thought avoiding the fight altogether to be the best. "What's happening out there?"

"Will's talking to them. So's the innkeeper."

"Good." The innkeeper was far more likely to be on their side than against them for various simple reasons. Not least among which was how much they were paying him. Plus, no innkeeper alive wanted this kind of trouble in his inn.

"They're not leaving, though."

Tuck could hear a raised voice. "No. We will search the inn."

"We have a *lady* staying with us." That was the innkeeper. "I won't have her privacy violated."

"These people are Marian heretics," the voice said. "We are sure of it."

"That's none of my business. That's between them and the Church."

Then there was the sound of a slap.

Clorinda used several words, quietly, that proved she was not a lady. "Gisbourne's man just hit the innkeeper."

Tuck wrapped both hands lightly around his staff. "Well, sounds like we might have to defend the poor man's honor." He headed for the stairs. Clorinda could be just as effective from here. He needed to be far closer to his opponent to do any good.

The servants were heading for the back door. Tuck felt the unworthy temptation to follow them. Any man would have, under the circumstances. Any sane woman, too. Clorinda, he had decided, was not sane by any stretch.

He stepped out into the courtyard, just as Gisbourne's men swept in. He could not see Will. No. There he was, still on his feet, but he had ended up behind them.

"We're searching the inn. For heresy and contraband."

"Heresy?" Tuck's voice was dangerously low. "What kind?"

"We received a tip that the lady staying here is a Marian."

Tuck arched an eyebrow. "News to me, if so."

"Who are you?"

"Her confessor." And thus, somebody who would know...although be obligated not to tell...if she truly was a heretic.

"Well, you're on the list too."

Tuck knew it was all invented...although perhaps Reginald had squealed. Perhaps the poor kid had been tortured, and mentioned the fact that several of the band were Marians. Had mentioned something that could, like this, be used against them.

"I'd rather not break any heads in the inn courtyard." Tuck actually smiled at the man. "There is nothing here for you. Go away before anyone else gets hurt."

Clorinda hadn't fired yet. So far, it seemed, the only casualty was the innkeeper, now standing behind Will sporting a black eye.

Tuck was not about to start a fight.

"We know who you are," the man said, dangerously quiet. His voice was not one Tuck wanted to hear again. It was heavy and gravelly. It sounded as if his vocal cords had been injured at some point. He had a scar across one cheek. Most definitely, this was a man who had fought and fought often.

Tuck did not back down. He could not afford to either back down or strike the first blow. He realized at that moment that Will and the innkeeper had both vanished again. Maybe Will was taking the man somewhere safe.

"Either cooperate or die. I'd honestly prefer you did the latter."

Tuck studied the man. "I'd prefer you disappeared." He felt no sense of anything. Not of God's presence, not of the Blue Lady's. As if neither could reach him here, in the heart of London.

Or as if they knew he did not need them. God did not have such limits on Him and Tuck suddenly felt buoyed up.

"I'm not leaving."

"But you aren't attacking, either." Did he think that doing so would make him look like the outlaw himself, with people watching? Likely. Tuck let out his breath. "This can be resolved in a better way."

"You could let me search the inn and then come with us. If you aren't who I think you are, you'll be released by dusk."

"Touch me and you'll have the Church down on you."

"If you're guilty, they won't care. If you're innocent, you'll be released before they can get here." Logical enough.

Then there were more hoof beats. More hoof beats and a sense of her presence. The Blue Lady, sweeping up the street.

Tuck could not see who was actually coming, but his grip on his staff relaxed a little. He felt reassured.

He felt that whatever was about to happen had to be for the best.

uck sat inside the wagon, his head on his hands, his elbows on his knees. He trusted her, of course he did, but there was a saying about frying pans and fires that came to mind.

They were going to the palace alright, but as prisoners. The royal men had decided to just haul everyone involved in and sort it out later. At least Clorinda was being given the courtesy of her own carriage. Which Tuck knew had weapons hidden in every nook and cranny.

For now, though, they were more or less heading in the direction they wanted to go. Escape was an option for the future.

They could still salvage this. John had to know what was going on, even if he found out through his jailers.

Yet, Tuck emphatically did not want to rot in jail or be hanged. He was going to escape somehow. Just after they had got the information where it would do the most good. If it did any good at all.

A bit of a bleak mood had come over him. He was not the only one. There was complete silence inside the wagon. Will was not there. Will had not been captured, it seemed. Which was some hope. The minstrel was competent. He might be able to do something about this disaster.

The disaster Tuck had caused. It was only he who had been bound by oath to a dead man.

The wagons pulled up into a courtyard. It was the prison at Fleet Street. Tuck's heart fell further. It reached rock bottom when he saw just who was talking to the jailer.

He knew that face. He knew that face entirely too well. What the man was doing in London, he did not know, but he could not deny that it was the same lord who had once imprisoned him and threatened to flog him. The same man. "Psst."

"What?"

"That man. He's bad news."

"Then we'll deal with him."

It was Much next to him, and Tuck relaxed, but only slightly. There was a big part of him that would cheerfully slit that man's throat. He pulled his hood up...knowing they would likely order him to pull it down again, but it might buy time before he was recognized.

How did they get to the prince now? They had to prove they were not exactly who they were, but Gisbourne was there first.

Gisbourne. Somebody else who's throat Tuck would cheerfully slit and take any extra time in purgatory it earned him.

If he was not...and he smelled the fragrance of roses. She was here, although he could not see her.

So, he thought, how do we get to see John?

Trust me. He heard her voice in his mind, not his ears. *Trust me.*

Trust an entity who had never been entirely honest with him, yet who had always bailed him out of the tough spots before. It was almost amusing. Yet, he would trust her. He had no choice about doing so. No other to whom to turn. He thought of God, but that presence seemed as far away as ever.

Or was it? Confusion flowed through him again. Fear. Doubt. Doubt of himself, of his own place in the world. Of his own being.

How could he trust anyone if he could not trust himself? Perhaps it was time to take off the habit after all.

He looked towards the tower lord again. The man whose name he had never obtained. He was turning to leave, but their eyes met.

That sense of evil returned, that sure and certain knowledge that this man was far outside of normal morality.

"Get behind me, Satan," Tuck murmured, out loud. A direct quote, translated, few non-scholars would have recognized it.

It seemed to work...a shadow passed across the man's face, and he turned to leave. Tuck felt himself relax.

Then they were being herded out of the wagons, but not into the prison. "So. We finally have the famous Outlaw of Sherwood. Impersonating a nobleman...and a noblewoman."

Clorinda. She shook off the hands of the men holding her, still wearing her gown. She had blood on her face, and he doubted much, if any of it was hers. "I *am* a noblewoman."

"You're a witch. Long overdue to be executed as such, according to Lord Gisbourne."

Clorinda just smiled. "And I escaped then, did I not?"

"From a provincial castle. Besides. We don't need to bother with a trial this time."

The man speaking was well spoken, his accent strongly Norman. His French, no doubt, was more fluent than his English.

He would probably have preferred to be on the other side of the Channel.

"A provincial castle?" That voice was oh, so familiar. Gisbourne himself.

"I see you came back again," came Robin's voice. Quiet, dangerous. "That is how many trips to the Holy Land?"

"It would be unwise to leave my lands long in the hands of a woman."

Clorinda looked like she was about to spit at him, but decided not to waste the effort. Tuck closed his eyes for a moment. With Gisbourne here, they were recognized. Will was the only one with any chance of getting to Prince John.

But Clorinda spoke again. "You are fully and completely mistaken. I am not the woman you seek. I am Lady Clorinda Locksley, and you think my *husband* is the Outlaw of Sherwood?"

Gisbourne stepped towards her and slapped her across the face. For a moment, she looked like she would hit back.

There were arrows trained on them all.

"When I talk to the prince, he will deal with you."

"The only person you're talking to is the executioner." Gisbourne lifted his hand to slap her again, but the jailer placed his own hand on the lord's sleeve.

"My lord. How do you know she is not who she claims to be?"

"Because I have seen her before, you idiot. She was not dressed as well, but it's the same woman, for sure. The same woman the Outlaw of Sherwood caused to vanish from my castle."

"And you think *this* man is the famous Robin Hood?" The jailer stepped towards Robin. "Pah. He barely comes up to my eyes."

Tuck still had his hood up. It was a reasonable assessment.

"He looks like a gelding or a mare." An insult that, yet in some ways true.

Tuck lifted his hand. He had not been bound, only disarmed...thoroughly, they'd taken his belt knife and the one he had had in his boot. But he was able to use his hand to hide his laughter.

All of those stories and legends...meant that Gisbourne would never be believed when he told people, truthfully, that this tiny, effeminate man was Robin Hood.

"Well, he is Robin. The tall one is his righthand man, John Little."

John, of course, was one of the most common of all names. Any flicker of reaction meant nothing.

"And I hear they call the friar Tuck. I suppose so that his mother house can't track him."

Tuck managed not to show a reaction. The jailer walked over and pushed back his hood, though, leaving him exposed. "A friar. A fat friar with a red face. You want me to believe this is the 'Friar Tuck' who is deadly with a staff?"

Red face? Tuck doubted his face was that red. He had not exactly had much ale today. But he was willing to take the insults.

"Believe it or not. These are the men. If you want to serve your country, you will lock them up very securely. In separate cells. I'd put Robin himself in the oubliette. See him break out of there."

Tuck shuddered a little. One did not put people in an oubliette one intended to release any time soon. Getting them out again was, after all, quite the logistical challenge requiring ropes.

Robin could probably still escape from one.

"You will have to excuse me, Lord Gisbourne. I would like to confirm their identity."

"I'm the Lord of Nottingham!" Gisbourne's face, most definitely, was red.

"You are in the Liberty of London. Your provincial title means nothing here. Don't worry. I don't plan on simply letting them go."

"Then at least take the precaution of separate cells." Gisbourne turned on his heel, stalking towards the entrance. His archers began to follow him.

The jailer walked up to Robin and looked him in the eye. "So. Are you Robin Hood, or Sir Robert Locksley? Or both, perhaps?"

Tuck realized he was holding his breath. He forced it out again.

"Or perhaps even neither. Perhaps a common thief. Well. We will straighten this out."

He did not, though, put them in separate cells. He herded them into one side of the common holding area. Except for Clorinda, who was dragged away literally kicking and screaming.

"Where are you taking her?"

"To a woman's cell. You would not want her shoved in with you men, surely."

Which meant she would probably be shoved in with the illegal prostitutes, have them eating out of her hands in seconds and stage a prison revolt that might get them all out of here. Tuck pinned some hope on that possibility. He pinned more hope on the Blue Lady. Had she influenced the jailer to see them as harmless?

Maybe. However, none of it got them closer to the prince. Or anyone who could talk to the prince. Gisbourne was on the outside spreading the truth about them. Tuck was...in a communal cell.

They had all been carefully searched, but he had seen Robin break locks without special tools before. He'd seen him do it with the tong of a belt buckle. Of course, they did have to worry about Clorinda.

Then a man came up to the outside of the cell. "Huh. You don't look the part."

Tuck shook his head. "That's because we're innocent."

"Everyone's innocent until they do something wrong. The first time is usually at about the age of two."

Whoever he was, Tuck felt an instant, strong liking for him. Which was almost embarrassing. The man was an enemy. "Good point, but we're innocent of the specific thing we're accused of."

Robin stood up, smoothly, moving over.

"So. Robert Locksley. A good choice, given there are no Locksleys left, even in the female line."

Tuck's heart dropped a few inches. The man, whoever he was, knew exactly who they were. "So, tell me. Why would the famous Outlaw of Sherwood and his most trusted men come to London in disguise? A little...risky."

The man was silhouetted against the light. Tuck realized he looked a lot like the king or the prince, but was younger and more slender.

"If I answered that, I would be acknowledging that I was him."

"Ah, yes. And then you would be hanged before dawn. Well, then." The man turned to leave. "In the morning."

Robin was frowning.

"Do you have any clue who that was?"

"From the color of his clothes and his face, I believe that may have been the Earl of Salisbury. Richard's bastard brother."

One of two acknowledged, Tuck recalled, the other, Geoffrey, having been given to the Church...a not uncommon disposition for royal bastards. "And why would such a personage come here to see us himself?"

"I do not know. But there is our line to the prince. If we can use it without earning ourselves a quick trip to the gallows."

Tuck nodded. "I should talk to him."

"Tuck..."

"They would have to go through a lot before they could simply hang me. I think I can convince him that Gisbourne recognized I, alone."

"It's risky."

"They're likely to hang us anyway. They clearly don't want to accept or acknowledge that they might be wrong." Tuck frowned. "Which would be very foolish."

"Yes, it would."

Tuck moved to a corner of the cell. Amazingly, he found he was quite able to sleep.

THE NEXT DAY, the jailers came and pulled Robin, Tuck and John out of the cell. "Come on, miscreants."

Tuck snorted. Of course, he might not see his friends again. Likely he was about to be handed over to Church custody. It was over.

The three were put in the same wagon, Tuck was sure, in which they had been brought to the jail. The horses, though, were different. He closed his eyes, feeling the rattle of it. Over.

But there was a part of him that thought it would be worth it if they could stop what brewed to the north. They could not, he knew, but maybe at least something could be done about Gisbourne.

He was dreaming. He opened his eyes as they pulled into a court-yard. A fine house, but not the palace itself.

"Get down. The earl wants to speak to the three of you."

And unlike Gisbourne, the earl had the respect of London. Tuck felt a slight hope at that.

He felt something else, too, as they were led into the house through the tradesmen's entrance. He saw, peeking out of the kitchen, a little girl who was clearly not a servant. Why she seemed familiar to him, he did not know.

No. He knew. The Blue Lady was here, watching over that child. Whatever she wanted, whoever she was, that child was important to her.

Into a sort of hall-like room. The earl stood there. "You three are three of the four ringleaders. They won't turn the woman over to me."

Tuck frowned. Clorinda. Well. With luck, she would escape. Perhaps she already had, and that was why they would not turn her over. Perhaps they were refusing to admit they had lost her.

"I know who you are, and there's no sense arguing. Tell me why you are here."

Robin spoke, softly. He knew all was lost, but he also knew, no doubt, that this was his one chance. "The Midlands seethe on the edge of revolt. The peasants starve whilst their men are taken for the levy and their food is taken in tax. Richard will not return, and half the lords are with him. Those left behind don't care."

"You don't speak of Gisbourne."

"That's personal."

Tuck listened in silence. He glanced over at the little girl. He wondered who she was. Who she would be. He supposed she was probably Salisbury's daughter.

"At least you admit it. I am trying to get the woman away from him."

Tuck smiled a little. But then he spoke. "Gisbourne is a problem. So is one whose name I don't know. He was at the jail last night."

"Unfortunately, I don't know who you're talking about. What did he do?"

"Tried to have me flogged...simply on virtue of me being a friar, and threw the Church from his lands."

"Well, he has sacrificed his soul, then, but..."

"He's dangerous." Tuck glanced at Robin for a moment, then back towards the Earl. "Gisbourne is simply a fool. The sheriff...is also dangerous."

"I have heard about that one. He hungers for power." The Earl frowned. "I think it would suit that one if Gisbourne were not to return from his next trip overseas."

"Or be killed by a bunch of rebelling peasants." Tuck wondered how much of the oppression was, in any way, Gisbourne's idea...what if the sheriff was provoking it.

"Indeed. How bad is it?"

Little John had dropped to one knee, so he was on the level of the girl...she was nine, and normally would not need that treatment. She was staying back, though.

It was Robin who spoke, sighing a little and reaching up to run a hand through his blond hair. "Bad. People can't feed themselves. They can't feed their animals. Gisbourne was hung in effigy last year. There have been a lot of arrests. He's now taken to burning villages."

The earl nodded. Slowly. "And thus, you risked yourself to try and get to the crown. What do you expect the prince to do?"

"Maybe his job." Robin let out a long, slow breath. "That's not quite fair. He's as stuck as anyone else."

"Our brother is determined not to return. I have often thought if he dislikes England this much..." He tailed off, as if remembering who he was talking to.

"He could, at the very least, censure Gisbourne. Let it be known that the crown does not approve." Robin frowned. He knew he'd thrown everything away on a fool's venture.

The look Tuck shot him tried to include everything. John, as always in these situations, remained silent.

"The Church is not helping...well, not helping the people. What these people need is food. Nothing else, at this point, matters." Clorinda might have said something impassioned about freedom. "The countryside is starving. Things don't seem to be much better here. If the tax was rescinded for even a year, they would have a chance."

Except that Gisbourne would not cooperate. Unless, of course, he was given something else to think about.

"Richard would not allow it."

"Richard," Tuck said boldly, "is not here. Prince John is here, and has powers of regency."

"But not full ones."

"Well, maybe if he did something Richard didn't like, it might actually get him to come back and open his eyes." Not that Tuck believed that would ever happen. He did not expect to ever hear from Richard 'Lionheart' again.

"Most of it was the ransom."

"I know. And I wouldn't have asked the prince not to pay it." He had to bear in mind this man, too, was Richard's brother.

Robin had developed the thoughtful expression he often had when he got an idea.

Then there was a tremendous commotion from the street.

33

*N*obody stopped Tuck from moving to one of the narrow windows, almost like arrow slits, on that side of the building.

Of course, nobody cared if he took an arrow from exposing himself, either. Except Robin...

"Gisbourne."

"I will talk to him." Salisbury glanced at the two. "You will stay here. If you don't, I'll lock you in the root cellar."

Tuck could not help but laugh slightly. The man didn't have an actual dungeon, but Tuck did not want to be locked in a root cellar. He stayed put.

Well, for a moment. Then a sense of strong alarm flowed over him. "Salisbury's in danger."

Robin had lifted his head at the same moment. He nodded.

"I think it's time to risk getting locked in the root cellar."

Gisbourne was so determined to rid himself of them that he was willing to also rid himself of the Earl of Salisbury. Or, perhaps, it was not quite that simple. Whether there was even a relationship between the two men, Tuck did not know.

There was no obvious weapon in the room other than an iron stick by the fire. Robin had already taken it. Tuck resigned himself to using the oldest weapon of all, should it be necessary.

Robin was on the move. He was out the door before Tuck could even move further, or finish that thought. John flowed after him, more like a great cat, right now, than the bear he more commonly resembled.

Tuck was left in their wake, but he followed, nonetheless. Onto the landing. The hall was on the first floor with steps upwards.

"Salisbury. I know you have them...and there they are!"

From the angle he was at, Tuck could see the archer on the far side of Gisbourne, the one that was circling. He would put a shaft into Salisbury and then they would get the blame.

If he got the chance. Tuck saw Robin hesitate and knew what caused it. The archer, or Gisbourne himself.

Both would have been ideal, but he had one weapon, the fire poker, sharpened to a point as it was. With a good throw, it could easily kill a man. A hesitation...

...then he threw it. Towards the archer as he lifted his bow towards Salisbury's back.

"On the contrary, I have..."

The man cried out, then crumpled into a small heap.

"Take them!" Gisbourne exclaimed.

The men started to launch up the stairs. Robin leapt, somersaulting to land on his feet between Gisbourne and Salisbury. "Excuse me, Your Grace."

Then another of the men grew a shaft and feathers. Tuck spared a glance and his eyes widened as he saw the pattern of the barbs. He did not know how she had done it, but he knew exactly who's hand had fletched that arrow.

Salisbury was just standing there. "Guards!"

"Your men won't come, Salisbury. I paid them off." They were coming up the stairs towards Tuck and John, but the latter kicked them back down again, into each other. They went down, bowling each other down the stairs.

Somebody tossed a length of wood upwards towards Tuck. He caught it. Too light...but Clorinda had got *everyone* out. That was Will...who had escaped the sting. Had he somehow broke them out?

He felt it more likely it was Clorinda's hand entire on the matter. The staff would serve. A second one landed in John's hands, and the big man broke it on a guard's head.

Tuck flinched, but then charged past the man. He was more careful, aware now that this stick would not take the sort of punishment a good oak quarterstaff would, knocking men out of his way.

Robin was still facing Gisbourne. "I suppose we should probably have let you assassinate him, but I don't accept a man's hospitality and then let him get killed."

Gisbourne drew his sword. Not a weapon Robin knew well to counter, but then the outlaw was pushed out of the way, a blade in Salisbury's hand. "And I don't let men under my protection be harmed."

The two blades met. Clorinda, in skirts, but with her bow ready, moving into the courtyard, but unwilling to fire into the melee. Robin might have attempted it.

The two men showed surprising finesse. This was no duel of hacking blades, it was a deadly dance. Tuck realized he was holding his breath, forced it out of his body as they circled one another. Light on their feet.

If Gisbourne won, he would destroy all witnesses to the duel. If Salisbury won, he might well do the same thing.

If anyone interfered... One did not interfere, not in such a battle. It was the utmost of dishonor to even consider doing so.

Tuck was an outlaw now. Did he care? He wanted Gisbourne to die.

Then Gisbourne broke from the fight, backing away rapidly. Tuck still only had the light stick, but he knew what was about to happen. He didn't need to see what was hidden.

He moved. Towards Salisbury. Out of the corner of his eye, he saw Robin stepping on the foot of one of the guards, but then he leapt...hitting the earl full on and knocking him to the ground. He did not hear the arrows...Gisbourne's men did not use whistlers...but he almost seemed to sense their passage. He felt a bit of red pain in his side.

Salisbury had stuck him with his sword as he went down. "My pardon, your Grace."

All that came from the rather squashed earl was a faint 'Oof'.

Tuck rolled off the man, quickly, coming up into a crouch, hands spread. As he did so, he saw Gisbourne's face. It showed surprise rather than fear. No less than three feathered shafts sprouted from his body.

As Tuck watched, he fell to the ground. It was a moment of almost anti-climax. That the man was dead, he was sure of.

Sure and certain. As the blood pooled around the fallen form, he felt an odd sense of emptiness.

∾

"I AM NOT sure quite what I am going to do with you."

Tuck sat on the chair rather gingerly. Salisbury's sword had cut a deep gash in his side and damaged a couple of his ribs. Not intentionally. He did not say anything. He was not sure what there was to say. Any word he spoke might somehow be used against him.

"Why did you bother?"

"Because Gisbourne intended to frame us for your death and then kill all of us. Neat and tidy."

"What does he have against me?"

Tuck sighed. "I don't know." He almost felt as if he was on the edge of becoming the earl's confessor. Or something. He also knew he was still in mortal danger.

Or was he?

"You saved my life. However, you are also an outlaw."

Tuck was no longer denying it. "And if nothing else, we staged a jailbreak."

"That woman. God, that woman. If we weren't both already married."

Tuck laughed. "I don't think Clorinda would be satisfied as your mistress."

"God knows I could use one." A pause. "I don't suppose you would understand. Or maybe you would."

"Your wife..."

"You met her."

Tuck's eyebrows both almost reached his tonsure. "The little girl."

He knew such happened. A political match, finalized legally years before it could be consummated. And a man like this could not seek release in the bishop's brothels. Except perhaps very carefully, in disguise.

"Blame my father. I sometimes think it's punishment for...you know the problems he had with his children."

And only the Pope could release the man from this chaste marriage. From the fact that he would be forced to bed her as soon as the midwives said it was safe for her to be with child, never mind that she was so young, never mind that he had raised her as a daughter or sister. Tuck shuddered.

"And still problems with Richard," Salisbury continued. "Tell me, Friar. Do you have brothers? Of the flesh, that is."

"Three," Tuck admitted. "But I never had the kind of conflicts with them some men experience.

"You're lucky. Richard is a fool and John is...narrow minded. I have to talk to him, but I'm not sure how."

He was definitely being used as a confessor. "I don't think I can help."

"You, right now, are just my evidence. Part of it. Unfortunately, I don't know if I can earn you a pardon."

Tuck frowned. "If you do not, we will likely be hanged."

"That I won't allow. Exiled, at worst. I promise."

An earl's promise, but what did it mean? And exiled...would be as bad as death for some. For Reginald, certainly. For Clorinda. Likely for Will. Tuck could live in an alien land. He could even go to Assissi.

But never to walk the greenwood again was harsh. On the other hand. Exile was preferable to some lengthy imprisonment. "What I care about the most is that something is done about the situation that gives us Gisbournes."

"And Wallaces...that is your other 'friend'." Salisbury frowned. "I've heard rumors about him. Rumors enough, if they are true, to earn him a stint in the tower at the very least. If I could get anyone to care."

"Rumors?"

"He likes his serving wenches young. Very young."

Tuck shuddered. "I'm glad to be out of all that."

"Don't tell me you keep your vows?"

"I've never had any inclination otherwise."

"You mean you've traveled with Clorinda for two years and not wanted to..." The man was astonished.

Tuck laughed. "She carries knives. So does her husband." He tried to make it clear which one of the two he feared the most.

Salisbury laughed. "Maybe I'll try and find a way to keep you."

"Likely the church will not permit me to remain a Brother."

"And? I still want to keep you."

Tuck actually felt warmed by that, and emboldened. "As what? A bodyguard?"

"Maybe."

Then the door opened. "Your Grace. It's time."

"I have to go. You will stay put, I trust."

"I don't like root cellars."

Salisbury laughed again, and then departed.

34

*R*obin looked surprisingly relaxed and comfortable. Tuck...did not share that feeling.

For one thing, they were in the courtyard of the Palace of St. James. For another, they were under heavy armed guard.

Tuck had fresh clothing. He had even managed that rare thing, a bath. He had managed to get his tonsure trimmed, but he wondered if he would now be expected to grow it out.

They could not get between him and God. Only he, himself could do that.

A woman stepped, for a moment, out of the palace. She looked almost like the Blue Lady...or as if she, too, had been touched by her, but she seemed to see the gathering in the courtyard and flee. A sensible departure. The tension was pretty high.

Everyone knew these outlaws were dangerous even when unarmed.

Then the doors opened again.

Prince John was instantly recognizable. His features were fairly similar to those of his half-brother, but somewhat more aquiline. He was flanked by two bodyguards, both of whom showed a clear readiness to do for him what Tuck had done for Salisbury.

He walked towards Robin. "I don't know whether to have you executed or give you a medal."

Robin's lips quirked into his usual ready grin. Even in this situation, he had that odd security. It was faith, Tuck knew.

Faith in Mary. Trust in Her.

If the Blue Lady was her. Tuck just let a breath out. And he tried to force all of his doubt out with it. All of his fear. If Robin could face the end with equanimity, then so could he.

"So. Tell me. To what are you loyal, Robin of Sherwood?"

"Myself," he responded, lightly, "England."

"In that order, I suspect." John's lips quirked in a not dissimilar pattern. "An honest thief."

"I have not said I'm not a thief."

"An honest thief, a roguish friar, and a bunch of thugs. Yet, you claim to know something of the governance of England."

"No." Robin let his hands fall to his sides. He had no weapons, but he could probably, at that range, kill John before they were all shot down. He did not move. "I don't claim to know anything about governance. What I know is the people."

He glanced around, then focused his attention to the prince. Then, deliberately, he dropped to one knee.

Tuck had never seen Robin kneel to anyone. He could not help but follow suit.

"What I know, Your Highness, is simple. I know that England is broke. I know that we can't afford to keep sending men and materiel overseas. I know because I see who is really paying the burden. It isn't you. It isn't Salisbury. It isn't the likes of Gisbourne and Wallace."

The hair rose on Tuck's neck. He knew that man was here, and had heard his name spoken in such an unflattering manner. His presence was very real.

And then he was striding towards the prince. No bodyguards for him.

"So, I see you are letting the outlaws talk. Why, your Highness, have they not yet been sent to Tyburn?"

"Because I am not done." John turned to face the man. "Why are you here?"

"To stop you from making a bad mistake. These men are pagans."

One of John's eyebrows arched. "Pagans?"

Tuck actually rolled his eyes. He could not help himself. It was all he could do not to speak, but he sensed that if he did... Besides. At some levels it was true.

"Goddess worshippers. The woman, at least, is a witch. Likely the supposed friar, too."

Tuck almost laughed.

"Is this true?" John half turned back towards Robin.

"The only Lady I honor is the Mother of our Lord," Robin said, carefully. "I believe this man may have mistaken my devotions to her for certain heresies."

Mistaken? Tuck knew that Robin followed those same heresies, but phrased as it was, it meant John had to turn it into an allegation.

"And your woman?"

"Some men will call any woman who does not cling to her stove a witch, your Highness."

"Indeed they will."

Tuck could see the look on Wallace's face. It was not yet the look of a defeated man, but definitely that of a frustrated one.

"I would appreciate it, thief, if you would finish."

"Men are being taken to the Crusades, leaving only women and children to handle the harvest. When it is not enough, the tax men take their food and even their seed grain. If we do not bring the soldiers back, there will be more deaths. And more violence." Robin's words were simply a statement of fact. Not impassioned, not emotional.

Almost as if he was giving a report.

"And what would you do about it?"

"Bring them back. End the levies. Give the people seed grain from the granaries."

It sounded so simple.

"And if Richard will not allow me to do so?"

"He's *your* brother."

That hung in the air, but those words did not come from Robin. They came from Salisbury, stepping up behind the prince, around the guards.

"And yours."

"But I did not share the same mother's milk."

John's lips quirked. "Neither did I. Do you think the queen would have damaged her figure with suckling? But your point is taken, brother. Still. He will not return. Am I to lie to him?"

The obvious answer was yes. But Tuck was keeping his eyes on Wallace. Who was now walking towards him.

Would the guards do something if he decided to attack? Tuck tensed. He was in a good position to stick some part of his body out and trip the man but elected not to. It would only cause him trouble.

All this man caused was trouble, Tuck thought, wryly. All he had caused Tuck, certainly.

Wallace stopped, then whispered to him. "She cannot help you. John will end this, because his brother will never forgive him if he lets any of you go."

"I escaped from *you*." Tuck looked towards the man. "Whatever force you serve has no power."

"And if I say it is God I serve?"

"Then I would know you to be a liar." Of course, he wondered who truly served God, in this time. Not most of the Churchmen he knew. The peasants? They worried about the survival of their bodies, not the health of their souls. The Crusaders? It was gold that shone in their eyes, not the cross.

The heretics were doing a better job.

"Would you?"

He walked away. Tuck prayed, focusing his thoughts on the image of Christ on the cross. The ultimate sacrifice and the ultimate redemption.

The Blue Lady impinged on his consciousness. Well. If she was Mary, she belonged there. If not...then he was already lost. Already doomed. He opened his eyes.

Salisbury was talking to Wallace quietly. He could not hear even the smallest snatches of their conversation, such as it was. Then the man started to turn on his heel. Started to.

Tuck remembered the demon outside the granary. In the corner of his eye, he saw another such creature.

It was heading towards the Prince. He stood, rising and turning towards it. For once, he did not care exactly who saw him acting so oddly.

He had blocked an arrow. Now he moved to put himself in the creature's path.

Wallace hit him. The blow hit his face, snapped his head to one side. "Get back in your place, scum."

With John gone, Salisbury would be regent. With them both gone, the only candidate was the princess Eleanor.

The demon was launching itself at the prince. Tuck spun, and with one quick shove thrust Wallace into its path.

It was an action born out of reflex, not thought. Yet, it was abruptly clear. Prince John could see the creature, his eyes widening as it struck Wallace's form, knocked him to the ground and then tried to leap again. Tuck launched himself, but contact with it was cold. So cold. "In the name of Christ I command thee, return whence you came and trouble us no more!" he found himself exclaiming.

And...the demon was gone. How could it have worked when he doubted his faith so much?

"I do not think we have any heretics here," the Prince said, after a moment. There was a murmur through the courtyard.

How many had seen? Had most of the men here been oblivious to the battle.

The Blue Lady was standing behind the Prince now. She was smiling at Tuck.

Why are you pleased? he asked her silently. I...

All gods are one God.

Those were the words that came into his mind. And then she was gone.

THEY RODE north out of London. Tuck had been offered a horse, but preferred his ugly, familiar mule. Tucked under his robes was a royal pardon. The others had something more.

A commission from Prince John, to 'patrol the Greenwood and ensure the safety of travelers'.

Unspoken was the knowledge that they would not obey the Forest Laws...and would get away with it.

Gisbourne was dead, and ahead of them rode a royal messenger. His wife would not be permitted to be regent. Instead, a certain spice merchant would get control of the lands until Gisbourne's son was mature. Of course, said spice merchant had two daughters, the youngest of a very appropriate age. The sheriff was to be fired.

He would no doubt cause further trouble. And no doubt they had not seen the last of Wallace, for all that he had had the symptoms of a stroke. The symptoms of which John had been meant to die.

Tuck knew it was the Blue Lady who had made the demon visible to all present, but the power of God which had dismissed it.

All gods are one God. He shook his head, then he set it deep aside. Deep into the back of his mind.

Into that place where you put things of which you know you cannot speak. It was spring and the sun was coming out, dappling the ground beneath the trees.

Cannot speak. Yet, there would be something from this. Just those words, voiced in rare corners to those few who were ready to understand.

Then there was a messenger. Tuck heard his approach, slowed his mount. The lathered horse, as swift as the ones that had spoken of Richard's imprisonment. He rode past, stopping alongside Robin.

"Lord Locksley."

The final irony...John giving the outlaw who had helped save his life and possibly his kingdom the very fake title he had claimed.

"What is it?" Robin turned, but there was something in his eyes.

"The king is dead."

They reined to a halt. Tuck could see Robin's lips move, but for a moment no sound came out of them.

Then, very softly. "Long live King John. Did he die in the Holy Land?"

"Nay. He fell in battle in Aquitaine itself."

So close. Yet, the prophecy that had hovered in Tuck's mind was fulfilled. "King Richard never came back to England."

"No. He did not."

Robin turned his mount, turning its head towards London. "We must do homage to our new king."

And Tuck wondered, just wondered, if John had known when he had given titles not his to give...if he had already known, in that way of brothers, that he was in that moment the King of England.

AUTHOR'S NOTE

Author's Note

I'm from Nottingham. Or rather, near Nottingham. So, it's somewhat inevitable that at some point I would want to write a Robin Hood novel.

Robin Hood tends not to be as popular as King Arthur. My introduction to the legend was *Tales of Robin Hood* by Enid Blyton (who also did a companion King Arthur book for kids). It was also rolling my eyes when Robin Hood's arrow was stolen *again* from the statue of him below Nottingham Castle Rock.

Rolling them harder when the actual real life Sheriff of Nottingham (a mostly ceremonial position) was caught embezzling county funds, to much amusement from the local press.

But I've also walked in what remains of Sherwood Forest, visited the Major Oak, and been profoundly disappointed to find out that Robert Locksley, if he existed, was probably a Yorkshireman.

So, this book. First of all, Robin Hood himself struck me as too enigmatic a figure to be the narrator of the story. (I felt much the same way about King Arthur in *The Lay of Lady Percival*).

I wanted somebody who made sense to be the one telling the outlaws' story, somebody who wasn't quite, *quite* a Merry Man.

My authorial gaze fell upon Friar Tuck. Friar Tuck represented to me, the struggle to be good within a mostly-corrupt organization, which the Church very much was at the time. The fact that both of my parents held St. Francis as a patron saint and were involved in the lay part of the Franciscan movement sealed the deal: Friar Tuck would be my narrator.

I then made another major, *major* change after doing some research into how the legend evolved over time: The removal of Maid Marian as a character. There is indeed some evidence that "Maid Marian" was a reference to the Virgin Mary. The Marian Heresy is a very old one within the Church. If Marian is the only woman Robin truly loves, then the next two decisions flow naturally: 1. Robin is a Marian heretic and 2. Robin is gay. So, yeah, it's probably *too* obvious to pair him off with Little John, but I couldn't resist.

Because I didn't want to leave us without a major female character, I created Clorinda out of whole cloth. Her name is the name of Robin's lover from one of the French tales, but given the circumstances I paired her instead with Will Scarlet. And I'm well aware there's a bit of Smurfette Syndrome going on, but I'm hoping the minor female characters somewhat make up for it.

Then I started writing. And the words "He was never tempted to break his vows" came into my mind. Friar Tuck in the legend is fat (and I definitely kept that), good with a staff, overly fond of ale, but never shows any interest in breaking his vow of celibacy.

I went over it in my mind, and over it, and slowly came to the weird dawning revelation that without any conscious thought I'd decided/realized that Friar Tuck did indeed have no interest in women...or men either! An asexual and aromantic man in the Middle Ages might well have entered Holy Orders to avoid pressure on him to marry.

The religious universalism in the book reflects a place I was in my own spiritual journey a few years ago before landing more into hard polytheism, although I'm still firmly of the belief that all gods are good and come, in many ways, from the same place. I also wanted to make it clear that while the Church in this book is problematic and corrupt, Christianity isn't necessarily so. Just like today.

Finally, I want to touch on the decision I suspect will piss off fans of the original the most. Richard Coeur de Leon (Lionheart) is generally portrayed as an example of the True King Trope we English are so fond of.

The man neglected his wife, barely spoke English, and nearly bankrupted all of his holdings going on crusades. It's this historical Richard who finds his way into this book, mostly because I am tired of True Kings.

ACKNOWLEDGMENTS

As usual, acknowledgments go to my wonderful editor, Jennifer Melzer, to my cover artist, Starla Huchton, and my husband and primary proofreader, Greg Pearson. I would also like to thank my sensitivity reader, who helped me make sure I didn't accidentally include any nasty asexual stereotypes.

All mistakes and problems are, of course, entirely on me.

OTHER BOOKS BY JENNIFER R. POVEY

⌇

The Silent Years (Mother, Crone, Maiden)

⌇

The Ky Federation novels

Transpecial

Araña

⌇

The Lost Guardians Series:

Falling Dusk

Fallen Dark

Rising Dawn

Risen Day

⌇

Daughter of Fire

⌇

The Lay of Lady Percival

⌇

Tales of Yirath:

Firewing

Made in the USA
Middletown, DE
31 December 2021

57239293R00157